THE

LONG

ANSWER

THE

LONG

ANSWER

Anna Hogeland

Riverhead Books • *New York* • *2022*

RIVERHEAD BOOKS
An imprint of Penguin Random House LLC
penguinrandomhouse.com

Copyright © 2022 by Anna Hogeland

Library of Congress Cataloging-in-Publication Data
Names: Hogeland, Anna, author.
Title: The long answer / Anna Hogeland.
Description: New York : Riverhead Books, 2022. |
Identifiers: LCCN 2021055899 (print) | LCCN 2021055900 (ebook) |
ISBN 9780593418130 (hardcover) | ISBN 9780593418154 (ebook)
Subjects: LCSH: Pregnant women—Fiction. | Motherhood—Fiction. |
Female friendship—Fiction. | Women—Psychology—Fiction. |
LCGFT: Pyschological fiction. | Novels.
Classification: LCC PS3608.O482675 L66 2022 (print) |
LCC PS3608.O482675 (ebook) | DDC 813/.6—dc23/eng/20211123
LC record available at https://lccn.loc.gov/2021055899
LC ebook record available at https://lccn.loc.gov/2021055900

Printed in the United States of America
1st Printing

BOOK DESIGN BY LUCIA BERNARD

for my family

CONTENTS

THE

LONG

ANSWER

Elizabeth

MY OLDER SISTER, Margot, called me and said, "You don't need to say anything but I wanted to let you know I had a miscarriage. Just an early one," she added quickly. "I'm fine now."

I was more surprised than saddened; I didn't know she was pregnant, or that she had been trying to get pregnant.

"The worst of it is over," she said. "I'm relieved that I lost it when I did, before I was any further along. I only thought I was pregnant for a week. So as far as miscarriages go, this was about as easy as they get." She and Nick had quickly conceived their son, Alex, now just over a year old, and there was no reason to believe they wouldn't conceive quickly again. It was unlikely that a miscarriage would happen a second time—even though the odds were higher now than they were before—and she knew she was fertile and her body could carry a healthy pregnancy to term. They just had to wait for one cycle to try to conceive again.

There wasn't anything more to say, she said, she'd just rather I hear it from her than from our mother. And she wanted to make sure that I would still feel able to talk to her about my pregnancy—I was nine weeks when she called—she had been hesitant to tell me any of this for fear that I would shield her from it, which was exactly what she didn't want.

"Truly," she said. "I only feel happiness for you. Please know that. How are you feeling, anyway? Any better at all?"

I wasn't sure if I should call her after that, if the miscarriage was something she wanted to talk more about, despite saying she did not. I was surprised she'd told me at all. We'd never been the kind of sisters who tell each other our most vulnerable secrets, and since this dynamic had always felt more like her choice than mine, I tried to honor it.

In the days following, I sent her texts saying, *how are you feeling?*; *please let me know if there's anything I can do*; and Isaac and I bought her a fifty-dollar gift certificate to Moose's Tooth Pizzeria. Her responses were curt: *doing OK today thanks*, or: *you're sweet but I'm fine*. Soon she only replied with an emoji of a flower bouquet or a yellow heart. When my last text, *just letting you know I'm thinking of you*, went unanswered, I decided to let her be the one to initiate contact next, whenever that would be.

Three weeks passed before she called again. I was walking back to my apartment from the library when I saw her name on my phone, and I felt a quick, sharp hope that she was calling to say she was pregnant, before realizing that she shouldn't be, not yet, not quite. But she had called to tell me about a conflict she was having with her friend

Elizabeth that had been causing her some distress; in the days following, what she told me came to dominate my thoughts as well.

"You sound out of breath," she said. "Are you all right?"

"I'm always out of breath now," I said, slowing my pace. "I'm seeing inclines I've never seen before."

"Just wait till it's pressing your lungs. And your bladder."

She was on her way to pick up Alex from day care, and she wanted to talk while she had some quiet. We were well, we told each other. I hadn't been writing much, finding it hard to focus on my novel while so exhausted and woozy, but teaching hadn't been too difficult to manage. Margot had just finished a stretch of long shifts at the hospital so her schedule would be lighter for the next few days. Husbands were well, Alex was well—he could stand on his own now, but he wouldn't yet take a step—and he was very into bananas and zippers. It was raining and cold in Anchorage, where she lived, and warm and lovely where I was, in Irvine, California.

A short silence fell between us. Her car blinker ticked, then turned off.

"Sorry," she said, though I wasn't sure why.

"Are you okay?"

"Yeah, I just—it's nothing real, not really. I don't want to bother you with this, but I'm not sure who else to talk to. It's about Elizabeth. Do you remember my friend Elizabeth?"

I'd only met Elizabeth once, at a barbecue at Margot's house in Anchorage the previous summer, when Isaac and I were there on our honeymoon. When Margot heard from our mother that Isaac and I were considering going to Alaska, she had insisted that we stay with them for several nights. They had a guest bedroom in the basement with its own full bathroom. The invitation surprised me, and I wasn't sure what to make of it; in the preceding several years we'd hardly spoken beyond short, obligatory calls on our birthdays and major holidays.

"You're living on a grad student stipend," she'd said to convince me. "I know you can't turn down a free place."

Elizabeth and I didn't talk much at that party; there were several other couples there, too, all with small children, and Elizabeth and her husband, Patrick, had spent most of the time trying and failing to quiet their four-month-old son's wails. They arrived last and left first.

But Margot had told me a lot about Elizabeth. During that visit to Anchorage, Margot frequently brought her up in conversation; she talked about her much more than she usually talked about her friends. She revealed intimacies of Elizabeth's life I knew were not meant for me to hear, and so I listened carefully. It was clear that Margot now had with Elizabeth the sort of female friendship I'd read about in novels and memoirs and I'd desired throughout my childhood and adolescence and even at present but had never found for myself, even for a short while—the sort of female friendship likened to sisterhood, but not a sisterhood like mine and Margot's, which for much of our lives had been distant and cautious.

Margot was nearly four years older than me, an adolescent when I was a child, and then she was in college, away, and forever after an infrequent houseguest. In the years we had grown up together in a pleasant Boston suburb, I often felt cut with the small, ordinary wounds an older sister effortlessly causes a younger sister—an eye roll, an incisive comment, or the silence of indifference, would leave me hurting for days, and for years after, whenever remembered. And if we'd been twins, perhaps it wouldn't have been so different. The world to her was an orderly and manageable place; her life was a set of small obstacles she could easily master. I felt always as if I were being sucked underwater, unsure if I was swimming toward the sand or the surface, desperate for breath. So I'd cast myself as a listener, wanting to hear how others lived their lives with the hope that I might learn how to live my own.

"Don't be so quiet," Margot once said, still in high school, after her friends had come over for the *One Tree Hill* season finale. I'd watched with them, ceding the couch and sitting on a pillow on the floor. "It makes it seem like you're stupid."

We hadn't ever repaired the rift between us, to know each other when we were older, when four years was hardly anything at all. I waited for her to make a gesture—it was her gesture to make, as I was sure I'd never affected her as she'd affected me—a gesture to show I was no longer a child to her, I was her sister and my life was of interest. It never came, and so years passed until we were adults living in faraway states, sharing little more than hazel eyes and a childhood home.

Margot loved Elizabeth, that was easy to tell, even though she wasn't sure how well she knew her. I developed, over that trip, an intense envy and something short of a fixation on this woman I did not know, who had so quickly come to occupy the space in Margot's life that had until then remained vacant. If anyone were going to fill it, I had thought it would be me.

I realized then, in Alaska, and I realized again when Margot called, that only when Elizabeth herself was the subject of her thoughts, was I the one she wanted.

"I met her at the barbecue," I said. "And Patrick and their baby."

"Phin."

"Phin, right."

"That's what I thought. Elizabeth didn't remember meeting you or Isaac, but I could've sworn she was there." Margot paused again. The air was quiet behind her. I imagined her pulling into a parking space at the day care, looking at the mountains capped with snow, keeping the car on and pressing her hands to the vents. I always imagined it cold there, but it was mid-October, and midafternoon, and so she may not have had the heat on. I crossed the intersection separating undergraduate housing and graduate housing, where I lived, trying to shield the sun from my eyes and the wind from my phone.

"I'm sorry to bother you with this," she said for the second time. "I think it's stupid but I just can't get it out of my head."

"What is it?"

"Elizabeth is pregnant again. Twelve weeks."

"Oh." I waited for her to speak but she was quiet. "I'm twelve weeks too."

"Already? Wow, I thought you were ten or eleven."

"Well, I'm almost twelve. I'll be twelve in three days."

She breathed into the phone. "So, yeah, she's pregnant again."

"That's great—I mean, that's great for her, I assume. But I'm sure it can't be easy for you, so soon after—"

"No, that's not it," she said. "Her pregnancy isn't bothering me. I mean, I'm genuinely happy for Elizabeth, like I'm genuinely happy for you. She planned it this way. She took out her IUD the week of Phin's first birthday and got pregnant right away. Didn't even have a period."

"Does she know what happened to you?"

"Yeah. I didn't really mean to tell her, but I was feeling so exhausted that I canceled our walk. She invited me and Nick over for dinner, but I wasn't up for that, either. I didn't want her to think I was upset with her so I told her. She was surprisingly sympathetic. She even left lentil soup on my doorstep the next day. I would've never expected her to do something like that.

"I'm glad I told her," she continued. "So it's not that. It's the way she told me she was pregnant. It's been bothering me more than I think makes sense."

"What did she say?"

A child cried somewhere near her, then quieted.

"It's nothing she said, really. It's more what she didn't say, I think, that's been getting to me."

I nodded in response, waiting for her to continue, forgetting she couldn't see me. I tried to recall then, in a flurry of images and memories, all that Margot had ever told me about Elizabeth; but I had already forgotten what, exactly, Elizabeth had told Margot directly, what Margot had inferred from what Elizabeth did or did not say, and what I had embellished myself.

Here is what I thought I knew about Elizabeth the day Margot called me and asked, Do you remember my friend Elizabeth?, though this would all be recast in the coming weeks (when Margot would learn more about her friend and share her new knowledge with me), not as lies—no, not so simple and deceptive as that—but as an artful curation of vulnerabilities and facts and omissions that gave the effective illusion of a complete truth, the kind reserved only for a close female confidant.

. . .

Margot and Elizabeth met after Margot's college friend Claire texted her to say that her friend from med school was moving to Anchorage, where Margot and Nick had just moved a few months earlier. *I can put you two in touch!* Claire wrote, and Margot accepted the offer without hesitation. The idea of a potential friend in Anchorage was so exciting to Margot that it made her aware of how lonely and isolated she'd already begun to feel in the small city enclosed by forests and cold salt water. Every time she'd moved in the past, it'd been for college (Hanover), med school (Ann Arbor), or residency (Philadelphia), and she'd been instantly and effortlessly surrounded with largely similarly minded people her age who were also new to their surroundings and looking for companionship. And though she didn't expect this community upon moving to Anchorage—hadn't she chosen to move there, of all places, precisely because of its detachment from everything she had ever known?—she was still disheartened when it failed to materialize.

Claire soon sent a group text introducing Margot and Elizabeth to each other, then sent Margot a text separately that read: *Elizabeth isn't the most warm and fuzzy. Don't know if you'll hit it off. But you should get together anyway and maybe you will!*

Margot was annoyed. She wished Claire had texted her this before the introduction text, so she could ask more of what she meant and determine if this woman was someone to whom she wanted to extend a gesture of friendship. Claire, Margot recalled with unease, was undiscerning in her affections, for both romantic and platonic relationships; she had chosen to live off campus her senior year with a clique of girls that Margot had found to be far more vapid and mean-spirited than Claire herself. But the introduction text had been sent, and now Margot felt an obligation, as the one who had been in Anchorage longer, to be the first to respond. So she texted Elizabeth separately to welcome her to town and to invite her and her husband over for dinner before she could think herself out of it.

To Margot's surprise, Elizabeth responded quickly, with two exclamation points and a smiling emoji, and the following Friday just after 7:00, Elizabeth and Patrick were at the door with pink tulips and a bottle of Malbec.

Soon after they stepped in, and Elizabeth removed her clogs with-out being asked—(Margot had the same ones, but in coffee rather than maroon and probably two full sizes smaller)—Elizabeth said, "Your home feels like a home already, it even smells like people really live here. In a good way, I mean. Our place smells like packing tape."

"Thanks," said Margot. "I don't know, it has a ways to go."

The house still felt bare to her, and her couch and bookshelves and lamps from college looked adolescent in the adult space.

"It's true," said Patrick. "We're using our boxes as a coffee table."

Though it was a small joke, maybe a true one, the laugher let Margot lighten a little. Soon they sat down for dinner, shakshuka with feta cheese and garlic bread, the plates already set on the fabric place mats Margot had bought at Target just hours before. They briefly talked about their respective connections to Claire. Elizabeth confessed that she didn't know Claire well, they had just taken a few classes together, which made Margot feel at once relieved and more wary. Then Elizabeth turned quiet, and she remained the most soft-spoken of the four of them for the remainder of the evening, often wearing a neutral expression that was difficult for Margot to interpret. She was pretty, perhaps beautiful, with a strong build and defined features and green eyes and black hair and light brown skin, a dark olive complexion. Margot felt pale and short and plain and sensed that Elizabeth didn't like her. As the dinner progressed, Margot watched Elizabeth's features, her skin under the recessed kitchen light, and she found herself both frustrated and ashamed that she was trying and unable to identify her race.

Patrick, however, seemed comfortable telling stories that lasted a little longer than they might have needed to, and Margot was grateful for his ease with conversation and how he directed his attention to Margot and Nick both, rather than only to Nick. When Patrick told the story of the day they moved in—the coldest day of the year, negative fifteen degrees, and he saw three figures in the dark that looked like monsters, and he thought he was losing his mind before realizing they were moose—Elizabeth added in a gentle interruption, "It was two cows and a calf, with no bull, not that I could see." Margot realized then that perhaps Elizabeth was simply shy, not aloof.

From then on, whenever Elizabeth spoke that evening, Margot sensed that she wasn't sure how much to ask, and how much to tell about herself, so she often elaborated on Patrick's stories rather than venturing to tell any of her own. Her compliments on the home and food ("How did you get the bread's crust so crispy and keep the middle so moist?") seemed to be inspired by anxiety, as if she had become suddenly aware that she had not spoken in too long a time. Margot wasn't sure if this meant the compliments were disingenuous, and she didn't really mind either way.

Margot's new theory of Elizabeth's shyness was undermined when there was a short, depressed pause after Nick had been telling them about the thawing permafrost, and Elizabeth broke the silence by asking, "Are your floors insulated?" Margot and Nick shook their heads, and Elizabeth sighed, making no effort to conceal her judgment. "If you insulate your floors less heat goes into the ground, you know. I definitely wouldn't buy a house without them, not here. It's expensive, but you can do it yourself. You should really think about it."

The dinner ended with Margot uncertain about her impression of Elizabeth, and even less certain of Elizabeth's impression of her. In the days that followed, Margot told me, she found herself checking her phone more than once, half-expecting a thank-you-for-dinner text, or perhaps an invitation to their place. When none came, she noticed a small deflation of her spirits.

It was three weeks after the dinner, when Margot no longer expected to hear from her, that Elizabeth invited Margot on a walk. She only invited Margot. *Are you free tomorrow?* Elizabeth texted. *There's a trail I've been meaning to try.* Margot accepted, elated and nervous to have a one-on-one with Elizabeth. It'd been several years since she had made a friend who wanted to see Margot solo, not Margot-and-Nick over for dinner. She hadn't realized how much she'd wanted a friend just for herself. There was nothing troublesome in her marriage that Margot wanted to discuss, but she liked the idea that she could talk to Elizabeth if there were. The date felt illicit, though also incredibly innocent, as if she were a child again.

On a trail outside of town, the edge of the wild, their eyes were fixed on the steep rocky path, not on each other, and this allowed them both to talk with more ease. Elizabeth spoke candidly about how she wasn't sure if she liked her new house, or her coworkers at the family medicine practice downtown, and as they hiked up the mountain, enjoying the illusion of the sharp peaks of Chugach Forest rising along with them, Margot spoke of the loneliness she'd been feeling now that the adrenaline of the move had worn off, and her feelings of ineptitude as she treated children at the hospital who had conditions she'd never heard of. By the end of the hike, their muscles warm and loose, they were speaking more comfortably and turning to look at each other for longer periods of time when the path was clear of roots and rocks. Though Margot was still not sure how to interpret all of Elizabeth's comments and pauses, she was more certain that she liked her, and that Elizabeth liked Margot in return.

Margot became pregnant that spring, and two months later, so did Elizabeth. Margot and Nick conceived after their second try—but Elizabeth and Patrick had been trying for eight months. Elizabeth had started to look into preliminary fertility treatments; her initial consult was scheduled for the day after her test was positive. When their friends from residency and med school announced pregnancies or births via Facebook or a mass BCC email—there seemed to be another one every week, Claire among them, now that they were all out of residency and quickly approaching their late thirties—Elizabeth and Margot would speak abstractly about wanting to start trying sooner than later. But neither had confessed that they had, in fact, been trying already.

Once Margot started to show, she and Elizabeth went shopping together at the 5th Avenue Mall, the only shopping center with Motherhood Maternity in all of Alaska. They split the price of a nice dress, black satin, that they could each wear to their work holiday parties. Elizabeth was three inches taller than Margot, with wider hips and shoulders, but the dress was loose enough with a string-tie waist that it fell well on both of them.

Pregnancy was harder for Elizabeth, I remembered Margot telling me. She was sick for most of each day for the first twenty weeks. She was exhausted and unable to nap in the afternoon or to calm her mind to sleep at night, so she spent the early morning hours trying to eat Cheerios in the kitchen and knitting a yellow yarn blanket on a beginner's loom. In the summer and early fall, those morning hours were the only moments of respite from the sun that never seemed to fully rise or fully set. She stayed awake to see night. Around 7:00 a.m., she'd wake to Patrick's hand on her shoulder, having fallen asleep for what felt like just an instant.

The only thing that made Elizabeth feel better was walking. By late fall, into winter, when there were suddenly only a few hours of dim daylight, Margot often walked to Elizabeth's house and they walked from there to the pond. Since they'd been pregnant neither Margot nor Elizabeth wanted to walk on the steep valley trails outside of town as they used to. Now they preferred the pond, with its paved walkway, where they could still see the mountains and smell the salt water and they would never be more than a twenty-minute walk from either of their homes or the hospital. Elizabeth brought a sleeve of saltines in case her stomach started to sour. The walking and the cold and the conversation made Elizabeth forget, for a little while, the nausea and how many days remained until her next ultrasound.

"Maybe I shouldn't have a baby now," Elizabeth said more than once. "Maybe I shouldn't have a baby at all. This may be the stupidest thing I've ever done."

Margot was never quite sure what to say when Elizabeth spoke this way, so she said little, but she sometimes shared some of her anxieties about her own pregnancy, and exaggerated, just slightly, any distance she felt between herself and Nick and her fears of him losing some love for her after the baby was born.

In those months they were both pregnant, Elizabeth often spoke about her past with Patrick as they walked around the pond, as if searching in her own narrative for an answer to a question she couldn't quite pose. Elizabeth and Patrick had seemed good together, to Margot—or not bad, at least. Patrick didn't cut Elizabeth off when she spoke. Elizabeth corrected or clarified Patrick's stories in a way that never felt like a challenge. They filled each other's wineglasses before they filled their own. Margot listened for evidence of unseen rifts, but Elizabeth's stories never revealed anything the least bit damning about either Patrick or their marriage.

Even so, when Margot called me that day and asked, "Do you remember my friend Elizabeth?" I immediately wondered if she was going to tell me that Patrick had left Elizabeth and the baby and he was not the decent man she thought he was. But if that was why Margot had called me—and it was not—I thought her voice would be different. Less harried, more saddened, heavy with concern for another but not for herself.

The vast majority of their relationship had been long distance, Elizabeth told Margot, as they'd been accepted to different residencies: Patrick to Chicago and Elizabeth to San Francisco. They hadn't been dating for very long when they had to decide whether or not to match as a couple, so they did not; but when the time came to move apart from each other, they decided to at least try to stay together, knowing full well that their chances of surviving three years of distance were quite slim.

They managed to visit each other on all breaks and sometimes just for a long weekend, taking turns flying to each other and splitting the fare. The first few days of the visits were as tense as they were exciting. Talking in person rather than over the phone, getting to know, again, each other's mannerisms, smell, affect, body, sarcasm, sounds they made in their sleep, made Elizabeth conscious of how much could happen in the short time they'd spent apart. Sometimes Patrick seemed to have changed to her completely, even his nose and hairline seemed altered, and she had to fight the impulse to break up with him right away. Sometimes she was terrified he would think the same of her, and she had to stop herself from proposing marriage to him or pausing her residency and moving to Chicago for as long as it would take him to love her as she loved him. He was from a very wealthy family on the Upper West Side, and she was from a middle-class family in Orono, Maine, and she worried he would realize that she was not the person he wanted long-term just as she realized that he *was* the person she wanted long-term. So as they hid from roommates in their narrow bedrooms, she would search for clues to what he thought of her in how he touched her and spoke to her and kissed her and lay next to her after sex.

After a few days, when they began to be calm together again, and Elizabeth became used to seeing Patrick next to her in the morning and enjoying their time rather than picking at it, the visit was at its end. She'd drive him to the airport, park in short-term parking and kiss and hug him before security, sometimes almost crying after he turned his back to her and walked away.

In their final year of residency, he proposed on a surprise visit over Memorial Day weekend. He placed the ring on the table at a crowded Thai restaurant they'd been to many times before, a diamond with a sapphire on either side. Too expensive, too garish, she first thought, she told Margot. Imagining him picking out a ring she did not like, and the shame he would feel if he knew, is what made her cry as she said yes. The visit had been a surprise, but the proposal wasn't. They'd been discussing marriage for months already—over Skype and the phone and late at night in bed during their short intermittent visits—and they both knew she would say yes when he asked her, whenever that may be. She'd already been offered a job in Anchorage, and Patrick would look for one, too. This time they would move together.

The ring was not heavy, but it caught on the threads of her sweaters and scarves. It reflected sunlight into her eye when her hands were on the steering wheel, or when she typed on her phone. She began wearing an old silver bracelet, a college graduation present from her uncle, so the ring did not look so out of place on her bare hands. (The bracelet, Margot noticed as she told the story, still hung on her wrist.) When her leather watch strap broke from wear and sweat, she replaced it with a silver link band. She took more care with her nails, filing them often and gently pushing down her cuticles. On a free and restless day a week or so after Patrick left her with the ring, she walked a mile to Essence Nails, a tiny salon in a strip mall she'd passed many times on her way to the hospital, and treated herself to her first manicure since her high school prom. She tested several colors on her thumbnail before finally deciding on a shiny scarlet called Tra-La-La!, and watched the woman clip, file, and buff her nails and trim the skin around them, then paint with the precision and focus of a surgeon.

Afterward Elizabeth's hands looked beautiful. They surprised her when she looked at them. She couldn't quite understand why she felt embarrassed when her colleagues and patients complimented them. She let the dishes pile up for two full days and an afternoon, afraid the harsh detergent would ruin the woman's fine work so quickly after it was complete.

As she looked at her nails and hands and the ring on her finger, she sometimes wondered if she became, in ways she was not fully aware of, a woman who would wear a ring like this. Becoming this woman felt easier than telling Patrick she did not like the ring and she was not this woman already. She never asked him how he chose it because she worried the truth was that he'd found it himself and was sure she'd love it. It would be better, she decided, to not know for sure, and to imagine instead that he had gone with his mother, who had picked it out of the glass case of some upscale jeweler across Central Park, and the salesman had convinced her it was perfect and then she had tried to convince Patrick. Even though he thought it may be too much for Elizabeth, he was persuaded by their expertise. In this story, it was hardly his choice at all.

Soon Elizabeth decided to like the ring, and soon after that, she hardly noticed it.

They married a few months later in Manhattan, a small ceremony in city hall with their parents and Patrick's two younger brothers and older sister, followed by a seven-course dinner at a dark French restaurant at Amsterdam and Seventy-Ninth. Elizabeth wore a cream cocktail dress she'd bought on sale at Macy's the week before. Neither of them wanted a big wedding, which relieved Elizabeth's parents and frustrated Patrick's. But his parents had hosted two lavish weddings for their children already, and his youngest brother would likely propose to his girlfriend soon, so they gave in without much trouble.

It all felt like a long time ago, now, to Elizabeth, though it wasn't at all. They'd just been married a few months when they moved to Anchorage, and in less than a year Elizabeth was pregnant, and in less than another year they had made parents of themselves. *He is my husband,* Elizabeth often thought now when she woke and found him sleeping next to her, when she had forgotten in her sleep that they now shared a bed, a house, a life. *This man is the father of my child.*

. . .

"What do you mean—what did you want her to say?" I asked Margot. Static ruffled our connection, and I remembered how far away she was, how much land and water lay between us. "What happened?"

"She just said, 'I'm twelve weeks pregnant.'"

They'd been walking around the pond, Margot continued, and Elizabeth told her in a short pause in their conversation, apropos nothing.

"Oh my god," Margot had said. Elizabeth had spoken so plainly, without charge or suspense, that it took Margot a moment to register her meaning. "Elizabeth! That's wonderful. Congratulations!"

"I hate being pregnant," Elizabeth said. "I feel like shit. I've felt like shit the entire time, before I even took the test. It's worse than it was with Phin, and it sucked with Phin, too. All I want to do is puke but I can't."

When she slept, she said, she dreamed of vomiting, and she'd wake herself up and hurry to the bathroom, unable to conjure up anything more than spit. Her digestion was so slow she felt like a whale. No foods sounded remotely appetizing, but she felt worst when hungry, so she forced herself to eat dry toast or crackers every thirty minutes. Nothing made her feel better this time, not even walking. She gagged as she ate and counted the bites left on her plate like a child she didn't want to raise.

When Elizabeth had been pregnant with Phin, she'd told Margot very early, just before six weeks. Margot was the first friend Elizabeth told—before she'd told her mother, even. So this time, as Elizabeth told Margot she was twelve weeks along, Margot wondered why she'd waited so much longer. Perhaps Margot should've suspected it; perhaps Elizabeth assumed Margot already knew. It was true that Elizabeth hadn't ordered beer the last time they went to Moose's Tooth with their husbands, three weeks before, and that she was seeming tired, and a little irritable, maybe, but Margot attributed that to Phin's difficulty sleeping lately and his new, sudden refusal of her breast milk. His refusal had made Elizabeth feel more hurt than she'd ever anticipated, as though this were the first of many things she would offer to her son that he would refuse until she could offer him nothing and he didn't need her at all.

"I just can't get excited about this one the way I could with Phin," Elizabeth said. "I know what it means now. I know what a chore they are. Two under two sounds like cruel and unusual punishment."

Margot resisted reminding Elizabeth that this baby was planned, this whole arrangement was planned, and that she was lucky, at thirty-seven years old, to have conceived so quickly and to have made it to twelve weeks with no complications. She was lucky to have a caring husband and health insurance and a stable, generous income to pay for everything they needed and day care and sitters and many things they didn't need as well, unlike the parents of so many of Margot's patients.

But Margot stayed silent as she listened, allowing her friend to speak of the fear and anger she would likely not express to anyone else.

As soon as Margot came home after the walk, she began to weep. She took Alex out of the stroller and lay him down in his crib, and he, mercifully, fell asleep with ease, as he watched her with more curiosity than sympathy as she wept and kissed him with wet cheeks. He was a good, sweet boy, like his father—she could tell already. Margot wasn't someone who cried often, even when she felt as though she should. She let herself cry. She sobbed until her stomach muscles ached. Her temples throbbed and her nose stuffed. Soon the crying no longer felt like emoting, but like a physical condition she couldn't stop on demand, like hiccups. She washed her face with cold water. She ran a hot shower. She made macaroni and cheese from a box, which she only allowed herself when ill and alone.

She fell asleep on the couch, and when Nick came home, he found her there, her eyelids swollen like she'd had an allergic reaction. Alex was whimpering from his crib with a soaking wet diaper. After Nick picked him up, changed him, and brought him out to her, Margot told Nick that Elizabeth was pregnant again, twelve weeks. He said, "Oh, I see, that's what's upsetting you"—and she said no, it wasn't that, and she truly didn't think it was.

By then she was done crying. Now she was angry. A new sort of headache came over her, so powerful she lay a hot compress on her forehead and swallowed three Tylenol and it did not cease. She wished she was still asleep and became angry at Nick for waking her.

She said to me on the phone, "Nick kept asking me why I was so upset, why I was so angry, it's okay to feel these things, and all that, but I wasn't really sure what was happening or what I was feeling. It didn't seem fair to have this response, and yet I was having it, against my will. When Nick said we're out of chicken so what are we having for dinner, I wanted to tell him shut the fuck up and leave me alone, figure out what to make for dinner yourself, don't always ask me as if it's my job alone, as if I don't work as much as you do, as if you're not a grown man—I thought you didn't want a wife like your mother but maybe you do so go ahead and find yourself one. I had the overwhelming desire to throw valuable things against the wall—vases and wineglasses, gifts from our wedding. I can't remember ever having that desire before. I wanted to see them all shatter.

"I think I just wish Elizabeth had said, 'I'm sorry about your miscarriage.' Or maybe not even anything about me, but something like, 'I know it will be hard and I feel like shit but I'm grateful to be pregnant.' It would've taken so little to say that. I think I would've said something like that to her—to let her know I was thinking of her, too. I feel selfish, selfish for thinking she's selfish."

Margot asked me what I thought she should do about it, if anything. I suggested that she talk to Elizabeth after her emotions settled. I said if I were Elizabeth I thought I'd like to know.

"I don't know," Margot said. "It might be best to just let it go. It'll be easier when I'm pregnant again, I'm sure. Maybe I will talk to her— I'll have to think about it."

"But tell me how you're feeling," she said after a heavy breath. "Excited for second trimester?"

A few days later, in a small exam room, I lay down in what looked like a dentist's chair and Isaac sat on the folding chair next to me, where I couldn't see him but I could hold his hand. A wide-screen TV was mounted on the wall for my view, and the tech, a woman no older than us with a round, pleasing face, spread warm gel with the wand over my slightly mounded stomach.

I wondered if Elizabeth was having the same test today, at this moment, in a room just like this.

At the first ultrasound, four weeks earlier, the baby had looked like a smudge in outer space. I had become convinced there was nothing inside me; it felt too good, too lucky to get pregnant on our first try. But there it was, a smudge in the right place with a beating heart. We hung the pictures on the fridge and were careful to protect them from splatter and finger grease. Now, on the TV, we could see the arms and legs and chin and the slightest suggestion of a nose. Its heart beat fast in the tiny chest. It kicked with both legs at a time. I tried to feel it move but I couldn't, not yet.

I thought to it, *Hey, baby love, it's so, so good to see you again.*

"Are its legs long?" I asked the tech. "They look so long to me."

"Maybe a little," she said, unconvinced. I knew if they weren't long now they would be long soon, long like Isaac's. No child of his could have short limbs.

"He's being uncooperative," she said. "I need him on his side."

"It's a boy?"

"Too early to tell."

Her face became less pleasing to me then, more sour and dull, and I resisted noting the pronoun or asking more questions, thinking, absurdly, that the more she liked me the healthier our baby would be. This was the ultrasound that, combined with my blood results, would tell us the chances it would have Down syndrome, or trisomy 18, or one of many other chromosomal abnormalities I couldn't name and didn't understand. Isaac was squeezing my hand hard, it almost hurt. I let him hold it.

He'd said to me late the night before, when I was unable to sleep, "There's no point in worrying, you know. Worrying protects against nothing. Just try to rest, baby, try to get some sleep." But he was awake, too, and he was awake when I fell asleep. He was still drawing light circles on my back.

I wondered what Elizabeth would do if her baby was not well.

In the parking lot of the medical center I texted the family group chat the results. From my mother, *What a relief!*; from my father, *great news thanks for letting us know*. Margot called and I let it go to voice mail: the third call from her in a month. Something had happened with Elizabeth, I thought, that's what she wants to talk about. I waited to call her back until we were home again. I told Isaac I'd just talk to her for a few minutes, then I'd help him with dinner, and I stepped outside where the service was better. I walked around the graduate apartment complex, peach stucco buildings and wide concrete paths. At that time, early evening, the air always smelled like sautéed garlic and burnt soy sauce, and children were calling out, but I could never hear what for.

"Anna? Can you hear me okay?" Margot asked. "I'm trying to link my phone to my car."

I could hear her, though I heard street sounds around her, too. She was driving home from work. She said she'd been thinking about me and wondering when the test was.

"It's wonderful news, really. That test terrified me. I didn't sleep at all the night before. I really didn't know what I'd do."

"Has Elizabeth had her test yet?" I asked.

"I don't know. I assume so. I assume she would've told me if something was wrong. But maybe not, actually." She laughed, but there was an edge to her tone. "I really have no idea if she'd tell me. Turns out I don't know her as well as I thought I did."

"What do you mean?"

I heard windshield wipers turning on, but the rain was silent. She didn't speak right away.

"The other day she told me a bunch of stuff about herself that she'd never told me before. Made me rethink everything."

"So you ended up talking to her?"

"After I talked to you about it, I knew you were right, I should talk to her. I thought at the very least it might just help get it out of my mind. Sometimes she just isn't very thoughtful, or she has a strange way of showing thoughtfulness—and I didn't want to resent her, you know, without giving her a chance to explain. I even rehearsed what I'd say to her," she said with a laugh, "but I couldn't figure out a way to say it that didn't sound whiny or unsympathetic, so I finally decided to just say that I've been having a hard time since the miscarriage, and how I'm worried about all the increased risks and I'm getting older, all that, and just see if maybe then she'd tell me a little more about what she was thinking, or not thinking, when we talked the other day. Then I'd just see how it went from there."

On their walk around the pond the day before, young sons in strollers, in the low afternoon sun after work, Margot told Elizabeth what she wanted to say, feeling nervous that it sounded as rehearsed as it was. When she finished, Margot waited for Elizabeth's response. Elizabeth had appeared to be listening, and listening sympathetically, but she said nothing after Margot stopped speaking. It was perhaps the longest silence, Margot told me, that had ever transpired between them. Margot wasn't sure what to say. She didn't know if the silence was hers to break. After a few more long moments, Margot laughed and said, "So anyway, how are you?"

"I'm all right," Elizabeth said, and they kept walking, their sons now quiet and still, maybe asleep. Elizabeth didn't say any more, and she looked ahead on the path, her face at rest, unbothered, as if she were walking alone. Margot walked alongside her in silence. An old man passed them, then a teenage couple, then the path was clear until the playground several yards ahead. Many children were playing there, screaming and running in circles, still manic from bright evenings, perhaps aware that soon the long nights would come. Their mothers watched from a bench, some in conversation with one another, others sitting alone. Few fathers. As they reached the jungle gym, Elizabeth said, without turning to look at Margot, "I've never told you about my old life, you know."

Before she was married to Patrick, she said, she was married to someone else.

As they walked around the pond, Elizabeth began to tell Margot some parts of her past that Margot already knew. She grew up as an only child in Orono, Maine. Her mother was a geology professor at the University of Maine in town, and her father was a journalist for the local newspaper until it went under several years ago. Elizabeth didn't hate Orono as much as all of her friends did. It was beautiful, in its way, with the old brick buildings, the Penobscot River to the east of town and the Pushaw Lake to the west, all the green in the summer and all the grays and whites and blues in the winter. Mack trucks from Florida, Alabama, New Jersey, drove past on I-95 on their way to New Brunswick and sometimes stopped for gas and rest in town. Orono was not far from the shore, but for most of the year the weather was too windy and raw for the beach, and it was too far from Portland for a day trip, so Elizabeth and her friends spent their weekends at discount movies on Sunday mornings or eating Chinese food in the mall food court while their parents shopped with younger siblings. Then, as Elizabeth and her friends grew older, there were bonfires in the woods in the summers and flip cup in basements during the winters.

In her small public school, Elizabeth was an excellent student and athlete—varsity in cross-country running, cross-country skiing, and track. She was good, even, by the state's standards, particularly in the 800, and hoped that she'd be able to run competitively in college, wherever that turned out to be. Her friends who hated Orono were not going to apply to the schools Elizabeth would apply to—the NES-CACs, some Ivies, maybe a few in California or Chicago. The fear of rejection alone seemed to discourage them from applying at all, though she wondered if some of them applied in secret, perhaps not even telling their parents. Only a few of her friends—the other sons and daughters of UMaine professors who didn't go to Gould Academy or boarding school in Massachusetts or Connecticut—would attend good and expensive private schools and come home to Orono only for school breaks and holidays until they married someone from any-where else. It was understood, though rarely spoken, that most of the students at Orono High would go to UMaine or Eastern Maine Com-munity, marry young, buy a three-bedroom clapboard and work at a small business in town and have two or three children as their parents steadily aged a few streets away, all living happily enough.

Elizabeth liked Orono because she knew she would leave and she would never return.

In high school, Elizabeth worked some weekend shifts at a café on the UMaine campus called Quad Coffee, in the building next to her mother's office. (This part, and the story that followed, Margot had never heard before.) Elizabeth liked working at the café. She had to wear a pin with her name on it and her hair up and shoes that covered her toes, but she could wear her trainers, jeans, and a hoodie, or a tank top if it was hot. The smell of coffee grounds and rooibos tea calmed her, and she found satisfaction in cleaning the kettles with vinegar and frothing milk into foam.

She liked watching the students work alone or gossip together at the small circular tables. They likely assumed she was one of them, and she let them assume it, not telling them that she was sixteen, then seventeen, and a local. Sometimes, watching the UMaine students study in the café, she felt a sense of superiority that she would never admit aloud, and then she'd feel ashamed for having felt superior for even a moment. Her mother often said that her students were brilliant—well, some of them—and Elizabeth believed her, but she assumed these were the exceptional ones, the ones who chose not to attend a more elite, private school anywhere else for some sympathetic reason. An ailing mother, perhaps. A gambling father.

The boy named Sam started coming into the café when Elizabeth was a junior. Elizabeth always asked his name for the order, though she remembered it the first time he ever told her. "Sam," he'd say, with his voice lilting up like it was a question. Or: "My name is Sam," as if he were about to shake her hand. He'd usually say, "How's it going," before he ordered, as many of the students did—but he, unlike the others, would wait for her response. He never said his last name, and she didn't ask. Sam. The name suited him perfectly.

He was her height, a little short for a boy, with hair between brown and blond that always seemed like it needed a cut, though it never grew past his ears or too far down the back of his neck. He wore a canvas jacket with red flannel lining and carried his books and laptop in a black JanSport backpack that was tearing at the seams, which made him look like the freshman that he was. He often came by in the late morning and ordered a light roast with no room for cream, and if he stayed into the afternoon, he'd order a decaf and an almond biscotti that he'd never finish. He sat at the table near the window, overlooking the quad, and if that table wasn't open, he'd sit near the front door. When he sat near the front door and she stood at the cash register, she could see his profile clearly. He had a bump on the bridge of his nose only visible from this angle.

One day in the spring, after Elizabeth was away for the weekend for the state track meet in Augusta, where she'd placed second with first only a half stride away, Sam came in at his usual time. He smiled and said, "You weren't here last Saturday. I was afraid you'd left." He looked instantly embarrassed that he'd said it aloud. She didn't tell him where she'd been, though she was proud of her performance. To tell him would be to tell him that she was a high school child. To tell him anything else would be to lie, and she didn't want to lie.

"I'm here," she said. "I'm not going anywhere." And in that moment she hoped this was true.

Every June for as long as Elizabeth could remember, her mother had hosted a party the week before graduation for the students she advised and some others who had taken several of her courses. Elizabeth liked to watch the students, who always felt much older than her, even as she approached their ages—but she mostly liked to watch her mother, her mother as professor, beloved, it seemed, and respected, maybe feared, by those who did not receive the grade from her they'd felt entitled to. These were the brilliant ones, Elizabeth knew. These were the students her mother loved. They were like her mother's other children, but in no way did they feel like Elizabeth's siblings; she never felt more like an only child than when they all came into her house and made it loud.

Elizabeth's father usually stayed in the kitchen during the parties. He was a quiet man, confident in his reporting and writing abilities but much less confident in social conversation, and he feared any awkwardness or misstep of his would make the students lose respect for his wife. So he helped by vacuuming and hiding piles of papers in pantry drawers and making sure there was always enough shrimp with cocktail sauce and crudités with ranch dressing and beers and wines and plastic cups.

Elizabeth liked to walk through the rooms, letting her mother introduce her as "my dear daughter." She wore a nice dress for the occasion, and a little makeup—mascara and tinted lip gloss and light cover-up under her eyes—wanting to show her mother's students, male and female, that she was prettier than the terrible portrait her mother had in her campus office of Elizabeth in seventh grade with braces and bangs. The boys, particularly after Elizabeth grew breasts, either avoided her altogether or spoke to her only when her mother was there, enforcing the interaction. When her mother would move to another group and abandon Elizabeth in conversation, the boys would flee back to their own kind with an embarrassment Elizabeth intuitively understood was their fear of her young, barely pubescent body and of their desire to possess it.

Sam came to the party the spring after he'd started to come to the café, one of the few freshmen invited. He was the first one to arrive. He wore the same jacket he always did, though it was hot, and a humidity was building that would break into strong storms the following evening. He wasn't wearing his backpack, and this made him seem, oddly, much younger and wider in the shoulders. He looked strange, and she tried to see if something else was different—but everything else about him was just as it'd always been. What was different was that he was here, in her living room. She'd never seen him outside the café, and he'd never seen her outside the café, that she knew of, without her hair up and a nametag on her chest.

When she saw him enter she was standing in the entryway to the kitchen, and she quickly took a step back so she couldn't see him and he couldn't see her. She heard her mother say, "Sam, welcome! Please, let me take your coat."

"Your house is beautiful," he said, in the way all the students said the house was beautiful, though it was modest, a university-owned

Colonial like all the others on the street, and all the art on the walls were prints. Elizabeth hid in the kitchen with her father, busying herself with putting away the dishes that weren't yet dry, suddenly hating her dress, a blue rayon sack, but she was unable to leave the kitchen to go to the stairs to her room to change without being seen. What dress would she change into, anyway? They were all awful, the dresses of children, of foolish girls. Her nerves coiled and she thought she'd have to use the bathroom—but that, too, was behind him, and she couldn't bear the thought of anyone hearing her, of him hearing her.

When more students arrived and her father said for the second time, "Really, Elizabeth, I've got this under control, why don't you go enjoy yourself?" she left the kitchen and walked through the living room. She poured herself a half glass of chardonnay—permitted to her on occasions like this—and she scanned the room, but she couldn't see Sam. Of course, he'd seen the picture of her on the mantel, the one of her running with pale legs and a slack mouth, and left. Of course, he wasn't thinking of her at all, didn't notice the picture, and he had somewhere else to be, with someone else, a brilliant Comp Lit or French major who was beautiful in a way Elizabeth would never be.

"Elizabeth."

She turned around.

"Hey," he said. "I hoped you'd be here."

"Sam. Hi. You're here. Why are you here?"

"Connelly's going to be my advisor," he said. "Well, I hope so. Professor Connelly, I mean. She invited me."

Elizabeth nodded and tried to think of anything to say. He was wearing a blue button-up that she'd never seen on him before; he might have bought it for this occasion. It was hard to look at him and hard to not look at him.

"I saw the picture of you in Professor Connelly's office," he said.

"I've seen it a lot before, it's right next to her computer. But for some reason it wasn't until the other day that I realized the Elizabeth in the picture was familiar and that it was the Elizabeth from Quad Coffee. I felt stupid for not having put it together before. There aren't a lot of girls named Elizabeth. I mean, I guess there are, but not many that go by Elizabeth—at least, none that I can think of."

He stopped talking and quickly took a sip from his beer. "I felt creepy," he continued, "like I'd stalked you without meaning to, and I didn't know how to tell you that I knew who you were without sounding even creepier. When Professor Connelly invited me to this party, I figured you'd be here, and I thought I'd just pretend that I made the connection right here. But I've already blown it by telling you. I'm a terrible liar. You'd think that would be a good thing but it's not, really."

"I didn't know you were her student."

"There's no reason you would know."

He sipped his beer again. He picked at the bottle's label with his thumbnail; small bits of paper fell on the floor, but he didn't seem to notice them. He was more nervous than she was, and this gave her a little thrill. She tried to straighten her spine without making it look like she was sticking out her breasts. They'd never stood so close to each other. One of his eyebrows was barely thicker than the other, and even though it was spring now and felt like summer, he smelled like winter, like old wood smoke.

They didn't talk for long. His friend soon came over to him, and before Sam could introduce them she fled again to the kitchen, where she tried to listen to Sam's voice below the others and could not hear it. By the time she went back out, he was gone.

"How do you know Sam Lemieux?" her mother asked her later, as they cleared the dishes and ate the last of the shrimp standing in the kitchen.

"I don't," said Elizabeth. "He just comes into Quad Coffee sometimes."

"I see," said her mother, her lipstick now pale and her shoes off. "He's a sweet kid. Smart, too."

Her mother ate another shrimp, and didn't offer anything more about Sam Lemieux, Sam Lemieux, Sam Lemieux, and Elizabeth did not ask.

"That was the last we saw each other before he left for the summer," Elizabeth told Margot. He went home to Presque Isle, she later learned, where he read ahead for classes he'd take in the fall and worked on repairing his father's old house so it'd be suitable to sell; he'd planned to use some of the profits to pay for whatever his scholarships wouldn't cover. After Elizabeth didn't see Sam for a few weeks, she thought of him rarely, and soon she was spending nights with a boy on the track team, a rising junior and the anchor in the four by four. He was cute and fast, and kind enough, but by early August she had grown tired of watching movies in his basement, and irritated with his inability and lack of interest in pleasing her as she pleased him. She spent the last days of the summer running early in the morning as steam rose off the river, and working on her college essays in the afternoon, trying to craft a narrative of her life so far and identifying what made her interesting, exceptional, and finding it increasingly difficult to tell what, exactly, made her different from all the other good New England girls applying to good New England schools.

When Sam returned in the fall, and she resumed her weekend hours at the café, they began talking more than they had before. He sometimes held up the line without meaning to, so when it was slow, she would go to his table to clear his cup, and they'd talk for longer there. She stood at his table, never sitting. "What are you reading?" she'd ask him, and he'd tell her about geochemical cycles or sedimentology with fluency and passion, and not as if he were explaining it to a child. He'd ask her, in turn, about track, and about how she was healing from her tendonitis, with what seemed like genuine interest. He was attentive to her, but she had trouble determining whether or not he was attracted to her, and if he even saw her as a viable romantic prospect. She was eighteen now, a high school senior, she reminded herself, and he was a college sophomore, and this distance began to feel less and less significant. She was probably older than a few freshmen, and certainly more mature than many of them, maybe most. Sam offered to look over her personal statement if she wanted, but she declined. She was afraid that he may find her to be a better writer than he was, and, if she were, she did not want either of them to be embarrassed by this.

By spring, she was accepted into most of the schools she applied to, some with generous packages and all with invitations to join the track team. She was deciding between Bates, Amherst, and Tufts, and after much deliberation, she decided to go to Amherst, which offered the best aid of the three. She would spend the summer in Orono and leave in late August, a week before classes started, to do the freshman hiking trip along a short stretch of the Appalachian Trail. Sam received a summer fellowship to research coastal erosions near Searsport, an hour south, and then he'd stay at Orono for his last two years; after he graduated, he would continue to live in Orono, if there was an opportunity for more funded research, otherwise he would move somewhere else. The opacity of the mid-distance future did not seem to concern him. Elizabeth liked this about him, she even envied it. She had always felt as though the years ahead had to be conquered with meticulous planning, or else her life would stall out and she would hardly continue to exist at all.

They did not speak of their futures in her last days at the café.

They spoke of anything else, though all she could think when she saw him was that this may be the last time.

"I still want to see you," she said on one of her last shifts as she cleared his mug. The café closed a week after the spring term ended, then only the large dining halls stayed open for the summer students. He had been coming in less frequently. Her nerves had gone, replaced by a new kind of bravery. Rejection no longer scared her as much as becoming a woman who does not say what it is she wants, who would live forever in discontentment, moved by the wills of others and never by her own. She feared that if she didn't become this woman now, then she never would—the self she was when she went to college may harden and calcify, grow resistant to change. Suddenly, that spring, for reasons she couldn't quite understand, she no longer felt like a girl. It was not difficult to say to him, in the end, after rehearsing it in the shower, on her drives to and from the café, in the moments before sleep. From then on, she'd always found it much harder to lie or silence her desires than to speak the truth.

"I still want to see you, too," he said. "I've been wanting to see you."

That summer they spent hours and hours on his futon mattress on the floor of his narrow single dorm room with a small window facing the parking lot and the low mountains behind it. They ate takeout burrito bowls from Green Gringo's on the futon, they watched movies on his laptop on the futon, they listened to music with closed eyes on the futon, always touching at least two points on each other's body. The room was stuffy and hot, and the drugstore fans they set around the room were loud and ineffective, so they dipped washcloths in bowls of ice water and pressed them against the backs of their necks.

It was so easy to be with him, but not so easy that the ease unnerved her. She enjoyed sex with him in a way she had never enjoyed sex before. Sam was attentive, and gentle, though just as eager and sometimes clumsy like the high school boys, but she didn't care. He touched her before he entered her, and she melted into his hand. He gave her the first orgasm that she didn't give herself. When she'd wake next to him in the morning, she did not worry about her breath or her naked eyes, the spots of orange pigment she always covered with concealer.

"You are so beautiful," he'd say as they woke together. "You have no idea how beautiful you are."

Some days she went with him to the coast, and as he gathered samples of sand and made measurements of schist outcrops with the other students on fellowship and his professor, an old friend of Elizabeth's mother, she would run along the rocky shore and skinny pot-holed streets, and when she grew tired, she read novels in the Searsport public library until Sam was ready to drive back. Elizabeth's parents weren't explicitly approving of her being with Sam, but they weren't explicitly disapproving, either. Her mother liked Sam and her father trusted her mother's assessment. And her parents probably figured that it would be a short thing, anyway, since Elizabeth would be leaving for Amherst by the summer's end, and Sam would stay here, and even if they tried to stay together it wouldn't last the distance and she'd meet another boy soon. Sam would become a boy of the past, perhaps only seen on winter breaks until he graduated and then never again.

Elizabeth also believed, in those first weeks of the summer, this was how it would unfold between them. It pained her to acknowledge that he was not someone she could be with, not in a true sense. His parents were not professors and journalists. He mended his peeling sneaker soles with Duct tape, seeing no reason to purchase a new pair when they still served their purpose. He had an accent, though slight, of the northern plains. His accent did not bother her—she adored it, when he opened his *r's*—but it served as an unsolicited reminder that he was not for her.

That is, until it didn't. The weeks passed them by, and his accent faded until she hardly heard it at all.

When Elizabeth packed, she wept, but she kept packing, and at the end of August, when it was already cooler and the nights longer and it smelled like fall, she and Sam said goodbye in a heat of kisses in his doorway at dusk. They had always known this would happen, they had agreed from the beginning, as if the agreement would prevent them from falling in love. She loved him, as best she could tell. She never told him aloud, and he never told her, either. He was not her boyfriend and she was not his girlfriend; they were something different, both bigger and smaller, but as she sat in the back seat of her father's Buick as her parents drove her to Massachusetts, with no radio on and the trunk and footwells full of books and shoes and new and old clothes, she believed she would never fall in love again.

"And I don't think I ever did," Elizabeth said to Margot with a small laugh, pausing to unzip her fleece halfway. The walk had warmed them even as the afternoon cooled into evening. "Not in the same way, anyway."

Sam sent the first email. Elizabeth had never read his writing before, and it wasn't what she expected. It was elegant in its simplicity, and at times beautiful; in all the emails that followed, she was newly surprised and pleased by this quality as he described his day, if it was raining or snowing or clear, and which friend he saw and what their conversation made him think about after the friend had left. *Dear Eliz-abeth*, they always began. As she moved through her day, classes and dining hall meals and track practice, *Gilmore Girls* with her teammates, hall parties with PBR kegs and box wine, she thought of how she would explain it to him in a way that made it sound less dull than it really was. Sometimes she did something just to write to him about it—took a drive to a lake she'd seen on a map, or run off trail, using the sun's angle and trees with distinctive roots to guide her way back. When she was running in the woods, she could pretend she was home, near him, she had never left; but the Massachusetts woods were not the same, more maple and fewer pine, and without the sense that you could run and run and never touch another town.

Though she met many cute, intelligent boys at Amherst who were humble enough, despite their wealth and talents, and she sometimes let them kiss her, she only wanted to be with Sam. When she missed him the most, at night after her roommate had gone to sleep and bass shook the ceiling above her, she'd read their emails to each other on the bright screen in the dark room. She savored lines he wrote that made her remember what it was like to lie with him on the futon, the way he looked at her when she woke.

There's a new barista on the weekends. His name is Jerry. I now do my work on the third floor of the library, next to the windows that look over the river.

Another: *I went to Deer Isle with my seminar on Saturday. We looked at the red marble beds. They are over five hundred million years old. It had been raining in the morning so they were slick and had a shine on them like gloss. I wished I could bring some back for you.*

And her favorite, the line she read over and over and over: *Every night before I sleep I think about you.*

One weekend, after fall midterms, he called her. They'd only spoken a few times by phone since she'd left—they both thought hearing the other's voice would make it harder—and it had, but not hearing it had been even worse. "Elizabeth," he said. His voice was clear and close, the only sound in her ear. "I miss you. I'm trying not to miss you but it's not working. I'd like to see you, if you want to see me. There's a bus from here to Boston that's only six hours. I can come next weekend. We can meet there, if you wanted to, or I can find a bus that will take me closer to you—" and she said yes, please, please come, I'll meet you in Boston, and they both bought bus tickets and began counting the days.

He kissed her at South Station with his bags still in his hands. They forgot to be tentative. Right there, she told him she loved him, and he said he loved her, too. They said it many times, the words were eager to escape their mouths. They spent the night in a discount hotel near Fenway and walked the city neither of them knew with gloved hands clasped. It was cold, and the trees in the city were bare and the restaurants expensive, so they spent most of the day in the double bed with scratchy sheets, where it was warm in the day and too hot at night.

They examined each other with their eyes and hands as they lay, in the evening, morning, and early afternoon, seeing how they had changed in their time apart—it'd only been a season, but they both felt older, to themselves and to each other. Sam had lost some of his boyish timidity. He kissed her and told her he loved her and had sex with her with less reservation than he had in the summer. Rather than feeling jealous of the women he must've kissed and slept with in their time apart to account for these changes in his touch, Elizabeth liked that he'd tried to be with other women and it had only made him certain that he wanted to be with her. She noticed that as she spoke to him, about anything—the social tensions on the track team, the professors who could somehow simultaneously make her feel gifted and ordinary—she didn't worry if she was being eloquent or interesting. This wasn't a change, exactly, from how she'd felt with him in the summer, but she had a newfound appreciation for this effect he had on her. In conversations at Amherst, both in and out of seminars, she often felt her peers were evaluating her on a rubric she didn't have access to, and she never knew her score.

As Elizabeth and Sam lay in bed in the morning before he left, she said, "I want to try to stay with you, if you want to try. I hate the distance but it can't be worse than not having you at all."

"I want to try, too," he said. "I love you too much to not try."

So for two years, they stayed together long distance, visiting on breaks and some weekends, calling and emailing whenever they could. As soon as Orono put up a cell tower he bought a Nokia mobile so they could talk in the unfilled hours between classes, over lunch, on her walk from practice at the field house to her dorm. When he graduated, he moved to her. He'd been offered a year-long fellowship to continue his research in Orono, but he declined it without deliberation. His father's old house had sold, after they lowered the price twice, and he had just enough money to support himself for the summer until he found a job.

She moved off campus and they rented the upstairs apartment of a small Victorian in Hadley, a one-bedroom with hardwood floors and a bay window in the kitchen. They went to thrift stores and found a desk, a bureau, a kitchen table, all different hues of wood with minor scratches. The place sometimes held the smell of cigarette smoke from the downstairs neighbor, a single man who was also the landlord, so Elizabeth bought many spider plants and terracotta pots from the nursery and placed them in all the windowsills. They bought cookware from Stop & Shop as they needed it, spatulas and measuring cups, and soon they had an apartment that felt like an apartment more than a dorm. He had his side of the bed and she had hers.

They rarely fell asleep or woke at the same time, and for the first few weeks they tolerated the disturbances. He assumed she'd adjust to his pattern and she assumed he'd adjust to hers. They never could get used to sleeping and rising at the same time, but soon they were not as disturbed by the others' movements, and they often took a brief nap together on weekend afternoons, hardly asleep. Elizabeth would lay her head on Sam's chest and his hand would rest in her hair, and when she closed her eyes she felt as though they were on that futon mattress in his narrow dorm room, in a summer that was quickly moving further into the past.

Sam applied to work in cafés and restaurants all over the valley, but he found that very few of them were hiring, particularly for someone with no food service experience. He applied to retail stores and eventually found a job at Pioneer Books, an independent bookstore in Northampton that sold both new and lightly used volumes. It was a fine job, with decent hours and pay a little above minimum wage, though his coworkers—all Smith and Amherst and Hampshire students or recent alums and all thinking of applying to English PhD or MFA programs—often made it clear to Sam and to themselves that their job there was just temporary, and soon they would become the intellectual professionals they felt entitled to become. Through subtle comments and gestures, it became clear that many of them spent time with one another outside of work, even those hired after Sam. The first and only question any of them seemed to care about was where he went to college, and when he told them, they all said, "oh," with the same expression of confusion. They didn't seem to know what else to say. They did not say: "I visited there and loved it," or "my best friend from high school went there, do you know Piper Green?" as he'd heard them say to others, when the answer was more legible, more satisfactory.

"They think I'm stupid," he told Elizabeth more than once when they were both home, making dinner. "Stupid and poor. And they're right."

"You don't know that. You don't know what they think. Maybe they sense that you don't like them so they keep their distance."

"I do know what they think," said Sam, and Elizabeth did not push back anymore. She knew this world and she knew he was right, they probably did view him with judgment and pity, they'd hear his accent and mistake it for character, just as she had, not too long before.

It was around then that Elizabeth began to notice Sam growing quiet. He was never a very talkative or outgoing boy, but when they were alone together, he seemed to forget his shyness and spoke to Elizabeth fluidly and vulnerably. But now he was quiet around her, too. At first, it was just in the mornings, as he brewed coffee and made instant oatmeal and she put away the dishes from the night before. It was as if he'd forgotten she was in the room, and didn't seem to hear her when she was speaking. When she asked him what he was thinking about he said he didn't know—and it seemed like he truly did not know, rather than hiding his thought. Then it was in the evenings, too, after he came home from the bookstore. He'd take a shower without first calling her name to see if she was home, and he always seemed surprised that she was, though her schedule had not changed. By her junior year, Elizabeth was sure that she wanted to go to med school. She was a biology major, but she would still need to take more courses and wanted time to study for the MCAT, so after college she planned to enroll in the postbac program at Elms College in Chicopee, about a half-hour drive south, before applying to schools.

"You can go wherever you want," he'd say, his support always earnest and effortless. "You'll get in anywhere. I say apply all over and pick the best one and I'll go wherever you go."

But it was after conversations about med school that he would become quiet, and sometimes a little short-tempered, though he always denied she'd upset him or that he was in a poor mood when she asked.

"It's not anything having to do with you," he'd say, holding his temples. "I'm just not sleeping well, I need to work out. You didn't do anything." He'd leave to go on a run, if it was warm enough, or to the gym, or drive to Stop & Shop to get ingredients for dinner. By the time he'd come home, his mood was normal, even pleasant. Elizabeth did not want to ask him about his sourness for fear the question might inspire its return.

Some days, when Sam fell quiet like this, Elizabeth thought about what he had told her about his family and his life before he came to Orono and met her in the café. She knew he grew up in Presque Isle and he hated it. When he was in middle school, his mother died of colorectal cancer after refusing all treatments. His father had quickly remarried another woman, the clerk at the post office—he was a mail carrier—who Sam suspected he had started sleeping with when his mother was ill but not yet dead. Sam's father then spent most of his time with his new wife, at her apartment, and so for his last two years of high school Sam lived alone in the house he grew up in. Living alone was preferable to living with his father without his mother, he said, but he never said more than that. Sam had a brother, Leland, who was eight years older. Leland had a different father—their mother's high school boyfriend who never knew Leland had been born—and he spent most of Sam's adolescence living in Boston and working as a chef. After their mother died, they stopped being brothers—that was how Sam put it. Leland stopped visiting and no longer spoke to Sam and Sam had little desire to speak to him. There didn't seem to be animosity between them, as Sam described it, so much as an understanding that they had been brothers because they shared a mother and now their mother was dead. Sam didn't know what state Leland lived in now, and if he had a family or ever became a successful chef. He could look him up, he supposed, but he had little interest in doing so because it wouldn't, really, tell him anything about his brother and what it might have been like if the loss of their mother had been the beginning of a stronger brotherhood rather than the end of a tenuous one.

Recalling this, Elizabeth gleaned little insight, and most often, by the end of the afternoon or evening, when Sam was again affectionate—there was never a night that he did not kiss her before he turned to sleep, that he did not tell her he loved her—her love for him was affirmed and strengthened, and she slept well.

Sam proposed the week Elizabeth graduated. In the morning, the day after her parents had left town, he lay in bed with her until she woke. He held her hand and pressed into her palm a ring from a hollowed quarter he'd seen at a garage sale the previous month, a temporary ring until she found one she liked. He'd bought one for himself, too.

"Are you sure?" she asked, slipping the ring on her finger.

"Yes," he said. "Yes, yes of course. You are the only thing I know I want for sure."

She loved the ring. The ridges were dulled, and it smelled like copper, and though it was a little sharp on the underside of her finger, it fit well. She wore it for several months, finding pleasure in watching her friends decide whether or not to comment on the ring, to ask whether or not she would ever get a real one. They hadn't been looking for a real ring, until one day she and Sam passed an antique shop in Easthampton with a gold band in the window. In the back of the store, in a drawer of jewels, they found a bigger ring, the gold slightly darker and the band broader than the other. It was meant for a man or a larger woman, they couldn't tell, and neither of them cared. His ring fit as it was, but the one in the window was still wide enough to fall off her finger when she shook it, so she sized it down, an expense that cost more than the ring itself. She liked knowing that it had once belonged to someone else, even if the marriage had been unhappy, or had been happy but ended with an untimely death—or maybe the death wasn't untimely, but they were both very old, and still in love, and the grown children did not want their parent to be buried with a metal that would not decay. She liked that she could give the ring another life, another marriage.

In the fall they wed in Orono at the town hall with her parents. Sam wanted the wedding to be small. He said his concern was money— he had none to offer and he felt awkward having her parents pay—but Elizabeth suspected he also wanted a small wedding because he didn't want to invite his family and he didn't want to be seen having no family. They didn't have many mutual friends they'd want to celebrate with, anyway. Most of her college friends had moved away after graduation, and those that stayed nearby she hadn't seen as often as she thought she would. She was saddened to realize that track and shared classes had been what bound them together much more than mutual affection. Her high school friends, too, were now distant acquaintances. So a small wedding was not a point of contention.

After the short ceremony they ate at the nicest restaurant in town, Blackboard Grille, a repurposed schoolhouse owned by an old couple from Prince Edward Island. The four of them ordered the artisan cheeseboard, lobsters with hand-cut fries, and two pitchers of Allagash White and chocolate sundaes for dessert. They all became a little drunk, and laughed easily—including Elizabeth's father, who, by this point, no longer feared that any fault of his would affect any respect for his wife, who wasn't Sam's professor anymore, anyway. "To you both," her father said, raising his drink, and they clinked their glasses. When the waitress brought the check, Elizabeth's mother asked if she would take a picture of the four of them together with her compact camera. They all blinked at the flash. Elizabeth and Sam spent the night in the upscale hotel in Bangor with a king bed, a gift from her parents, and the next morning they woke early, hungover, and drove the long drive back to their apartment in Hadley, married and giddy.

The wedding was not dissimilar to her wedding to Patrick, Elizabeth said to Margot, though Patrick didn't know that. As she stood and recited her vows to Patrick, almost three years ago now, she was overwhelmed with vivid details of her wedding to Sam that she had not thought of in many years. Sam had combed his hair in a different way than he had ever before, so that his forehead and brow seemed too wide, and his navy sports jacket was a little too long in the arms. He'd seemed nervous like he had when they spoke at her mother's party and he hadn't seemed since. Her parents wore the outfits they'd worn to work events—her mother in a floral cotton dress and her father in a fishbone blazer—and they did not seem unhappy. Elizabeth wore a lavender summer dress she already owned, but new shoes, beige espadrille wedges, on sale as the warm season was now coming to an end. Her feet were cold but she loved how her crimson-painted toes looked against the canvas.

As she married Patrick, remembering her wedding to Sam, she looked at the Manhattan courtroom, newer and smaller than Orono's, her diamond ring with sapphires on either side, her cream dress from Macy's, her new husband with dark hair cut with clean lines and a suit that fit him perfectly, and her parents, markedly older in the thirteen years since their daughter's first wedding, both wearing new clothes with finer materials to impress Patrick's parents (a silk tie on her father, a fitted satin dress on her mother), and she was able to return to the self that she was now, even if it was not so different from the self she was then.

———

As Elizabeth told all this to Margot, she was steady in her telling. She would sometimes pause for a moment, as if unsure what to leave out and what to share. In some places, Margot felt she moved too quickly, or too slowly, and she wanted to ask a question but did not want to interrupt. Margot had the sense that Elizabeth had never told the story as she told it now. The version she'd told to Patrick was different—not untrue, but maybe condensed, the particular nature of her affection for Sam redacted. They had finished the loop around the pond, walking slower than they usually did. Margot feared that when the walk ended, so would Elizabeth's story, and if she didn't finish it now, she never would. Margot had often sensed that Elizabeth enjoyed their time together, she told me on the phone, but that she was ready for it to be over when it was over, if not a little while before. But when Margot walked Elizabeth back to her house, Elizabeth invited her in for tea, and Margot accepted.

Their small sons were still asleep in their strollers. Though the naps were late in the day and likely to disturb their nights' sleep, their mothers let them sleep where they were, sometimes pushing the strollers back and forth in the living room if they stirred. Elizabeth and Margot sat on the couch, speaking more quietly now, as the hot mugs of peppermint tea warmed their cool hands, and Elizabeth absently touched the mound of her stomach, barely visible under her cable knit sweater.

"I can hardly believe," Elizabeth said to Margot, "that Sam was only twenty-five then. I think of him still as so much older. I thought he should know what he wanted in life by that point. I began to ask him what he would do when I went to med school. He never had an answer, so he wouldn't respond at all. I asked if he regretted not taking

45

the post-grad fellowship in Orono, and he always said no, of course not, why would I even ask that? It was clear I was annoying him, so I stopped asking. If he was ever jealous of me for going to a good school, for knowing what I wanted and knowing I could get it, if he ever thought I was just like his coworkers at the bookstore, then he never said so. I never sensed he wanted me to be lesser than him. I would never have married him if he did.

"There were times when he wanted to do so many things—apply to PhDs in geology, or try working for the Massachusetts Department of Environmental Protection, or the parks, or a startup that had something to do with sustainability. He even mentioned a few times that he could go to med school with me, that maybe he would have the mind for it, and I agreed that he was certainly intelligent enough to go. He just needed to take the courses. But he never applied to anything. He acted as if everywhere had already rejected him. He'd say he didn't want to work anywhere, he wasn't qualified for anything, he'd have to start from scratch, maybe he was stupid for majoring in geology at UMaine, a useless major at a shit school, as he called it. He should've majored in economics, or engineering, something that could actually get him a job. But he made enough at the bookstore to pay his half of rent, and my parents gave me some money to help me pay for my post-bac classes. They gave me a little more than he knew. I also did some tutoring for my professor's kids, and they paid well. So we were making it by just fine. It would all be temporary, anyway, I kept reminding him. We'd just stay in Hadley for two more years, and then I'd be in med school and we'd be in a new city. We'd figure it out there, I'd tell him, and he always agreed that we would. Then he started talking about wanting a baby."

Elizabeth wanted a baby, too, at some vague point in the future when she was done with med school and Sam had found a job that he liked and they had a house and some savings. Well, she thought she wanted one, when asked, though she could be fine without one, too. A baby wasn't an object whose absence she felt at present, and it wasn't a thing she thought she would need to be happy, or even content and fulfilled, when she was older. She rarely thought about it. She and Sam hardly ever talked about babies while they were dating, and even when they were engaged, but he seemed to want a baby at a similar vague point in the future, maybe two babies—possibly three, if all went well. They would discuss that all in the years ahead. Not now, not anytime soon.

But now he was talking about having a baby soon—why didn't they just try to conceive in the next few months, he started to say, while they were still young and energetic, and weren't yet tied to long work hours. "Babies are cheap. Kids are expensive," he reasoned one night, as they brushed their teeth before bed. "By the time we have a kid we'd have enough money to support it. You'll be a doctor. I'll be something, too. I say we start trying tonight," he said, kissing her cheek, then neck, under her earlobe, the place where the slightest touch made her instantly wet.

Elizabeth was becoming increasingly uncertain if Sam meant what he said, or if he was trying on standpoints, seeing how they felt on his tongue before fully subscribing to them. She was unsure if he had always done this and she was just now noticing. "I think being a father is the thing I'm meant to do," he'd say with excited conviction. "This is the job I've been looking for. I just don't know why it took me so long to realize it. But now that I see it, it's the clearest thing." And it soon became clear to Elizabeth that he was serious about this, it was not an idea or a joke now if it had ever been at all. If he had his way, she would stop taking the pill right away. So Elizabeth tried to be firmer when she told Sam that though she loved the idea of having a baby with him, and though she loved his excitement about fatherhood, now was not the time, and they would still be young and energetic for several years to come.

Rather than retreat from the topic then, as she expected him to do, he continued to talk to her about the baby as if it were already decided, as if she'd forgotten an agreement. When she was pregnant, he'd put in an air conditioner in the bedroom. When the baby came, they'd need to buy a bigger car with more safety features, maybe a Subaru Outback. Elizabeth recognized this tactic of persuasion: fantasizing a reality into existence until the other could no longer see the previous vision with as much clarity. She had sometimes seen her father employ this on her mother when purchasing a new computer, or deciding where to go on vacation, and, much to Elizabeth's irritation, it was always successful—they bought the Macbook Pro, they went to Sanibel Island, and the Lenovo and San Diego were forgotten or now seen as ideas that were never really going to pan out, anyway. But she'd never seen Sam try it.

And it worked. Despite her awareness of his strategy, she began thinking about babies and seeing babies and pregnant women and women with toddlers and school-aged children. She began dreaming about babies and pausing over baby clothes and toys at sidewalk sales and thrift stores, though she never bought any, more out of a newfound superstition of buying clothes for an unconceived baby than because of the encouragement it would give Sam. If she were going to have a baby, she wanted to have more than one baby—she never wanted her child to be an only child as she had been—and since it wouldn't be wise to have another baby until after residency, several years and years in the future, perhaps it did make sense to have her first baby now, (she thought as she passed a woman on the sidewalk with an infant strapped to her full breasts and her husband, she assumed, pushing a sleeping toddler in the stroller), when she and Sam both had time to care for it, and her parents were in good health to help out. She could have her second child, then, around thirty.

Her first child would have the pleasure of their parents' attention and then be able to be an older sister (she imagined it as a girl), and her second child (also a girl), would be younger by enough that the girls would not compete with each other over friends, teachers' affections, boys. They would be able emerge into whatever sorts of women they desired to become—not out of opposition to or emulation of each other.

And her fertility was not something she took for granted. Her parents had had difficulty conceiving; the details of this part of their life had always remained oblique, though her mother had said a few times how she wished they had started trying much earlier than they did. Elizabeth's mother was raised by her Italian father and Indian mother in Brooklyn, the middle of five siblings, and her father was an Irish-Catholic from central Maine, the second oldest of seven. They'd both wanted a large family saturated with the love and clamor of their own childhoods, only with more money and less chaos. But it did not appear. Perhaps, Elizabeth thought in those days of contemplation, if her parents had started trying at the age Elizabeth was now, rather than waiting until her mother finished her PhD and her father was salaried rather than freelancing, Elizabeth would have the brothers and sisters she and her parents had so strongly hoped would come.

In the end, what she believed really convinced her, she said to Margot, was not the fantasy of a baby itself so much as what this fantasy had already done to Sam. He seemed happier than she'd seen him in years. He signed up for the GRE and studied at night, though he was not even sure what type of grad program he would apply to, and he worked longer hours at the bookstore without complaint, wanting to save up more money. He seemed to even look at Elizabeth in a new way, or, rather, in the old way, the way he would look at her at the café or at her mother's party or in that summer on his futon mattress in his narrow dorm room. It was a look that she hadn't realized had departed until its return.

They started trying in the spring. She stopped taking the pill and then counted fourteen days back from her expected period and checked the texture of the mucus in her underwear, and when it looked like raw egg whites, as all the websites described it, she and Sam tried to have sex at least once a day for a week. Elizabeth tutored in the evenings, mostly, and Sam worked at the bookstore during the day, so they woke early for sex, though neither of them would prefer sex in the morning. By the end of the week, it took him longer to finish, and she had to sigh in new ways and whisper into his ear desires she would never repeat to help him come faster, before she began to chafe. They only had missionary sex, and afterwards, rather than getting up to pee to avoid a UTI, Sam slid a pillow under her hips and she lay there for twenty minutes as he showered and dressed, made eggs for both of them, and kissed her on the forehead and lips before he left for work.

As she lay, listening to the shower, to the spatula scrape the skillet, she imagined sperm like she'd seen in her high school textbooks swimming fast with frantic tails up into her body, a sea of deep magenta, and she'd press her hand over her uterus, making sure her hips were lifted, trying to relax her cervix, trying to feel for the sperm's pointed head burrowing into her egg, trying to feel the chromosomes' clasp, feeling both a thrill and a terror at the thought that her body might be making a person and she did not know what that person would become.

A day after her period did not come, she walked fast to the Rite Aid three blocks away, bought a test and peed on the stick in the bathroom at the back of the store. She lay the test on the sink and watched. Two pink lines appeared almost immediately. Dark pink, uncompromising.

She stared at the test for a long time. This didn't seem real. Her body felt no different. It had not betrayed a hint of disturbance or infiltration.

It didn't matter if she felt pregnant or not. She was pregnant.

She threw out the stick and covered it with paper towels and washed her hands. For the rest of the day, as she attended her postbac class and tutored a new student on algebra equations she barely remembered, and a knot in her left shoulder radiated red up to her temple, Elizabeth repeated the thought, *I'm pregnant, I'm pregnant,* willing herself to believe this, unsure what emotions accompanied it. It was not as simple as relief that they could and had conceived, and it was not as simple as regret, or dread, of what she had done to herself. Of what could be undone.

She waited to tell Sam until he came home in the late afternoon. After he set down his backpack and took off his coat and drank a glass of water, she stood in the kitchen and said, "I'm pregnant."

"Are you sure?" he asked. Tears filled his eyes and his face turned crimson.

"Yes, I'm sure," she said. "I took a test this morning."

He kissed her deep, lifted her up, then put her down, terrified to shake the little thing loose. It was then that she began to feel happy more than anything else, a happiness that felt like her own rather than a happiness on behalf of Sam. Her body was indeed making a baby and she did not know what that baby would be, and she would spend her life wanting to know this baby, child, teenager, adult, learning to know this baby again and again.

That night, in bed before sleep, with his hand on her flat stomach, she tried to imagine this baby's face, hair, hands, feet, and she was unable to see anything other than babies she already knew, composites of babies she did not know, not resembling herself or Sam in the least.

"Can you see it?" she asked. "Can you imagine what it will look like?"

"Yes," he said. "I can see it perfectly. I can't describe it, really, but I can see it so well—I wish I could show you."

Soon she began to feel ill. First in the afternoons, then the evenings, then the mornings and all through the night. She spent her twenty-fourth birthday in a dizzy daze, half-asleep and half-awake, watching episodes of *How I Met Your Mother* she instantly forgot. Sam rented movies from the library he thought would make her laugh, *Little Miss Sunshine* and *The 40-Year-Old Virgin*, bought all the groceries, sometimes going to the store twice in one day if she felt suddenly unable to eat anything in the house. He never made a critical comment about her clothing, now all leggings and loose sweaters, and the lack of makeup and the growing pimples on her forehead and chin and the dark veins in her breasts.

She began to show early. First, the mound seemed like bloat, and then it rose and hardened. Her breasts grew and hardened, too, but as her stomach rose, her breasts fell, the left a bit more than the right. They were tender as new wounds.

If anyone noticed the change in her shape—the students she tutored, their parents, the college friend who had spent the night on their couch on her way from Burlington to New York—they said nothing, and so Elizabeth said nothing, too. But very often she wanted to confess it, to tell everyone she saw on the street. The knowledge felt too big to fit inside her. It didn't feel natural to contain her excitement, or her fears, when she had them. She nearly called her parents several times, but she was unsure how to tell them, how much to tell them. They hadn't known she was trying to get pregnant, and they very likely would have advised her against it.

On the days she wanted to call her parents she experimented with telling strangers. When she bought three boxes of Saltines and a liter of ginger ale from the gas station, Elizabeth said to the young boy cashier, in response to nothing more than a nod at the presentation of her credit card, "I'm pregnant."

"Cool," he said.

A few days later she went for a haircut, to a stylist she had never been to before. As the stylist parted her hair with acrylic nails, Elizabeth said, "I'm pregnant."

The stylist looked delighted in the mirror.

"How far along?" she asked.

"Nine weeks."

The stylist's delight fell.

"That's very early," she said. Then she started talking about when she was pregnant with her own daughter, now five years old and an absolute tyrant, she threw up the entire nine months and spent Thanksgiving in the hospital hooked up to an IV. She didn't mention Elizabeth's pregnancy again.

Elizabeth would tell her parents when they came to visit next, she decided at that moment, she'd invite them for the weekend when she was sixteen weeks, at which point she hoped the prospect of a grandchild would thrill them more than the knowledge of her early pregnancy would scare them.

Though she felt ill, fat, constipated, and sore, and terrified of all that could go wrong, she loved being pregnant. She loved seeing what her body could do, what it knew how to do all along, without her instruction. She loved how much Sam loved it. When she pulled off the leggings and loose sweaters, revealing herself and what she was becoming, he ran his hands over her body with great tenderness and care, as if she were made of porcelain.

"Look at your body," he'd say. "I can't tell you how much I love your body."

When her nausea subsided, which it started to do as her first trimester came to a close, she began studying for the MCAT and making a list of where to apply. Sam would apply to PhD programs in geology to schools in nearby cities to those she applied to. She would still be a med student and then a doctor, just a med student with a baby, a year later than she'd planned. The undergraduates would babysit and the faculty kids would be playmates. She liked the idea. It brought her comfort. She wished she could promise this baby inside her that she would not be alone for long, that she would have another baby in time, maybe two more, and they would be a family.

"I lost it at fourteen weeks."

That's how she said it to Margot, as they sat in Elizabeth's living room, drinking her peppermint tea. Elizabeth kept her eyes on her hands, wrapping and unwrapping the teabag string around the mug's handle. She didn't say what happened, or how she learned the baby was dead, if she woke up in bloody sheets or heard it from the doctor while lying on her back in a dark room, and if she then had to wait weeks or months for the dead baby to leave her body or if she let the doctors take it out themselves.

Margot watched her friend and resisted her questions; Elizabeth would tell her what she wanted to tell her, no more and no less. Their sons' sleeping breath filled the silence.

"I lost it at fourteen weeks," she said again. "And Sam fell apart."

Elizabeth and Sam only spoke about the loss as they lay in bed before sleep—she came to bed with him now, not wanting to stay up in the dark kitchen alone—when they couldn't see each other's faces clearly, but they could feel the heat of their bodies and they were no longer able to distract themselves with any small tasks the day demanded.

Sam once said, "There isn't anything wrong with you, you know. You didn't do anything wrong," and she said, "I know that." She wasn't sure either of them believed this.

He often kissed her forehead or touched her shoulder when she passed him, and offered, as he had when she was pregnant, to buy all the groceries and wash all the dishes. But she was no longer ill, the hormones fell hard and fast, and she was unsure what to do with free afternoons and free hands. She insisted on doing the chores herself, though they gave her little satisfaction, and when she had excess agita and energy she'd go on walks around the neighborhood. Running no longer appealed to her; she was not as fast as she had been, her bones felt heavy, and she didn't want to be so aware of her own breath and her own heart.

During those weeks, she talked to her mother on the phone for long stretches of time. Since Elizabeth had left for college, she rarely spoke to her mother in great depth, and a neutral distance had settled between them—but in the weeks after the miscarriage, her mother was the only person she wanted to talk to.

"I had a miscarriage," Elizabeth told her. Then: "I was pregnant. I'm sorry I didn't tell you."

"Oh, honey," her mother said, in a way she'd never said it before. Honey like lead.

Her mother told Elizabeth about her own miscarriages, both before and after Elizabeth was born. Until then, Elizabeth had thought her mother had only had one, but there had been four: two early and two not so early. "My one regret," her mother said, "was that I told no one. No one knew what was happening. Not even my close friends. They had losses, too, they must have, though they never told me about them, either. We all went through it alone."

Then, one day, Elizabeth didn't feel like talking about dead babies anymore, and the distance resumed between her and her mother, though from then on it would more easily collapse into closeness.

When the house was empty and quiet was the only time Elizabeth felt she could sob, sometimes screaming into her pillow until her throat was coarse. Her grief felt more like fury than sadness, and she let it rage when she was alone. But when Sam was home, or when she was out in the world, the fury subsided and numbed, and she felt cold and calm. Elizabeth and Sam went out to sushi dinners and ordered wine they didn't want. He bought her a wedge of expensive raw cheese from the south of France that they never opened and didn't throw out until it was covered in green mold. For a month they did not talk about trying to conceive again, and she often forgot she was no longer pregnant. When she wanted to turn over at night, she was slow and careful, bracing for the strain of her ligaments. She avoided the meat aisle in the grocery store and cooked her eggs until the yolks looked like yellow clay. When she showered, she rubbed soap over her belly in gentle circles and looked down to see if her stomach now eclipsed her toes.

Then she would remember.

It was fall then. The air was still hot, but no longer heavy. Fall in Maine was like winter but fall in Massachusetts was like spring. Her applications were due. She sent them off and Sam sent his off, too. She was done with her postbacs and restless at home so she began to tutor more and more—she had a great reputation, now, and was soon busy helping high school seniors with their personal essays for their college applications. She found some pleasure in helping the students find a story to tell about themselves, to curate a shape to the lives they'd lived so far, and she came to see the hours with students at their kitchen tables as the time when she felt most at peace.

Time passed steadily, then quickly. After the month was over, she no longer forgot she was not pregnant. Now she forgot, sometimes for a day or two at a time, that she had ever been pregnant at all. It all started to feel like a story she'd heard about someone else, the daughter of a friend of her mother's, maybe—those were the women who lost babies. Her bras fit again, then her jeans. All of her maternity clothes and prenatal vitamins and onesies from Salvation Army and stretch mark oils and the baby food cookbook Sam had brought home from the bookstore were all in an opaque plastic bin on the top shelf of the closet. She didn't see them; she didn't think of them.

"Maybe we should start trying again," Sam said one weekend morning as he made pancakes. He faced the stove, showing her his back.

"I'm not ready yet," she said.

"What does ready mean?" he asked, turning to her. "Maybe trying again will be the thing that makes you feel ready. You seem to be feeling better—you say you're feeling better." And she agreed that she was, but the idea of trying again made her feel a pressure in her temples and filled her with an anger she couldn't explain. That morning he did not press her further, but after another month passed he asked again, more persuasively this time. He began to talk about this baby as he had about the first baby, speaking it into existence to weaken her resistance. But the technique was not so effective now. Now the timing was terrible, when it had been manageable before; if she became pregnant again soon—and carried this one to term—then she would be in her third trimester when she started med school, going on leave after only one or two semesters. She thought they should wait at least until she was in residency, three years from then, and perhaps they should've always waited. Perhaps the miscarriage was a sign, of some sort, from some deity or cosmic wisdom, though neither of them believed in that kind of thing, and she knew it. She never spoke this thought aloud.

Sam's sadness became anger. He accused her once, late at night, of tricking him.

"This was what you wanted, wasn't it?" he said.

"What? No, of course not. You can't be serious!"

He rolled on his side and faced the wall and said, "It doesn't matter," and she was too stunned and infuriated to engage further. She was afraid of what else he might say, what else she might say. In the morning he kissed her rigid cheek and said many times that he was sorry and he knew he had been unfair. She forgave him and meant it. But she began to think more about whether or not he was changing, becoming harder, more mercurial, less forgiving of himself and of her, or if he had always been this way, and she had never noticed it before. Both possibilities disturbed her.

Elizabeth again began to turn over what she knew about Sam's life before he met her, what he'd told her about his parents and his brother and his life in Presque Isle. When she thought it over now, as she watched him not talk to her, not look at her, not touch her, it felt like very little. She wanted to know more. She wanted to know if Sam's father had been merely unpleasant and irritable, or if he was in any way abusive. She wanted to know if his brother Leland was as distant as Sam described, or if the silence between them had been imposed by Sam, and Leland was only honoring it. Most of all, she wanted to know what evidence Sam had for believing that his father had been sleeping with his second wife before his first wife died. Had Sam seen them together, heard them together, or had he been so enraged with grief after his mother's death that he cast his father as a villain, his father who was himself grieving?

She turned the questions over in her mind, though she knew she'd be unable to bring herself closer to any answers without talking to

Sam. And that, she felt, was not an option, not anymore. The time of lying next to each other in the afternoons, noses almost touching, talking about their families and the years before they had met each other had passed long ago. To ask Sam about his father now would betray that she was seeing something in him that scared her, something she couldn't explain, and she didn't know what he'd say then.

One afternoon in the winter, on her way home from tutoring her old orgo professor's daughter, Elizabeth drove out of the way to the women's health clinic in Northampton for an IUD insertion. She didn't tell Sam she was going to go or that she had gone. After the appointment, she spent the evening on the couch watching *Friday Night Lights* with a hot water bottle on her stomach and an eight-dollar bottle of merlot. The pain of the insertion, so deep and primal that she thought she'd faint, had passed soon after the plastic was inside her, but the angry cramping that followed hardly eased. If Sam, finding her laying like that when he came home, suspected it was not her period that was causing her pain—if he had started tracking her period since it returned and knew that it was one week too early for that—then he said nothing about it.

A few nights later, when he came inside her, (he didn't ask if he could come inside her and she didn't tell him he couldn't), he hit her cervix and she flinched away in pain. He was still for a moment, then pulled out of her. The expression on his face was odd, somewhere between anger and surprise and knowing, but he said nothing. He had felt the strings, she was sure of it. He didn't kiss her or lie next to her after as he always did. He took a long shower and said good night and fell asleep.

A week later he again began speaking about the miscarriage as if it had been an act of deception.

"You never really wanted a baby," he said. "I know you didn't."

"That's not true," she said, "how can you say that?"

"*You* said it. You said you didn't want a baby and you were only doing it for me and now the baby is dead so what am I supposed to think?"

"I never said that," she wept. This man speaking to her, in this way, was not a man she knew. "I never even thought that. I swear. How can you say that? I hate that it's dead. I loved it as much as you did and you know that I did."

"I don't know that." He laughed bitterly. "I don't know anything—that's what you think, right?"

He slept on the couch. He did not apologize to her in the morning.

By spring she had been accepted to Stanford, Columbia, and Michigan. He was only accepted to Orono. She hadn't known he'd applied there. Orono wasn't anywhere near any schools she'd applied to. When she told him this, he said flatly, "I thought I told you," and this did not convince her.

"I'm going to go there," he said a few nights later over a late dinner of rice and beans. "Back to Orono. Go wherever you want and I won't follow you if you don't want me to."

They lived together for one more month. They both tried to spend as much time out of the house as they could. They were awkward together, quiet and polite. They shared a bed and sometimes still had sex, in the middle of the night, with his face pressed against hers, never looking at each other or acknowledging it in the morning. She insisted he keep most of the things they had bought together—the desk, the spider plants, all the kitchenware—she wouldn't bring it with her, and he agreed to take it and sell or donate what he didn't need. They didn't officially divorce for another two years, and the process was simple and cheap. Nothing material remained between them; they had no money and no children.

"I didn't mean to keep all of this from you," Elizabeth said to Margot. "I don't think of it as a secret, really, so much as a story that's hard to tell in sections. But it's also hard to tell in its entirety. It's just easier not to. I think people can know me without knowing all this about me."

"I'm glad you told me," said Margot. "Thank you for telling me."

They were quiet for a little while. Margot finished what remained of her tea, cool now. She thought of how she would tell Nick later, at home, what she would include and what she would leave out, what parts of the story she had already forgotten or unwittingly manipulated in her recent memory.

Margot asked, "Who else knows?"

"Of the people you know, nobody. Just Patrick. That's it."

Her friends at Stanford didn't know she was married, she said, and that she was going through a divorce, much less that she'd been pregnant and had lost a baby she had come to want and love very much. Patrick didn't even know any of it until they'd been dating for over a year, when she thought to keep it from him much longer would be more like deception rather than passive omission. She was barely twenty-six when she started Stanford, a similar age to most of her new peers—but she felt impossibly old, so much so that she was often surprised when she looked in the mirror or saw a picture of herself, and the face was without wear, and she was most perplexed when others told her she looked younger than she was, sometimes assuming she had come straight from college.

And she also felt very young, almost like a teenager, more of a teenager now than she had been in high school. Often she felt immortal rather than fragile. She had survived what most people were terrified to experience, and here she was, at a bar in Palo Alto flirting with the cute boy who would become her second husband, among all these young and brilliant minds who likely believed that what had happened to her would not happen to them, that they would not divorce or miscarry. That was what befell other people—sympathetic people, people who were certainly not to blame for their misfortunes—but still, people who had been marked, at some point early in their lives, as unlucky. These new friends of hers were the daughters of brain surgeons and corporate lawyers. They were high school valedictorians and Phi Beta Kappa scholars from the Ivies. These friends had talents beyond their prowess in science and standardized tests—they were former opera singers, all-Americans in lacrosse and swimming, one was a Miss Idaho Teen USA, she admitted, embarrassed, after two glasses of wine. She'd danced *The Swan* en point. Miss Idaho was not the only beauty, either: many of them were well-dressed with fine features, and they were made prettier by their social grace and wit. These were not the dorks and indoor kids that she had expected. They were incessantly likable.

Elizabeth knew, like a reluctant prophet, that in the coming years they would also divorce, or miscarry, or both, or worse. They would lose a spouse or a child to a car accident or some degenerative autoimmune disease or a quiet but quick cancer. Or they themselves would be the victim. But a few would remain untouched by the common tragedies that struck those around them, until perhaps they believed they were not just lucky—they were superior.

So there she was, sitting among them, drinking her IPA and smoothing her hair as she laughed, not acting like one of them but *being* one of them. And she was okay.

"I didn't know if I was stronger from what I'd been through," she said to Margot, "but I knew I wasn't weaker."

Elizabeth stopped talking again. The sun outside the bay window was low, almost set. Nick was probably already back home and texting Margot, starting to worry. Her phone was on silent in the back of the stroller. Her breasts were starting to ache—she needed to nurse Alex soon, or pump—it was unusual for him to nap so long, and she watched for the small rise of his breath in his chest, resisting the desire to feel the proof of it under her palm.

She wasn't sure if Elizabeth's story was over, and if she should mention the other day. She thought about saying that she understood a little better, now, why Elizabeth had told her she was pregnant in the way that she had, why she hated being pregnant, how it terrified her, and though Margot felt her friend could still have understood this effect on Margot and acknowledged it, just a few words would be all it took, Margot was no longer upset.

But it didn't seem as though Elizabeth was thinking about the other day. That was not why she told the story. She didn't mention it, and so neither did Margot.

She was glad the marriage ended, Elizabeth said after some time. If she hadn't lost the baby, maybe they would've had another child, maybe two more, and they probably would've had a much worse divorce several years later—right around now, maybe, and she'd be a single mother of three at forty, living who knows where. And without the miscarriage, she wouldn't have gone to Stanford, and met Patrick, and moved to Alaska, and she would never have had Phin, or become pregnant with this baby now. She saw now that she and Sam had been children, terrified of the world around them and of being alone in it, and everything they did—from spending that summer lying on his futon to staying together long distance to moving into the apartment in Hadley and buying spatulas and marrying and getting pregnant— all of these had been desperate gestures to not be alone, to not be left, perhaps more than they were inspired by love for each other. She didn't know him, really, not even at the end. And he didn't really know her, either.

And yet she still grieved the death of the baby that made this better life available to her. If given the option to go back and save it she thought that was what she would do. Some days she thought that. Though it was a foolish thing to think about. It wasn't an option then, and it never would be.

"I've been thinking about that baby a lot lately," she said. "More even than when I was pregnant with Phin. Phin felt different to me, but this one reminds me of the one I lost, it has a similar feeling. It's hard to explain, and I don't fully understand it myself. I've been thinking about it a lot this week especially, the fourteenth week."

After Margot hung up, I went back inside, one ear hot from the phone and the other cool from the wind. It was dusk, nearly night. Isaac was making a tofu stir fry and listening to a podcast from his laptop, a voice I recognized but couldn't name, saying something about robocalls.

"There you are," Isaac said. "I was starting to wonder." He dried his hands and paused the podcast. "Do you think this hoisin is still good?" he held the open bottle under his nose, then mine. My sense of smell, always finer than his, had in the past few weeks become so attuned we used it to determine the health of all questionable ingredients. I could smell salsa and curry paste through sealed jars, and garlic and onion juice in the grain of the cutting boards, no matter how many times they'd been washed.

"Smells perfect," I said, and kissed him on the cheek.

"Everything okay? You were talking to her forever."

"She was telling me about her friend. Do you remember her

friend Elizabeth? We met her and her husband Patrick at the barbecue at Margot's. They had a boy about Alex's age who cried the whole time."

"Was their kid the one in the tribal suit?"

"No. That was the Finnish woman's son."

He added the hoisin and garlic to the tofu in the cast iron skillet, a wedding gift from our teacher, and stirred it in. He ate a piece of tofu off the spatula and added more hoisin. I suddenly became acutely hungry, but I didn't want tofu. I wanted red meat with mayonnaise and tablespoons of sea salt.

"Elizabeth had dark hair," I said. "She was kind of pretty, she came late. Her husband told us marriage was about doing more of what you don't want to do."

"Vaguely."

"Anyway, Elizabeth used to be married to someone else, this guy she met in high school, and she had a miscarriage at fourteen weeks and then they got divorced. Margot had no idea."

"That's awful. What happened with her baby?"

"Don't know. She didn't tell Margot."

He lifted another tofu cube with the spatula and blew on it before tasting, added a little more soy sauce.

"I really only remember that kid in the tribal suit," he said as he stirred. "That kid and his father."

That night I lay awake and tried to remember meeting Elizabeth, searching for signs in my memory of her life before. The barbecue had been Margot's idea, a way for Isaac and me to meet her friends and have her friends meet us, and to give us an occasion to plan and shop for, something to fill the day. By that point on our honeymoon, Isaac and I were beginning to sleep better in the long, light evenings but were growing tired of wearing the same clothes, musty from the suit-case, and sleeping in sheets with unfamiliar fabrics and scents.

I was nervous to meet Margot's friends, particularly Elizabeth. I wore the most presentable blouse I'd brought, a white linen. It was wrinkled from rushed packing and smelled like the sweaty socks tucked next to it. In the basement bathroom I applied mascara and light lipstick and simple stud earrings, trying to look pretty—prettier, I admit, than Margot—but without betraying vanity. Margot would likely wear the same outfit she'd worn during the day, when we'd been out to Costco and vacuuming and putting Alex's toys in the closet, a loose flannel and no makeup. She'd never shown any indication I posed a threat to her, no matter how silly and small, never took even minor pains to impress me. I took off the earrings. I wiped off the lip-stick and applied tinted lip balm instead, fearing my efforts were too visible.

The first to arrive was a couple and their son—a man in his fifties, maybe, with a wife slightly younger, both blond, though his hair was thin and turning so light it was almost white, and hers was thick and pulled back in an intricate design. She had a short name I couldn't pronounce then and I didn't recall now, and a slight accent I couldn't place.

She was pregnant. I didn't notice the curve of her stomach under her loose chambray blouse until Margot said to her, "All the cheese is pasteurized, and I bought a whole carton of coconut Le Croix with you in mind."

The woman said, "Oh, you are always so thoughtful!"

The couple's son seemed about four years old. He wore a matching top and bottom set of black and yellow triangles in a design that looked like a poor and probably offensive imitation of traditional African tribal clothing, but I couldn't say from which tribe or region. The clothes were a thick canvas material and cut like nursing scrubs. The boy had an odd look about him, apart from the outfit: his skin was so pale you could see the blue vein by his temple, and his light gray eyes focused sharply on each adult around him. He stared at me for several seconds without blinking, expressionless. He didn't look away until Margot said, "I like your outfit, where did you get it?" He stared up at her, still unblinking and expressionless, until Margot looked up at his parents and laughed uneasily.

"It's a present from my sister," said the boy's mother. "She was on vacation in Johannesburg and brought it back for him."

"He insisted on wearing it here," said the boy's father, rolling his eyes. "He's worn it every day this week. I keep telling him it's hideous but he doesn't seem to care." The son cut his eyes to his father. "He'll grow out of it soon, anyway. We're running out of clothes for him. And if this one is a girl, we'll have to buy a whole new set. It never ends! I feel like we're always buying more shit. We never have enough shit, do we, darling?"

He looked at me and Isaac then, as if he hadn't noticed us there before. We introduced ourselves and shook hands.

"I'm Margot's sister," I said.

"I can tell," he said. "You're the same person."

Margot and I looked at each other. We'd been told we bore a strong resemblance to each other many times as young girls, but rarely since. I never knew if it was meant to be a compliment or a slight, and I didn't know how Margot felt about the comparison. We both smiled.

"She's taller," Margot said. "And younger."

"Not really," he said.

"Anna and Isaac just got married," Margot said, breaking the short pause that followed. "They're here on their honeymoon."

"Congratulations!" said his wife warmly. "What a special time. I hope you are liking Alaska so far?"

"I knew you didn't have kids," he said, more to me than to Isaac. "You have that look about you. Here's what no one will tell you: *don't*."

He laughed, and his wife hit his arm a little harder than seemed playful. His son walked onto the porch, where Nick was preheating the grill.

"What?" said the boy's father, sounding more earnest than mocking. "They'll have kids anyway. Everyone does."

Soon another couple arrived, then another right after them, then another, all with small, beautifully dressed children, none older than age five. I couldn't tell which child belonged to which couple; they were all white with hair the color of wheat or chestnuts. One couple brought vanilla cupcakes, generously frosted with pink sugar flecks on top, and another brought a growler of hoppy beer from a local brewery and fresh corn to grill. Margot's friends were all kind and polite and had a similar sensibility about them, like they all knew they were only playing at being responsible parents and adults and doctors, but their performance was excellent, as excellent as their grades had been their whole lives. Our friends, Isaac and mine, the friends who were also in the MFA program, were brilliant, too, but without this aura of ease and adjustment. Margot's friends displayed no sense of hardship, past or present, that had made possible their successes. Their hair was shiny, they laughed easily, but they did not—and this is what impressed me most—convey a hint of phoniness or superficiality. I liked them.

When the cheeses were half gone, and the first round of burgers were ready, Elizabeth and Patrick arrived with Phin strapped to Patrick's chest. Phin was wailing so loudly he could be heard before the door opened, over the din of Father John Misty and children and conversation. They smiled and said hello as they came in, with the same grace as the other couples, though Phin's cries and the fatigue in their faces betrayed the labor that was less visible in the others.

When I realized that this woman was Elizabeth, the Elizabeth I'd already heard so much about, Margot's closest female ally, I felt at once resentment, relief, superiority, inferiority, and affection.

"I'm sorry we're so late," said Patrick as they walked into the kitchen. "I swear it wasn't me who pooed my diaper three times in thirty minutes."

It was easy to imagine the chaos that had ensued just moments before their arrival: both of them confessing to the other that they didn't want to come to this thing, but they had said they would and it was too late to say no now, besides there'd be food and they were starving, so they'd go for just a little while and leave as soon as they ate. They were both attractive, despite their harried appearance. Patrick was the same height as Elizabeth, which made him seem smaller and her seem taller. He had dark curls and a slight beard, a big boyish smile, and a thickness to his chest that didn't seem quite natural on him. Elizabeth had dark hair too, with green eyes, and skin that was a little darker than his. I couldn't tell if she was tan, maybe from hiking in the long days, or if this was her natural complexion, and I found myself trying to place her skin tone, her hair, her eyes, to name her race. I felt ashamed as I did so, knowing she must recognize this look and know what it meant and resent it, and then resent me. She was dressed casually, cotton nursing shirt and cargo shorts, which drew attention to her engagement ring, a large diamond with sapphires on either side.

Margot introduced them to us, and our names ignited recognition across their faces.

"This is the little sister!" said Elizabeth. "You look even more like Margot in person. We've heard so much about you; it's wonderful to finally meet you."

"Nice to meet you, too." I resisted saying that I had heard so much about her, too, I probably knew much more than she wanted me to know, and asking what, exactly, did Margot tell her about me?

Phin continued to wail. Patrick patted his head and kept saying *shhh, shhh*, firmer and firmer, barely containing tears of his own, it seemed. With a warmth and interest that surprised me, Elizabeth congratulated us on our wedding, "the pictures were stunning," and she asked how we were enjoying our honeymoon, what we'd been up to in Anchorage, until Phin's cries became so loud it was difficult to talk over them.

"He needs a change," said Elizabeth.

"We *just* changed him," said Patrick.

"I know, but I think he still needs one. That's what that cry is."

"I thought that cry was the hungry cry."

"No, the hungry one is the sharp one."

"They're all sharp," said Patrick, looking to me for confirmation.

"I'm going to change him," said Elizabeth. She moved to undo the carrier.

"No, I'll take him—Margot, do you have a diaper we can borrow and never return?"

As he passed us to follow Margot down the hall, he said to us, laughing and looking at Isaac, "Welcome to marriage! Turns out it's just doing more of what you don't want to do."

When Patrick went to change Phin, Elizabeth sat down and poured chardonnay into a plastic cup. She spread brie on crackers and ate them. She nodded and smiled at what the mothers around her said—they were talking about how now that they all have strollers they are newly aware of how inaccessible so many places are for anyone in a wheelchair, how terrible it is—but Elizabeth did not contribute. Isaac had gone to the living room to watch Alex and the other babies and toddlers. He was sitting cross-legged on the carpet, looking enormous next to the children, building a tower with painted wooden blocks. I was about to stand to join him when Elizabeth turned to me and said, "I'd love to hear more about your trip. Where are you going next?"

"We're going to Homer tomorrow. Have you been there?"

"Patrick and I went soon after we first moved here. It might be pretty crowded there now, but it's really beautiful. There was a restaurant there that we loved. Alice's Champagne Palace, I think it's called. It's fun. Do you remember Alice's Champagne Palace?" she asked Patrick, who just then returned. Phin was flopped horizontal in his arms, now quiet but looking no less miserable than he had before the change.

"Where is that?" asked Patrick.

"In Homer."

"Is that the bar covered in dollar bills?"

"No—that was down by the pier."

"Don't remember."

"Well, anyway, they're going there next."

"Cool," he said, distracted. "You'll enjoy it. Elizabeth, he's hungry."

She took Phin in her arms. "I just had some wine."

"There's milk in the bag. Remember? You said you wanted to have some wine so I put the milk in the bag."

"Where's the bag?"

"Did we bring it in?"

"I don't see it there."

"It must be in the car," he said. "I'll get it."

"I'll get it. I'll just feed him in the car."

Elizabeth rose, holding Phin pressed to her chest, and walked out and Patrick went to the cooler of beer. The last I recalled of either of them at the party was a while later, after Elizabeth had returned from the car and Phin was sleeping in her arms. The mother of tribal-suit boy had brought Elizabeth a burger, and the two women spoke quietly with serious expressions as Elizabeth tried to eat with a free hand.

My impression of Elizabeth by then, if I remembered correctly, was that she was a nice woman, surely a smart woman, but an unremarkable woman. From my short time in her presence, I could not yet see why Margot had chosen her, above all the other nice and smart women at the barbecue, and above me, to become her closest friend.

Like Isaac, what I remembered most about that party wasn't Elizabeth or Patrick, or any conversation in particular, but the tribal-suit boy and his father, and how, throughout the evening, the boy often left the room with Isaac and the children and came up to his father on the porch to show him a small scratch on his palm, then an orange thumb tack he'd found in the carpet. The father would nod once to his son while continuing his grown-up conversation. A few times the boy took his father's hand and tried to lead him into the kid's room—to show his father the tower, I presumed, that was now over two feet tall thanks to Isaac. But the father shook his head at the requests, then ignored them altogether. The boy stopped approaching his father and started crawling under the chairs and pinching guests' Achilles' heels, including mine, with impressive force, then turning the dials on the grill when Nick was looking elsewhere. Then the boy stood on a plastic chair that had recently been vacated and used it to gain the height necessary to reach the top of the porch railing. On the other side of the railing was a drop off of about fifteen feet, and under it were rakes and shovels and a wheelbarrow. The boy started to climb over the top.

I didn't see him, and I didn't think anyone else did, until his father yelled "*Hey!*" and ran to the boy, who had by then one leg swung over and was lifting up the other, with a smile on his face of feigned innocence. It was the only time I saw him smile. Before the father could reach him, the mother was there, pulling her son down and into her arms. The paper plate of crab legs and corn had fallen from her lap and the food was scattered around the porch. She spoke to her son sternly in a language I couldn't identify. The boy's face hardened but he did not cry. She set him down and took him by the hand and kept speaking to him as she led him inside, neither of them looking at the father as they passed.

Later, in bed in the basement, after the dishes were done and the guests were gone, Isaac and I talked about the boy and his father. Isaac said the boy was definitely weird, but he'd been very sweet, it turned out, when they were building the block tower, and he played well with Alex. He kept picking up a block and telling Alex what color it was. The boy had told Isaac about how he was excited for his mother to have another baby and he didn't care if it would be a boy or a girl because he liked both the boys and the girls in his day care. I told Isaac what I'd seen on the porch and what Margot had told me after they'd all left and we were doing the dishes, while Isaac cleaned up the blocks and Nick was putting Alex to bed.

I'd asked Margot where the boy's mother was from, and what the father was like.

"She seemed lovely," I said. "But he's one of the few people I've met and immediately disliked."

Margot told me that the son only spent time alone with his mother when he was very young. The father was a neurosurgeon and made a lot of money, so after her maternity leave the mother took some more time off, and she'd recently started working part-time as a pediatrician at the hospital again, which is how Margot knew her. They'd quickly become friends. The boy and his mother spent so much time alone together that the boy's first language was Finnish. He'd been speaking Finnish for several months, and the father didn't know it. He thought the boy was just making odd sounds. He didn't realize the boy was speaking Finnish until he was speaking in complete sentences and the wife would respond, using the same sounds and inflections. This infuriated him. He was mortified that he couldn't even recognize his wife's native tongue. He felt as though his wife and son had developed their own secret language without him, to spite him, perhaps, and so he began to spend as much time home as he could, playing talk radio and podcasts all day and reading to the boy at night, and insisting that his wife stop speaking Finnish at home and go back to work as soon as she could.

Now the son spoke English better than he spoke Finnish, and his mother feared he would forget the language entirely and never be able to speak to her parents without her translating. The people she loved the most in the world would never be able to speak to one another with fluency, and so they would never be able to know one another, not with any sort of intimacy.

"I didn't like him when I met him either," said Margot, drying dishes with a dampened cloth. "But he isn't really that bad. I've noticed he puts on an affect when he's at parties like this, like he's over being a father, but he loves his son a lot. It was his idea to have a second kid. She'd had a loss with her first pregnancy, before her son; I don't know the details, but I got the sense it was pretty traumatic. She told me her entire pregnancy with her son was joyless and she didn't want to go through it again. I'm not sure what he did to convince her, but a few months after she told me she never wanted to be pregnant again, she was pregnant."

I wondered, as I lay next to Isaac, recalling that evening the summer before, if the boy still dreamed in Finnish, the language of his mother, and if he knew that these sounds existed beyond her, in a country very far away, surrounded by cold salt water, near the top of the globe, where the summer days and the winter nights were just as long as they were in Alaska, the only place he'd ever known, or if he believed that his mother spoke one set of words and his father spoke another and so they would never be able to do more than guess at each other's meanings and only rarely be correct.

Corrie

ON SATURDAY MORNING, I walked to the ten o'clock prenatal yoga class, through graduate and undergraduate housing and into University Town Center, the small plaza with Trader Joe's, Del Sushi, Peet's, In-N-Out, and Shakti Yoga. I'd never done yoga before I was pregnant, besides a few twenty-minute videos of Yoga with Kelly on YouTube during restless hours. I'd found it, in turns, too easy and too challenging, and it made me feel mildly embarrassed whenever Kelly spoke in Sanskrit or referenced the third eye.

The Shakti classes had been a present from Margot—I'd turned thirty just a few days after telling her I was pregnant, and I soon received an email from her, a forwarded confirmation that a ten-class pass at Shakti Yoga had been purchased for me and I could redeem it at the front desk before my first class. I hadn't expected anything from her; we hadn't given birthday presents for years.

"I'm not a yoga person either," Margot had said when I'd called to thank her, though I hadn't said anything about my own aversion. "But I loved prenatal. Just try it. Maybe you'll even make a pregnant friend."

The yoga studio was painted soft turquoise, and it smelled strongly of feet and incense from the class before, a pleasing combination. The pregnant women of Orange County soon arrived, claimed their spaces around the room at a respectful distance from one another and gathered the supplies from the closet—two foam blocks, a Mexican blanket, and a bolster for shivasana. The women were all at least my age but no older than forty, by the look of them, and all with pedicures, dark reds and oranges, autumnal.

Once the room was settled, the instructor entered, a very petite woman with a slight German accent. "Good morning, beauties!" she said, and lay her mat down at the front of the room. She synced her phone to the speakers and began to play music with flute and chimes, then asked that we all go around the room and introduce ourselves, say how far along we were, and what sort of discomfort we were experiencing today.

"Let's start with our Queen," she said. "Who is our Queen today?"

The two women with the largest bellies, one short and one tall, looked at each other.

"I'm thirty-eight weeks," said the short one.

"Fifty-eight," said the tall one, and the room laughed. "Feels like, anyway. I'm forty-one," she amended, smiling apologetically to the thirty-eight-week woman. "My due date was last Friday."

The Queen was never Queen for long. Since coming to the class for the first time several weeks ago, I looked for these former Queens, Queens become Mothers, pushing strollers through the plaza parking lot, nursing on the benches outside In-N-Out. But I never saw them. I looked, too, for the seven-to-ten-weekers, ladies-in-waiting, the ones who came to class a few Saturdays in a row and then never again. I never saw them in the world, either.

The Queen was feeling intense pressure, she said, pushing down, sciatica and lightning crotch and constant Braxton Hicks, but never the real thing. She was anxious she'd be induced and it would be as intolerable as it'd been with her first delivery, but she was trying her best to stay mindful. The women each spoke in turn: Laura, Hae-Won, Deepa, thirty weeks, twelve weeks, twenty-five weeks, heartburn, round ligament pain, fatigue, nausea, lower back pain, lower back pain, lower back pain. After I spoke (fifteen weeks; heartburn and round ligament), the instructor asked, "And you?" directing her gaze to the last woman in the circle, the woman next to me. I had not looked at her until now, as I'd tried in the minutes before class to keep my eyes lowered, to not show my inspection of each woman's belly, comparing their enlargement from the week before as they took off their sweaters and unfurled their mats. But still, I was surprised I hadn't noticed the woman next to me.

This woman was a girl. No older than twenty. And she was tiny. Her stomach was flat under her white cotton undershirt, the kind sold in plastic packs of six at pharmacies, not the sweat-wicking blends like the other women's shirts and like mine. Her legs were twigs coming out of her pink running shorts, and her breasts were barely visible. She didn't look as though she could carry a pregnancy, much less was currently carrying one and far along enough to know it.

"I'm Corrie," she said. "This is my first class."

"Welcome, Corrie," said the instructor. The women, all sitting with crossed legs and straight backs, smiled at her, though I noticed their eyes, like mine, were scanning her sharp figure.

"I'm ten weeks. And I'm feeling fine. No discomfort or pain or anything."

"No fatigue?" asked the instructor. "No nausea?"

"Nope."

The instructor watched Corrie expectantly, almost challengingly. Corrie said nothing and kept looking at the instructor, meeting her gaze without wavering, until the instructor finally broke her stare and said, "Well, that's wonderful! You may just be one of the lucky ones." Then she smiled and brought her hands together and turned to the room.

"Okay, let's all come to a comfortable seated position, if you aren't already, and begin to bring awareness to your breath."

Throughout the class, my attention was on Corrie's body more than on my own. She moved gracefully, and she was strong, stronger than her thin arms suggested, though it was clear from her frequent glances at the instructor and at me—once, for an instant, we made eye contact when I was supposed to be facing away from her—that she did not know what the instructor meant when she said puppy pose, pigeon, lizard, rag doll. She did not emanate wealth, which meant she very likely did not come from around here—but she also didn't have the look of the UCI undergraduates, my composition students, many of whom wore heavy foundation and bold lipsticks and dressed in designer athleisure. Her face appeared entirely bare of makeup, and her hair was so blond it was almost white, dry from harsh shampoo. It was naturally blond, judging by the hair on her arms and unshaven legs, incidentally and accidentally blond, unlike the blond of many of the women in the class.

The only suggestions of vanity were the silver loop in the cartilage of her right ear and the tip of a tattoo, maybe a leaf or vine, on her shoulder, mostly covered by her undershirt. Her toes and my toes were the only unpainted, if not unpedicured, toes in the class.

Her appearance, in this expensive yoga studio in this affluent California town, seemed in itself to be an act of defiance against the dominant culture around her, whether or not this was her intention. By the time the instructor dimmed the lights and we were propping the bolsters on our blocks to prepare for an inclined shivasana—a structure Corrie watched me arrange before arranging herself—my appreciation of her presence here had eclipsed my initial unease. I liked having her next to me.

As we all lay together in the dark, and the only sounds in the room were the slow instrumental music and the breath of women, my attention shifted, not to my own body and the "feelings of the benefits of the practice," as the instructor had encouraged, but to the conversation I'd had with Margot the night before. I'd been thinking about it all night and morning, until the class began, and the moment my eyes closed it returned to the front of my mind. She'd called when Isaac and I were on the couch, deciding which TV show to watch before bed. It was the first time we'd spoken since she'd told me the story about Elizabeth, and I again assumed that she was the subject of the call.

But when I picked up she said, "Did Mom call you already?"

I said no, she hadn't, as I took the phone into the kitchen, and before I could ask why, is everything okay? she said, "Good. I told her not to."

She waited for me to understand.

"You're not," I said.

"I am. Nine weeks."

She'd had her first ultrasound last Friday. The embryo was the right size and in the right place with a beating heart—viable, so far.

"Last time we talked," Margot said, "the whole time I was telling you about Elizabeth, I kept wondering if I should tell you that I was pregnant. But I wanted to wait just a little longer."

Isaac was looking at me questioningly from the couch. *Pregnant!* I mouthed, miming an orb over my own swollen belly. His face brightened.

She had been planning on telling me after her second ultrasound, she said, when she'd be nearly done with her first trimester, but her most recent walk around the pond with Elizabeth had changed her mind. Elizabeth had told Margot that at her last appointment, they'd learned the baby's heart rate was steady, but too slow. The baby was most likely fine—the OB had assured them that this was not so unusual, though still wise to monitor—but Elizabeth's wan complexion and distracted stare on the path ahead made it clear that she was not optimistic her baby would be well. As Elizabeth spoke about the ultrasound, Patrick's insufferable optimism, and her difficulty concentrating on anything else since, Margot realized that if she were to lose her own new pregnancy, a loss she'd been preparing for since she'd felt the familiar ache in her breasts weeks before, she would want Elizabeth to know. She would tell Elizabeth right away. There was no reason, then, to withhold any longer.

"So I told her I was pregnant too," said Margot, "and she laughed and was like, 'Yeah, I know, I've been wondering when you were going to tell me, you already have the same adorable little bump as last time.' After I told her, I felt I had to tell Mom and Dad, and you."

Margot had told Elizabeth before she told me, and I noted a small flare of envy, but it soon faded, I was too delighted by the news of her pregnancy. It felt good to be genuinely delighted for her. And anyway, telling Elizabeth first seemed spontaneous, and contrary to her precontemplated plan.

"It feels good to say it aloud," she said. "It really does make it feel more real, like something exciting. I have no idea what will happen, and I hate waiting to know what will happen, but I know I feel better being pregnant and waiting than not being pregnant and waiting."

After we hung up, I felt, along with happiness and relief and an alleviation of guilt about my own pregnancy I hadn't realized I'd been feeling, an unpleasant sensation distinct from but not entirely unlike the nausea I'd felt for several weeks and had only recently subsided, a nausea like seasickness. I felt it again as I lay in the dark yoga studio, recalling the phone call. An image came to mind, just before the instructor invited us to bring some movement to our fingers and toes and to return our attention to the room—perhaps from a dream I had the night before that I'd forgotten, or perhaps not—of Margot and Elizabeth and me on a dinghy in rough open seas, a boat so small that the only way any of us would survive the swells was if one of us jumped out of the boat and volunteered herself and the baby inside her to drown. Or else we'd stick stubbornly in the boat, clutching our bulging bellies, and all drown together, our bodies never found in the wide black sea.

After the class came to a close with a brief guided breathing and choral namaste, Corrie was the first to put the blocks and blanket and bolster back into the closet, and she left the room quickly. I saw her standing on the sidewalk outside, the sun high and bright now, without a mat under her arm; she must have rented one from the studio for the class. She was looking toward Del Sushi, then toward campus, then across the plaza parking lot. The other women now came out onto the sidewalk in twos and threes, talking together and sipping from their insulated water bottles, as they always did after class before parting ways. The Queen and the thirty-eight-week woman stood close to me, laughing with each other, their popped navels almost touching.

That was what Margot wanted for me, I thought. A pregnant friend. She wanted me to have what she had with Elizabeth. I wondered how

Margot, if she were here, would have managed to become half of one of the pairs.

I stood alone and watched Corrie for a few moments, to see if she was going to walk in the same direction as me, but she just stood there, wayward, but not distraught. She now wore a long-sleeve black cotton shirt that somehow made her torso seem even more narrow than it had before.

I approached her and asked, "Do you need directions somewhere?"

She turned and smiled at me.

"Yeah, actually, thanks. I know I came from that way," she gestured toward Del Sushi, "but I got lost on my way here. There's got to be a faster way back."

In the sunlight, she looked a little older than I'd thought, maybe closer to twenty-three, twenty-four. I looked at her pink running shorts: no pockets. No purse or tote. No phone.

"Where are you going?" I asked, taking my phone from the outside pouch of my yoga bag.

"Briarcrest Drive. Or Briarcrest Street, maybe. It's in University Hills."

"I know University Hills," I said. I often walked there, the neighborhood where faculty and their families lived. It was an easy place to get disoriented, if you didn't know it well; all the streets were nearly identical, all the houses were beige bungalows with rock gardens, hybrid cars, and Radio Flyer tricycles in the driveways. I'd never seen anyone who looked like Corrie in University Hills.

I was walking toward University Hills, I told her, my apartment in graduate housing was on the way, (which was almost true), and I could walk her as far as that, or I could give her directions. I indicated to my phone that I could show her the way on the map. To my surprise, she said she would actually like the company, if I really didn't mind. Besides, she was terrible at remembering directions; if left on her own, she'd likely find herself wandering the streets of Orange County until nightfall.

So we began to walk.

We walked through the parking lot onto campus and through Aldrich Park, past the sycamores and jacarandas and other drought-resistant trees, holding our hands up to shade our eyes. Perhaps, from afar, we looked like close female friends, maybe close female friends like Elizabeth and Margot—and, perhaps also like Elizabeth and Margot, only one of the two pregnant women appeared to be pregnant, as any expansion of Margot's belly at this point would look more like bloat than bump to anyone who didn't know her figure well. But nobody was taking note of us; no one even glanced at Corrie's extreme thinness, which struck me anew every time I turned to look directly at her. It made me feel significantly bigger than I maybe was, even now, at the biggest I'd ever been.

"Are your parents professors?" I asked her as we began to walk.

"No," she laughed. "No way. I don't live here."

I asked where she was visiting from, and she didn't answer directly, but said, "I'm staying with my sister."

She didn't like it here, she told me, and she didn't want to stay any longer than she had to—but, as of now, she had nowhere else to go that seemed more appealing.

"This place is too weird," she said, gesturing to the manicured park around us. "It's like a movie set. I haven't seen one piece of litter. I haven't even seen bird shit."

She went on to talk about how in the past, staying with her older sister Leah had always felt like a relief, but not this time. The dynamic between Leah and her daughters, thirteen-year-old twins named

Graciela and Natalie, had been more difficult to witness than ever before. Nat was two minutes older than Grace, she explained, but Grace was a teenager and Nat was a child. Corrie hated watching Grace chastise her mother; she wore tops scissor-cut to show her barely-existent cleavage and she spent hours on her phone with an amused smile, the only smile Corrie had seen on her since she arrived a week ago. Nat, alternatively, affected a baby voice, saying "please Mommy" when she wanted permission to watch *Riverdale* before dinner, or for frozen waffles for breakfast. Corrie had unsuccessfully tried to support Leah as she attempted to be more authoritarian than she was by nature during the nightly arguments over screen time in bed; on this matter, the twins were of the same mind. When Grace snapped at Corrie the other night to stay out of this—"It doesn't have anything to do with you, you know," Corrie mimicked—she retreated to the guest room, listening, letting her sister be outnumbered and worn into submission by exhaustion.

"But it's Paul," she said, "who makes me want to leave the house."

Paul was Leah's husband, I inferred, but not the twins' father. There were a few moments throughout the day when Paul and Corrie were home alone together that Corrie had come to dread: when Leah walked the twins to the bus stop in the morning and Paul had not yet left for campus (he was a tenured professor in organic chemistry), or when he came home after his classes and Leah was at the bank, or Target, or Trader Joe's, and he'd walk in and see Corrie sitting on the couch watching YouTube clips on Leah's laptop or making herself a cheese sandwich in the kitchen. He'd say, "Oh, hello! Didn't expect to see you here!" in such a way that made it obvious he was terrified of being alone with her.

Corrie didn't dislike Paul. He was fine. He was nice, if dull, apparently smart in his field, and probably a competent professor. And he seemed to treat Leah and the twins well, though not as if they were his own daughters—he never touched their shoulders as he passed, never joked with them, never scolded them—but he didn't show any animosity toward them, either. It were as if they were a tolerable but slightly unpleasant smell that, if he wanted to be with Leah, he would have to bear without showing a hint of aversion. And he loved Leah just enough to do so.

"So it's not Paul, really," she said, pulling a strand of hair behind her ear, "it's more that he is so obviously uncomfortable with *me* that it makes *me* uncomfortable with *him*, and when we're both uncomfortable and it's painfully clear, it makes it all the more awkward."

Corrie couldn't always predict when she and Paul would be home alone together, but this morning, she saw it coming: the night before, Leah had said she was going to take Grace and Nat to their tennis lesson at eight, and Paul had announced no plans of his own. When Corrie woke, she began to immediately search for somewhere to put herself. She saw the Shakti schedule on the fridge while filling a glass of water from the filter. She'd never done yoga before, but she knew that Leah loved it since moving here, and, for the most part, what Leah loved, Corrie loved.

The prenatal class was at ten. It was only seven-thirty, but she wanted to be gone by the time Paul came downstairs, so she dressed and took a long walk through University Hills and campus, circumscribing the park we walked through now, and eventually she made her way to Peet's for a coffee, (she didn't specify if it was decaf or regular, if she were concerned about caffeine with her pregnancy), and then she walked next door to Shakti.

We were walking quickly, more quickly than I would alone, since I'd been pregnant, and my breathing was heavy and audible. She was breathing easily and talking at a fast clip. I had not expected her to be so loquacious, and there was a pressure and urgency to her voice that made me suspect she was someone who enjoyed an audience, no matter how small and fleeting. It wasn't until then that I began to wonder if she really was pregnant, or if she had just wanted to go to yoga this morning and prenatal sounded like the most accessible class.

Lying to strangers, she may have reasoned, was hardly lying at all.

"So you have no nausea or anything," I interjected into a brief pause. "I'm jealous. I'm fifteen weeks and I just started feeling a little better."

"Yeah," she said. "I feel fine."

Though if she were trying to deceive, I thought, she would likely come up with a symptom or two to avert suspicion. So it might be true, what the instructor said. She may just be one of the lucky ones.

"Where is your OB?" I asked.

"Don't have one yet. I think I'll just get one wherever I go next."

I thought of saying, you should really go and make sure the embryo has a heartbeat and is implanted in the right place, missed miscarriages aren't so rare and ectopics can be quite dangerous, the OBs at UCI Medical Center in Orange have been really wonderful to me so far, and you are so, so thin, did you know you are so thin?—but she was already speaking about how the discomfort she felt in the house, in addition to Paul's discomfort, had to do with the house itself.

"It's so big and clean I don't know where to sit and what to touch," she said. "And the house is brand new, it even has this new smell, and there isn't even any grass on the lawn yet."

Corrie and Leah grew up in Riverside, she explained, in a small, boxy apartment in a complex right next to the 215 with three bedrooms for the six of them. Leah and Corrie shared a queen bed, and their little sisters shared a double. There was no space designated just for one person: no dining chair, no couch cushion, no work desk. Even the bathroom was frequently crowded, and the lock, like all the locks in the house, had been busted out by the previous tenants and never repaired. Privacy was not a luxury she'd even thought to desire.

Corrie had often wondered what their lives might have been like if they had been rich growing up, how they would decorate their home, what shade of curtains they would buy, which paintings they would hang from the walls, etc., and now here it was before her, here she was inside it, how Leah would live if she had the money. Grace and Nat each had their own bedroom with their own double bed, closet, window, desk. They had their own dressers and vanities, their own tablets and phones and headphones. Corrie was staying in the guest room, and this room, too, had its own closet, with some heavier coats and formal dresses pushed to one side, and an empty dresser. She had only brought enough clothes to fill one drawer, but she kept them in her suitcase, ready to leave whenever the instinct struck.

Leah and Paul had met on Match.com, Corrie said. They dated for less than a year before Paul proposed.

"How long have they been married?" I asked.

Being around Grace and Nat, she said, ignoring my question, now barely teenagers, had been making Corrie think more about herself when she had been their age, or a little older. That was a time in her life which she now saw, in retrospect, as the point at which everything that had transpired since had been set into motion, if not determined outright. She was now thinking nearly constantly about this boy named Danny, whom she had already been thinking about more than usual, now that she was pregnant again.

"You've been pregnant before," I said.

"A long time ago."

She didn't look at me as she spoke, keeping her hand shading her eyes. A girl passed us on the path, speaking what I guessed to be

Vietnamese on her phone, not looking at either of us. On that Saturday on campus, like most weekends, the park was quiet. Across the green, an older couple stood next to each other in silence with hands clasped behind their backs.

It wasn't a story she'd told many times, she said, and when she did tell it, she only told people who she knew she would never see again. Patrons at bars in towns she didn't live in. Seatmates on long bus rides. She has a talent, she thinks, she said, for identifying strangers who want to hear a story like this, though it is much more difficult for her to identify which strangers want to tell a story in return.

"With you," she said, turning to look at me, "as soon as you offered me directions, I knew you were one who wanted to listen. But I couldn't tell if you had something to tell."

"I don't."

"I didn't think so," she said, perhaps with an edge to her voice, a judgment. She smiled and then looked back straight to the path, and she did not look directly at me for the rest of the walk, until we parted on Briarcrest Drive, knowing but not acknowledging that we would more than likely never see each other again.

Corrie began her story by telling me how, in the midst of her parents' constant arguments, or what felt to her more like one argument that lasted for the entirety of her childhood, her mother had often threatened to leave her father if he did not stop sleeping with other women. Her father always adamantly denied these accusations. He'd demand evidence that her mother refused to provide; she'd just say, "I'm not an idiot," and he'd call her a bitch, whore, cunt. They never hit each other, and they never threatened to—but Corrie and her three sisters feared violence as soon as they saw the heat rising in their parents' faces. The girls would huddle under the sheets of Leah and Corrie's bed, singing Spice Girls to drown out the shouts.

Many times, her mother made good on her threat. She'd leave early in the morning, before anyone else was awake, and she wouldn't return for several days, sometimes up to a month. Corrie's father was a long-haul truck driver, and the girls were accustomed to his absence, and for most of their childhood their mother would stay home while he was away and wait to leave until he had returned. But by the time Corrie was thirteen, her mother was leaving more frequently, and more often while their father was also gone, so the girls were alone for up to three weeks at a time.

Corrie didn't know where her mother went and if there was a man she visited there and whether or not she would return. Just when Corrie would become convinced that she had left them for good, her mother would call from an unlisted number, speech heavy and slurred, unsure which of her daughters had picked up, and say, "I miss you baby, I'm just in the desert, don't mind that father of yours, be good, take care of your sisters, I'll be back soon." She always did return—until the night she did not—late at night after the house was asleep. Corrie would find her at the kitchen table in the morning, looking haggard but happy, smelling stale, wanting a hug and a kiss and promising to never leave them again.

It was unclear who caused the accident. Both her mother and the other driver, an eighteen-year-old boy on his way home to Twenty-nine Palms from visiting his girlfriend in Chino, had high alcohol levels in their blood. They were both pronounced dead at the scene.

After her mother's death, her father took more shifts, driving across the country and back, sometimes deep into Canada. At least that's where he said he went. He would come home for a few days, do his laundry, sleep most of the afternoon, and then go on the road again. One day he took Leah to the bank downtown and made a separate joint account so Leah could pay rent and utilities while he was gone. He sat Leah down at the kitchen table that night after dinner and showed her how to write a check. Corrie watched closely, envious of the attention, and practiced her own signature with C's of various heights and depths on the back of her homework.

"That's my good girl," her father said when Leah had written her first check correctly without needing his guidance. "Look how grown up you are."

His trips stretched longer and longer, and then he didn't come home at all. He had not forgotten his daughters—by the end of each month the account would have just enough to cover rent and utilities and groceries—but he no longer wanted them. The pain of this realization, which occurred not on one day in particular but steadily, over the accumulation of weeks, then months, was far sharper for Corrie than the pain of her mother's death. Her mother had chosen to leave them, over and over again, but she had also chosen to return over and over again. She may have hated life, but she did not, from what Corrie could tell, choose her death that separated them forever. Corrie began to suspect that her father had been unfaithful to her mother, as her mother had likely been unfaithful to him, and that he had another woman, in some faraway state, perhaps a woman he loved, perhaps a woman with whom he had fathered more children.

That was the story that Corrie chose to believe, anyway. She would rather he chose to leave them for love than for anything short of it.

The girls called no aunts, no uncles. All grandparents were dead, save their father's father who lived in rural Oregon, and they didn't want to call him, either, given what little they'd heard about their father's childhood. They did not call DCF on themselves; DCF was not called on them. They forged their parents' signatures when needed, affected older voices on the phone, kept out of trouble. They were on their own, and they wanted it to stay that way.

For Leah and Corrie, seventeen and fifteen, their new roles as caretakers for themselves and for the twins, Jenna and Bella, who just turned nine, were not so new, but they had a different feel to them now, heavier for their apparent permanence, but also lighter, in a way, since the time of anxiously awaiting their parents' return was behind them. They bought food on their way home from school from Albertson's. They tried to buy what didn't need cooking: rotisserie chickens and boxes of mashed potatoes, black forest ham from the deli counter, peanut butter and grape jelly for lunches. They never bought milk or juice or any liquid; that was too heavy to carry home with all the other groceries and the books and folders in their backpacks.

At home, at night, after Jenna and Bella had come home from their afterschool program at the youth center, they'd all eat the food bought earlier that day, always the meat first. Their fingers and cheeks would be greasy with it. They'd eat on the couch in front of *Wheel of Fortune* and *Jeopardy!* with paper towels protecting their laps. When they were still hungry, which they often were, they'd eat the deli meat wrapped around thick slices of cheddar cheese. For dessert they walked two blocks along the freeway to Chevron, one older sister holding one younger sister's hand, and they ate Twizzlers and jelly beans in the gas station parking lot, watching the sun lower and the sky pink behind the stream of cars moving east toward the desert and west toward the ocean.

As Corrie and Leah lay together at night, wearing their mother's old shirts, they confessed. They confessed to each other horrible thoughts they'd had during the day, or a secret they'd been told in confidence, a friend's first period or first French kiss or first blow job.

Corrie could never remember a time when she was not in love with boys, when she did not think of them as she touched herself late at night after Leah was asleep. Latency had not quelled her, and adolescence had only intensified her appetites. She told Leah about the boys she wanted, often older boys—men, in her eyes, high school men, men repairing the road on Sherman Street, her elementary and middle school teachers. "Mr. Everett," she'd sigh in the dark. "Don't you just want to bite him? Or maybe I'd rather have him bite me."

Leah never had any desires to confess in return. Corrie had asked Leah more than once if she maybe liked girls, and Leah had always paused, giving the idea consideration, before saying no, she didn't think so. "I just don't think about it," she'd say. All that didn't concern her, and it shouldn't concern Corrie so much, either.

It seemed radically unfair that Corrie was the one afflicted with infatuation for men she could not possess, both because she was too young and not pretty enough, while Leah herself was both older and prettier. They undeniably resembled each other—both had their father's almond face and ski-jump nose and their mother's fair complexion—but the few subtle differences between them had made Corrie wiry and plain, while Leah was slight and refined.

What Leah confessed to Corrie in bed before sleep was how she sometimes believed she was a genius, but not in any subject taught in school, so she might never learn her true talents. She'd confess that she thought her best friend Rachel Beck wore way too much makeup, and she didn't know whether or not to point out the line of foundation along her jawline that betrayed her neck was an entirely different, and lighter, pigment than her face. When the girls tired, and their confessions of the day ran dry, they fell asleep, and Corrie dreamed of tidal waves and paralysis, of her lungs filling with black tar. She'd awake gasping.

The first boy's name Leah ever spoke at night was Danny Rosario. "You know Danny Rosario?" she whispered to Corrie in the dark, saying his name in a way that sounded like she'd been turning it over in her mind for days already. Corrie had heard the name Danny Rosario, but she didn't know him or have any association to his name.

"I think he likes me," said Leah. "Maybe, I don't know. It's so stupid."

Though Corrie couldn't see her sister's face in the dark, she felt her smile as she said so.

At first Leah was amused by Danny's feelings for her, she told Corrie, how eager he was, though she wasn't sure if she liked him in return. They were in the same grade, juniors, but they had taken few classes together—he mostly took honors and AP—but they had shared art, tech, and health. It was in health class in their junior spring that they began to talk; they'd been paired together to do a presentation on how marijuana effects your memory, and by the time the presentation was over, Danny was leaving notes in Leah's locker saying, *Hey, can I take you to the movies?* Or: *Hey, you look extra gorgeous today.* It didn't take long for Leah's amusement at Danny's affection to become reciprocated affection, and for the affection to become a feeling so strong it had convinced her it was love.

Once she mentioned his name, Leah's nighttime confessions became exclusively about Danny, what note he had left her, how he had smiled at her—then how good a kisser he was, how he gave her shivers all over when he touched her hair, and how, on the last night of school, he had not gone out to party with his friends but had instead driven Leah to Box Springs. He'd already packed a blow-up mattress and pillows from his bedroom with clean pillowcases and a tent and electric lanterns. Leah had been nervous when she realized what this night might become, but she wanted him as much as he wanted her. It was Leah's first time, of course, but it wasn't Danny's. It was well known that he'd had sex with Nicole Goodwin the year before, and Molly Tan, though Leah remembered only hearing that they'd had sex, with no negative charge associated with it—nothing forceful, nothing disrespectful; she heard no rumors about how their pussy smelled like cod, or how they couldn't suck dick for shit, rumors that stuck to girls like Post-its on their backs for years. Danny, all evidence showed, had been good to the girls he'd slept with, and he kept the details to himself.

That night, in the pop-up tent in the cold air, they had sex together for the first time. And the second, and the third.

"Did it hurt?" Corrie asked the night she returned, listening rapturously to Leah's confession. "Did you bleed? What did you do with the cum?"

Leah laughed, and she gave off an air, for the first time, that she was older than Corrie, that she had lived what her little sister had not. Her hair still smelled like woodsmoke. But Corrie pressed, refusing to be left out, especially now, when her sister had touched the world that she'd been craving so badly to touch herself: the world of men and sex.

Danny was gentle, Leah told her, though it was still painful, especially as they were just starting. It took a while for her body to get—"ready," she said. He always stopped when he felt her wince or clench and asked her if he should go on. She always said yes. Sometimes he moved faster and harder than he meant to, and though these were the moments that hurt Leah the most, she loved that her body could have this effect on him. She could make him lose control. He'd offered to give her pleasure in return, and after some time, once she got over her shyness, she let him touch her with his hand, and then, after he begged, he went down on her.

"It tickles at first," Leah said, "but then it feels good, then *really* good."

Corrie vividly imagined everything Leah told her in the dark bedroom. She could almost feel it: the weight of him on her, him inside her, massaging her with his tongue. The image of Leah in pain pained Corrie, but what disturbed her more was how the thought of them together—Leah, moving rhythmically, gasping, moaning, the image she had conjured of Danny sweating and his face concentrated, transported—aroused her.

Once they started having sex more regularly, Leah stopped telling Corrie about it in so much detail, and soon she hardly told her about it at all. Leah was now a woman in love, not a girl with a crush, and her most intimate secrets were given to Danny. Corrie no longer asked her sister for details; rather, she felt some relief at being spared the scenes Leah had described and the unsettling sensations they'd inspired deep within her. Corrie stopped telling Leah about the boys she liked, too, in part to mirror her sister's retreat and in part because she no longer saw her unrequited feelings for boys as feelings at all, but as the whimsies of a child.

"Did she ever bring him over?" I asked.

Corrie seemed annoyed at the interjection, or perhaps at the question itself, as if I had suggested an alternative course of the narrative that she'd so thoughtfully plotted. We were walking now past the cluster of brutalist humanities buildings, through the cool shade they cast on the concrete quad. She pulled the sleeves of her black shirt over her hands.

"We never had anyone over," she said after a few steps of silence. "We were afraid they might figure out our father had left, report us, go and tell their parents, something like that. But after Leah and Danny had been dating for a few months, she'd already told him everything and he'd sworn to secrecy. She insisted that we could trust him. And since she'd told him, we didn't really have a choice."

Corrie paused again and looked in my direction, though not directly at me, in a way that seemed to say, *so may I continue?* I didn't say anything in response, allowing her to go on. After a moment of thought, recalling where she had left off before I'd broken her stream of memory, she began to speak again.

They spent that summer together, Danny and Leah, nearly every day and into the evenings, which were warm and dry; it was always dry but it was especially dry that summer. Leah's curls fell flat and straight and the brown hills to the east burned, and the city smelled like smoke and the sky always had a yellow hue. They parted when Danny had to go to his house in Sierra Grove, the wealthy neighborhood, before his curfew at 10:00, which he never broke. Leah was working morning shifts at the checkout at Albertson's, where she got a fifteen percent discount, and Danny had an unpaid internship with his father's colleague, a real estate developer with an office just one plaza over from the Albertson's on Calabasas Avenue. When they were both out of work, Danny would drive Leah to the Santa Ana River, or to Box Springs, or, most often, especially when the dry heat was too harsh, they spent the afternoons and evenings at the house with Corrie, who all summer was tasked with watching after Jenna and Bella.

He came over for the first time one painfully hot day in early June. "Hey," he said as he entered, with Leah's hand in his. "Corrie, right?" Corrie nodded, suddenly mute. Leah had said many times that he was handsome, that he was "so, so cute," but Corrie was still struck by the way all his features seemed to be in harmony. His eyes and smile and cheeks and lips had a softness to them that complimented the firmness of his body, and his lashes were long, almost feminine. He shook her hand. Corrie felt the muscles in his palm—no calluses, clean nails. She was surprised she hadn't already noticed him in school, big and crowded as it was, and that he was not already a member of the cast of men who populated her fantasies.

He seemed instantly comfortable in the apartment, though not entitled. He sat on the couch and draped his arm over Leah's shoulders; he tossed Corrie a pillow when she wanted to sit on the floor. Once he started to come over more often, he was helping himself to glasses of tap water and offering some to all the girls, and placing his empty glass in the top shelf of the dishwasher before he left. Some days he brought them liters of lime soda, the kind he said they sold everywhere in the Philippines, it was the drink of all his childhood summers, but here he'd only found it at the gas station on Buscador Boulevard; he had to drive ten minutes out of his way to get it. He'd pour it evenly into cups with a cube of ice and they'd drink it while watching TV, waiting out the heat, a heat that Corrie now wanted to last all day and night.

When Danny was in the house, the space shifted, it seemed, in two directions simultaneously. The smell and sounds from the freeway were louder, the brown stains on the carpet and couch and countertops were all more glaring, the ceilings were lower and the footsteps from the upstairs neighbors were angrier. It felt like the kind of place children live when their parents no longer wanted them. But the space also seemed cozier and livelier when he occupied it. It was a place she wanted to be. Corrie imagined Danny's house in Sierra Grove as silent, clean, odorless—except, perhaps, for the scent of lavender laundry detergent on towels and sheets. She imagined fresh lilies on the kitchen table in crystal vases, picked by no one, and whole milk and fresh-squeezed orange juice in the fridge. Corrie had never been to

Sierra Grove, and as far as she knew Leah hadn't either, and though it was just fifteen minutes south on the 215 with favorable traffic, it remained to the sisters a forbidden, mythic place that existed only to take Danny from them at night to shower, brush his teeth, sleep, and change into another pair of khaki shorts and another short-sleeve Polo.

Leah had said a few times that Danny's parents were very strict and very Christian, that they had specific expectations of Danny's future that he often felt he would be unable to fulfill. He would go to USC. He would take over his father's real estate company. He would transcend the wealth he had come from, marry a devout Filipina girl, and raise his family close enough to his parents to have dinner together every Sunday. But Danny did not begrudge his parents, as Leah had expected. "It's weird," she said, "but I think he wants all those things, too." Corrie didn't know where Danny's parents thought he was in the hours between his internship and his curfew, but she was sure it wasn't in the Tabors' living room with the Tabor girls. It was understood that Danny's family would not approve of him dating a girl like Leah: white, secular, motherless, and poor. That Danny chose Leah, against what his parents wanted for him and what he thought he wanted for himself, made his feelings for her seem that much closer to true, movie love.

"I feel like we're Tony and Maria," Leah said to Corrie one night in the dark. *West Side Story* was one of the only DVD's they owned, and they'd watched it so many times they could nearly recite it by memory in its entirety. "Except, you know, that nobody's in a gang or anything. *But you are not one of us*," she said in a dramatized accent.

"*And I am not one of you*," replied Corrie.

Corrie soon came to crave Danny's laugh, how it filled the room, and she'd do whatever she could to summon it. He laughed liberally, at what was on TV, at how the younger sisters were always mimicking

Alex Trebek and the sound effects of *Daily Double*—but when he laughed in response to a joke from Corrie, she glowed. She'd try to keep her face turned to the TV to hide her satisfaction.

"That guy looks like a sad cross between George W. and Santa Claus," Corrie said one day when they were all watching *Jeopardy!* in the living room.

Danny laughed and said, "Yeah, you're so right. Or like Bush and Mr. Navarro."

"Oh my god, totally," Corrie agreed, though she didn't know what Mr. Navarro looked like, only that he was the AP English teacher who had taught Danny but not Leah.

"What are you, a standup now?" Leah chided Corrie. To Danny: "She's not usually like this. Only when you're around."

They were all sitting on the couch together, Leah between Corrie and Danny, Jenna and Bella on the floor, laying down on their stomachs, propping up their heads with their hands to see the screen, a weak fan inches from their faces. Corrie's thighs were sweaty against the couch.

"That's not true," said Corrie. "Like what, anyway?"

"So giggly," said Leah.

A rage rose up in her, a rage she had felt often before, at her parents, at herself, but very rarely at Leah.

"Leah," said Danny, in mock-discipline, "you don't know Corrie like I do. We go way back. We're super tight."

Leah rolled her eyes and Danny brought her under his arm. His arm, tanned from the sun, darker in his light blue Polo shirt, was strong and toned, though he never mentioned working out. The boys Corrie's age were children, she thought. It wasn't fair. They had thin, hairless arms and legs, bird necks and cracking voices, braces with purple and yellow rubber bands for the Lakers. Danny seemed completely unaware of his beauty and the effect he had on all the Tabor girls. Even Jenna and Bella were constantly asking him for piggyback rides, which he always gave. They squeezed his head between their legs.

Leah's beauty, however, clearly transfixed Danny. Corrie figured that she and Danny were the only ones who saw Leah for how beautiful she was; it was the kind of beauty that grew stronger the more you looked at it. Danny stared at her—aware, at all times, where she was in relation to him, and always moving himself closer.

"Yeah," said Corrie. "We're super tight," but Danny was no longer paying her attention. He was watching Leah flip her long, cucumber-and-melon hair over her head and smooth it back into a high knot. She gently lifted up the fine, blonder hairs on the back of her neck. He touched the spot with his fingers, then his lips.

"Whatever," said Leah, warmed now, leaning into Danny. "I think he looks more like a cross between Bush and Barbara Walters."

Leah rested her head on Danny's shoulder, then he whispered in her ear, and they stood and Danny said, "See you guys later," and he followed Leah down the hallway, toward the bedroom. Corrie turned off the TV, though it was in the middle of a question, and told the protesting twins that it was time to go on a walk and get some snacks from Chevron, no matter the heat, no matter what food she'd already bought.

Corrie had caught Leah and Danny together only once. It was a Saturday in early July, and Corrie had taken the twins to the playground behind the elementary school in the morning before it became too hot. Leah had been gone when Corrie woke in the morning, and she'd assumed Danny had come to pick her up and they were now out, somewhere, without her, as they often were. While at the playground, just around the corner, watching Jenna play Hot Lava while Bella talked to girls on the swings, (Bella was the more cautious of the two), Corrie felt a wetness between her legs, and she knew her period had come. She'd had her period just for six months, and it always came when she didn't expect it. Six weeks, then seven weeks, then four weeks, and each month, it had been heavier than the last, the blood now red and thick rather than stains of pink or brown. When it came on this day, she panicked, afraid she'd ruin the one pair of jeans that had been a present to her alone from their mother, not a hand-me-down from Leah. Corrie quickly made sure there were enough older siblings and parents around that could collectively protect her sisters for a short time, then ran the few blocks home.

Corrie didn't call to see if anyone was there. She didn't see their sandals in the doorway. She walked quickly to the bathroom, and as she passed her bedroom door, she saw it was not open, as it always was, but not completely shut, either. The air from the window always blew it open, so when Corrie really wanted privacy, in the short periods of time when the room was her own to inspect her body, her breasts that never seemed to grow, new pubic hairs, she placed a book in front of the door to keep it shut. There was nothing holding the door closed, no foresight of a witness.

Corrie saw, through the open sliver, Danny's long, tan back, and the top of his ass, the muscles clenched, and her sister's pale arm reaching above, gripping his black hair. The only sounds were their breathing. Corrie hurried to the bathroom and sat on the toilet and pressed one of Leah's pads into her underwear—already stained, ruined, but her jeans were spared. She walked back down the hallway and from this direction she could not see inside the door without stopping and turning, and she did not, she kept walking and went out the front door, closing it quietly, and ran back to the playground, where Jenna and

Bella were still playing as they had been before, hardly aware that Corrie had left until she returned.

Corrie had seen it all only for an instant, but the image was strong in her mind, and she replayed it, repainted it, until it seemed as though she had watched for several minutes and been much closer to them than she actually had been. She wanted to see it again, to watch them for longer, to hear them sigh and moan, to know the sounds they made when they came. Still, when Corrie was having trouble climaxing, alone or with someone else, the image that always helped her come was the scene from another angle, one that showed Danny's face, tense with pleasure, and he was fucking not Leah, but another, altered woman, Leah-but-not-Leah, wishing he were fucking Corrie.

Leah learned she was pregnant in September, Corrie said as we passed by the bougainvillea covering the western wall of the engineering library. The first week of her senior year. She told Corrie in bed before sleep, the first confession from either of them in several months.

"Are you sure?" asked Corrie.

"My period is six days late. And I took four tests."

Corrie's lungs filled with ice. She was grateful for the dark, that Leah's face was the one lit by the yellow streetlight.

"Have you told Danny?"

Leah shook her head.

"You're not going to?"

"Of course I'm going to. I just haven't figured out when yet." She searched Corrie's silence. "You don't think I should tell him."

"No—I didn't say that."

"You don't think I should keep it."

Corrie paused, considering, still absorbing the idea that Leah was pregnant. Corrie realized she had instantly assumed Leah had decided not to keep it. She'd assumed that's what the confession really was, that she was pregnant and she was not going to keep it and she might or might not tell Danny. Just the week before, Leah had started talking about college for the first time. She'd printed off applications at the school library. She'd been talking about maybe wanting to study psychology and becoming a therapist eventually, she thought she'd be good at that. She wanted to help foster children and orphans. Danny would go to USC, in all likelihood, and Leah could try for CSULA, or Santa Monica College. They could still see each other all the time, maybe even live together. When Corrie thought of Leah leaving in a year, less than a year, she always felt both dread and relief. Now she felt only the cold in her chest.

"I don't know what you should do," said Corrie, and it was the truth.

"I don't know what I should do either," said Leah. "I mean, I don't know what the right thing to do is. But I want it. I know that I really want to keep it. Is that stupid? I can't help it. I don't think I can get rid of it even if that is the right thing to do."

Leah told Danny a few days later, sitting in his father's pearl-white Prius in the parking lot after school. He was shocked, Leah told Corrie. He kept saying, "Are you sure? You're not joking?" and when she said that she wasn't, she wouldn't joke about this, he just stared into space out the windshield, rubbed his temples, took long breaths. Then he started to try to convince her to keep it, but Leah cut him off. She told him she didn't need convincing; she had already decided that she would. He became weepy, and giddy, he took Leah's hands and said he loved her so, so much, and said over and over that he would never leave her and their baby, whom he already loved.

For several weeks Corrie observed no change in her sister other than a new alertness. Leah and Corrie had always walked the mile to school, along the 215, and through the corner of UCR campus, dropping Jenna and Bella off at the elementary school on the way. But now, Danny picked them all up and drove them together, Leah in the front. Leah always wore her seatbelt now without being prompted by Danny, and she warned him when there was an erratic driver ahead, or when the stoplight turned yellow. When she cooked burgers, she cut them into bits with the spatula to make sure the insides were brown, without a hint of pink, and she checked the expiration date of the ketchup before spurting a pile next to the meat and passing it to Corrie. But that was all. She did not vomit, she did not expand, and she did not glow.

Until, one morning, Leah's flat stomach had protruded out, as if it had remembered its condition overnight, and she could no longer fit into her jeans, which she had always worn looser than Corrie wore hers. In a panic before school, Corrie and Leah ran upstairs to their parents' bedroom, where neither of them ever went, and looked for jeans of her mother's, who was only slightly bigger than they were. The room seemed eerie, as if it, too, had given up on their parents' return, and it was more spacious without the bed: the girls had dragged the mattress out to the dumpster that summer, when it developed an awful yeasty smell. Her closet was almost empty, just a few shiny dresses they'd never seen her wear, and her dresser was empty—their father had donated most of her clothes the week she died. Leah wore leggings to school that day with a long flannel, and she wore the same thing the next day. She kept her jean jacket on to hide that she was wearing the same shirt twice, though it was still as hot as it'd been all summer. Leah told Corrie it was at school, in the middle of lunch, that she became overcome with disgust of the smell of the turkey chili Rachel was eating and she had to run to the bathroom to vomit. The taste of bile was on her tongue the rest of the day.

When she started vomiting at school every day, multiple times a day, Leah went to the nurse's office, hoping she would be able to convince her it was just a stomach bug, and that she just needed to lie down for a little while, have some saltines and ginger ale, skip gym. But the nurse was not easily fooled. She insisted that Leah take a pregnancy test. Leah pushed back, but the nurse pressed, until finally Leah said, "I don't have to take a test, I've taken four already." To her surprise, she began to panic, there on the cot in the back room, for the first time since she learned of the pregnancy herself. The nurse coached her to slow her breath and squeeze her toes, until Leah was able to speak coherently. When Leah told her the day of her last period, the nurse took out her own cellphone and helped Leah to set up her first prenatal appointment, one she should have had weeks before.

"Tell your mother," the nurse said. "I won't call her for you, I can't do that, but you go home and you tell her."

A few days later Leah and Danny left school early to drive to the ultrasound at UCR Medical Center on University Avenue. When Leah came home later, she was alone. Corrie was opening a thawed package of chicken for dinner, and she turned to Leah, who sat at the kitchen table with her backpack still on. Danny was at his parents' house, she said, telling them that they were dating, that she was pregnant, that she was keeping it, that he loved her. She was waiting for his call.

"So you'll never believe it," she laughed flatly with her face in her hands. "I'm having twins."

Corrie didn't know what to say. She repeated the sentence in her head, let it settle into meaning.

"That's what I said," said Leah, laughing again. Her eyes were strained, tired.

"What do you mean," asked Corrie.

"What do you mean what do I mean."

"What did they say?"

"They said, 'Looks like you're having twins.' They run in the family, I guess. So watch out."

Danny had wept upon hearing this, Leah told Corrie, there in the ultrasound room in front of the tech, and Leah couldn't tell what emotion was inspiring his tears. She felt only a churning inside her, something between elation and terror, as she saw the two gray smudges against the black backdrop of her uterus and blood.

She hadn't realized until then that a part of her, a tiny part, a part she hadn't wanted to recognize, had hoped that today they would learn something was wrong. She didn't want to have an abortion, but she wasn't entirely sure she wanted to have a baby, either, even with Danny, for whom she felt a love she believed was the most love she would be able to feel for any man for as long as she lived. Maybe she didn't want an abortion because she didn't think Danny wanted her to have an abortion, Leah reasoned aloud to Corrie, and maybe Danny only said he didn't want her to have one because he didn't think she wanted to have one, and they were now plummeting toward teenage parenthood because neither of them wanted to be the one to say: I don't know if we should do this.

But now, with two tiny heads with two heartbeats and four arm buds and four leg buds on the screen before them, the possibility of an abortion instantly became an impossibility.

To end one, Leah believed, was one thing, but to end two was another.

Corrie listened sympathetically to her sister. She made chicken and rice in soy sauce for dinner, washed all the dishes and wiped the counters, helped the girls with their homework and put them to sleep, letting Leah lay down in bed, keeping her phone by her bedside, still waiting for Danny's call. And Corrie kept to herself, that night and for all the years that followed, that she thought Leah was making a great mistake.

Danny came over late that night, long after all the sisters had gone to bed. Corrie was still awake, restlessly ruminating, when she heard the knock on the door. She stepped out of bed, careful not to wake Leah, terrified it may be her father. When she saw it was Danny through the peep hole, she became aware that all she was wearing was underwear and an old shirt of their mother's, one that showed the loose suggestion of her breasts underneath. She crossed her arms to hide them, then uncrossed them, letting the fabric press her nipples, and opened the door. He smiled when he saw Corrie, an apologetic smile. She had never seen him so serious, so tired.

"Hey," he said. He was wearing his school backpack and held a roll-along suitcase, and in his other hand he carried his running shoes by the shoelaces. "Is it okay if I stay here for a little while?"

That night, and for many nights that followed, Danny and Leah slept together in the bed and Corrie slept on the couch. Corrie slept terribly. The cushions were too soft, so she sunk into them, and the fabric was rough and smelled like old popcorn. She had let Danny use her bed pillow, slipping a clean case over it and putting her own pillow case over a throw pillow on the couch, hoping the familiar material and scent would help to recreate a sense of her bed, but the throw pillow was too thick and stiff, and the embroidery underneath pressed into her cheek. The lights from the street were a bright, sick yellow, even brighter than those in her bedroom, and the footsteps from the neighbors above were loud and unceasing, sometimes syncing to the pulse in her temples.

After a week of sleeping fitfully with restless dreams and waking with a sore neck and locked knees and being unable to concentrate in school, at nearly 3:30 a.m. by the stove clock, Corrie went to the bathroom as she often did around this time. As she passed her bedroom on the way back to the couch, the door was open more than it had been on the previous nights. She hoped and did not hope to see what she'd seen that day in the summer when she came back from the playground—the thought of it alone again aroused her against her will—but she only saw them sleeping, Leah on her side as she always was, facing the door, and Danny on his back in the space Corrie had slept. His bare chest moved with his breaths.

She opened the door a little more and walked into the dark room. She would not go to her old side, putting Danny between them, even though there was more room next to him than there was next to Leah. Instead she sat on the edge of the mattress, on Leah's side, and as quietly as she could, she lay down and filled the small space next to her sister.

"Corrie?" Leah lifted her head. "You okay?"

"Can I sleep here? Just for a few hours?"

They were whispering, but Danny awoke. He lifted himself up and looked over at the sisters. His face was dark, backlit by the yellow streetlight through the window behind him.

"Corrie," said Leah, "go sleep on the couch. You shouldn't be sleeping in here."

"It's all right," said Danny. He moved over closer to the window. "There's room. It's no problem."

Leah paused, then moved toward him, making space for Corrie, and soon Corrie fell asleep listening to her sister's breathing and to Danny's breathing and to her own.

The nights went on like this. Corrie started on the couch, then moved into bed with Leah and Danny, sometimes stirring them as she crept in and pulled the sheets up to her chin. She never started off in bed with them. It was important that Leah and Danny have time together before sleep, to lie next to each other, to stroke hair and hold hands, kiss, have sex (if they were still having sex), to press their hands on her growing belly and breasts, to confess to each other in the dark.

What they confessed, Corrie could only guess. Which features of the other they hoped appeared on their children's faces. If they wanted boys, girls, one of each. Their fears about what may be happening inside Leah, what could happen after the babies were born, and as they were born. Where they would live, how they would make money, the shape their lives would take as a family.

These confessions were not meant for Corrie to hear, and she didn't want to hear them. So she waited until well after midnight, when she was certain they were asleep, then she'd walk down the hall and slip into their bed.

As her pregnancy progressed, Leah's sleep deepened, and she no longer woke in the middle of the night as often to pee or to vomit, and the odd pains and cramps did not alarm her as they once had. In the mornings, she spoke of the most intense dreams she'd ever had—of drowning, of bursting open, of the babies sliding out of her uterus and getting stuck in her arms and thighs. Soon she did not stir at all when Corrie lay next to her, and Corrie always lay next to her, until one night, when Corrie walked into the room and saw that Leah's body was pressed against the edge of the mattress, leaving Corrie no room. Danny was sleeping on his back as he usually did, bare chest rising and falling, close to Leah. Corrie stood there, unsure what to do, knowing what she wanted to do, before quietly, as quietly as she could, she walked to the other side of the bed and lay down on her old pillow, which now smelled like Danny, like his shampoo she smelled in the shower. Sea Breeze, salty and turquoise.

When she shifted her weight to her side, toward him, he woke. He looked at her. His face was lit by the yellow streetlight, and she saw him smile sleepily when he saw her, his eyes barely open.

"Hey," he whispered. His face was close to hers, his breath like milk, but not sour.

"Hey," she said.

"Do you have enough room?" he asked. He moved closer to Leah.

"Yeah, thanks."

"Good night," he said.

"Good night."

When she woke in the morning, Danny and Leah were still sleeping, and if Leah knew Corrie had slept on Danny's side that night, she never spoke of it.

Nothing happened, Corrie said as we walked over the green bridge over Anteater Drive that connected the graduate housing complex to campus, until some time later, after a few weeks of sleeping in their bed, sometimes on Leah's side, but more often now next to Danny. Leah was growing by the day, it seemed, and by the winter she slept with a pillow behind her back, between her knees, and soon, another small one wedged under her belly. The space between them narrowed. Sometimes Corrie woke with Danny so close she could feel his wet, warm breath on the nape of her neck, the place he used to kiss Leah on the couch when she gathered her hair. She'd feel his chest against her back, sometimes her feet lay against his. His feet were always cooler than hers, and she loved the sensation of his feet warming and the knowledge that it was her doing, a silent communication between their bodies. Whenever she lay next to him, he'd wake, and he'd say *hey*, his eyes squinting from the streetlight, and he'd move an inch or two closer to Leah and fall back asleep.

Corrie loved how he said *hey*. She replayed it over and over in her mind. It made her wet, the way he said it, it made her think of his mouth, his lips and his tongue, how they would move on her. It felt to her like a code to an agreement that whatever was happening between them was okay, and it was their secret—though nothing, really, was happening at all. The small touches at night gradually, then quickly, moved from being sources of comfort and satisfaction to agonizing temptations. She came to loathe as much as she'd once craved when his chest found her back, because then the night of sleep was ruined, she wanted so badly to turn around and kiss him and do anything to him that he would let her do, and she, in turn, would let him do anything to her that he pleased.

She had made out with plenty of boys since she was in middle school, and had given Harris O'Riley a hand job after spring formal as a freshman and a few times in the summer that followed, in his bed when his parents weren't home, and he had tried to finger her, but his hands were dry and clumsy, and she preferred to do it herself, later, back at home. Harris had asked her, once, if she would have sex with him, and she said maybe later, and she meant it, but then they lost interest in each other and she had rarely thought of him since. She was glad she hadn't had full sex with Harris. Now there was nobody she wanted to have sex with but Danny—all the other boys and men she had desired before were forgotten—and she found herself fantasizing constantly about a feeling she had never felt before, that she could only imagine from Leah's description, a feeling of fullness from a man's body, of Danny's body.

The night it happened, she lay next to him as she often did, but on this night he did not wake. She waited, moved to her side, facing him, and the movement still did not stir him. She studied his face in a way she hadn't been able to before. His nose was smooth and the tip round and pleasing, his nostrils almost perfect circles. His eyelashes were long and dark and lay lightly against the top of his cheek. His lips, at rest, angled downward, and in the corners were small creases she hadn't before noticed.

"Hey," she said, just above a whisper. She touched his shoulder under the covers, the first time she had touched him like this in the bed, with unmistaken intentionality. He opened his eyes, smiled, said *hey*, and this night he did not move toward Leah. He kept his eyes open and she kept watching him.

"You okay?" he asked.

She moved closer to him, and he let her. Closer, slowly, then closer, until their lips touched. She kissed him, and after a moment of stillness, he kissed her back. She kissed him again, and did not pull away, and he found her tongue with his, and she pressed her body to his body as she pressed her lips to his lips, his chest touching her breasts, loose under her cotton shirt. She moved her hands down his back and then over his torso, moving lower. He was hard under his boxers, and harder as she touched him, above the fabric, then below, skin on skin. His hands were on her now, too, cupping her breasts and making their way to the frayed elastic of her underwear. They moved quickly and frantically and silently. She nearly moaned with anticipation. He moved on top of her, his weight heavy above her, a heaviness she'd been craving for weeks, for months, forever, and he swiftly slid off her underwear and his boxers and kicked them into a bunch at their feet under the covers. He entered her, breathing a long breath out as he did so. She bit her lip, the pain of him inside her unexpected and sharp, and though the pleasure she had felt as he touched her had evaporated into pain, she did not want him to leave her body. She felt more full than she had imagined, too full, and she feared that she could not fit him. But with a few deep breaths her muscles eased and he bore his forehead into her shoulder, hiding his face, and moved and breathed in a way that let her know that this was what it was supposed to feel like, she was doing what she was supposed to do. She lifted her hips and tried to move against him, and nearly as soon as she did so, he jerked awkwardly. She wanted to see his face, to see if his eyes were open, but fearing, too, that if she saw him, if their eyes met, that all of this would stop and the spell would break and it would be as if it had never happened. Then he pushed further into her and she winced as he touched a red tenderness, the deepest point inside her.

He became still. His skin went damp, and he breathed against her neck, longer breaths now. He moved out of her and lay on his back. He pulled his boxers up, and she pulled up her underwear, cold now from her wetness. She looked over at him, and their eyes met, just for an instant. She kept her face neutral, then she smiled at him, about to move to kiss him. He turned to his side, away from her, toward Leah.

Corrie lay still as a corpse. She felt his spit on her tongue, his cum dripping from her. The pain and satisfaction of the fullness inside her was already a memory.

When she woke in the morning, Danny wasn't in bed. Leah was lying asleep, her new, full breasts saggy under her shirt. Corrie examined the sheets in the dim morning light. She straightened the pillows, pulled the blankets taut. Her underwear was dry now and a little stiff. She looked inside it, and then over the sheets once more. No blood.

Corrie slept again in their bed the following night, next to Danny, fearing that if she went back to the couch, it would be both an admission to Leah of what had happened and a signal to Danny that she did not want to do it again, and she did want to do it again. He didn't touch her that night, or the night after, but when she kissed him on the third night, he responded as he had before. As Danny moved on top of her and entered her and the pain seared inside her, he made a low, grunting sound. Leah, still facing away from them, toward the door, said "Danny?" and with incredible speed Danny slipped out of Corrie and lay next to Leah, kissed her shoulder, and said, "I'm here, baby, you okay?" and he never turned back to look at Corrie.

After staring awake for some time and waiting for Danny to move toward her again, to touch her in any way, Corrie went back to the couch and lay there awake until morning. She didn't go to their room the next night. On the couch, her neck cramping and the cushion smells giving her a headache, she forced herself to keep still and to not allow her feet to move her toward him. The hours passed, the upstairs neighbors fought, stomped, and silenced. She didn't think she'd fallen asleep, if she'd fallen asleep it must have just been for a moment, because she woke to a strong sense that someone or something was near, watching her. Her eyes opened and her heart sped. Danny was there, standing by the couch in his boxers and an undershirt she'd never seen him sleep in.

"Hey," he whispered. "I didn't mean to scare you."

"You didn't scare me," she said. The space on the couch was more narrow than the space on the bed, but Corrie lifted up the blanket and moved herself against the back cushion, inviting him to lie down next to her. He paused, as if he had promised himself he would only come out here to tell her that what they had done was wrong and that it could never happen again and they could never tell anyone about it, ever, they both loved Leah too much to ever hurt her more than they already had.

But he said nothing. He stood still and so Corrie moved toward him. She sat up on the couch and looked up at him, and he looked back at her, his eyes seeming to take her in for the first time. She slowly pulled his boxers down, waiting for him to object, but he did not. She bent over to take him into her mouth, and once he was fully hard he touched her chin and pulled out of her, and in a few swift movements he was on the couch with her, she on top of him this time, pressing her face into his shoulder as he had pressed his face into hers, now hiding their eyes from each other as they rocked.

Then he stopped, suddenly, just as he had started to enter her.

"We have to be careful," he said, his lips hot on her ear.

"I won't tell."

"That's not what I mean."

He stayed inside her, moving slowly deeper, the pain of restraint in his breath.

"I'm on the pill."

He paused and looked at her for a moment, but did not ask for whom.

"For real?" he asked.

"I promise. I don't lie."

He waited a few seconds longer, looking at her, then began to move again, clutching her hips. The sex no longer hurt as it had the first two times, and she had come to crave when he touched the tender spot deep inside her. After he came, she moved off him and they lay next to each other, close on the cushions, and without a word he kissed her on the forehead, found his boxers on the floor—he'd kept his shirt on and she'd kept hers on too—and he pulled them up, then walked down the hall. Corrie waited there for several breaths, long enough for the time to pass for him to lie next to Leah and for her to wake if she were going to wake. Then she walked quietly to the bathroom, clenching until she sat on the toilet. She relaxed her muscles, letting him seep out of her until she was again empty. She wiped what remained, then flushed and washed her hands.

This gesture, which became ritual, allowed her to almost believe that she was good by her promise, and she was not someone who told lies.

Those quick minutes in the dark with Danny were all Corrie thought about during the dull hours on the couch without sleep, the dull hours at school, the dull hours grocery shopping and walking Jenna and Bella to Chevron and back and making them dinner and tucking them into their bed. Her mind replayed over and over the last time he'd been with her on the couch and anticipated the next time. She could never accurately predict when the next time would be, there was no signal during the day to suggest that after they went to bed that night, he would wake and walk to the couch and touch her hair and say *hey*. Two nights in a row he came to her, then two nights in a row he didn't come, then every other night, then every three, then twice in a row. The dark, the half sleep, the yellow light from the street on his face, made all the sex feel surreal, dreamed, a fantasy she was telling herself that she hardly believed could be true.

Sometimes she hoped it was not true. On weekends and sometimes on weeknights the five of them all still watched *Jeopardy!*, but since the night visits to Corrie, Danny rarely joined them. He stayed later at school, doing his homework at the library, he said, though Corrie suspected he was sometimes with friends at parties Leah wasn't invited to, and driving to his house in Sierra Grove when he knew his parents weren't home to get more clothes and do his laundry. He never brought his clothes to the laundromat with the girls; and his shirts always smelled fresh, even through the sweet-sour scent his body revealed at night. When they did watch TV or eat all together, Danny and Corrie did not speak directly to each other. Their eyes danced apart, before they'd meet with an unpleasant intensity when they each thought the other was looking elsewhere. Their eyes met, too, when he came out of the bathroom just as she was about to knock (now that Danny was in the house, the girls knocked on the bathroom door and closed it as best they could), or when he looked in the rearview mirror on their way to school and she had been watching his gaze on the road, his dark eyebrows moving as he spoke to Leah in the front seat.

It was when their eyes met like this and they both looked away and she felt a pull deep in her gut that Corrie knew without a trace of uncertainty that what was happening between them was indeed happening, it was not an imagining or a recurring dream or a fantasy, and that he remembered it, too.

"It was so brief, and strange, and always in the dark," Corrie said as we walked past the empty lap pools in University Hills, the water stagnant and peppered with yellow leaves. "I still think about it. I remember each night more vividly than entire relationships I've had since. I still compare men to him, even though I know we weren't right for each other. If Danny and I had been able to be together, if he'd never been with Leah to begin with, then it probably would've been a pretty brief thing, not some great love story, not even a love story like his and Leah's. It would've run its little course in a few months and I wouldn't be thinking about him now."

She paused in thought, and I let her think. In her pause I thought of Vince Balsamo; the memory of him had been surfacing throughout Corrie's story, and was now sharpening into focus. Vince was Margot's high school boyfriend for a brief time, a gangly boy, a top runner who, in his senior year quit the team and went for the school play. He gave a heartbreakingly earnest performance as John Proctor in *The Crucible*. Whenever Vince came over, Margot treated me like a pest—"Can't you be literally *any*where else right now?"—but he'd look at me with his light eyes as though we shared a secret, a look I reciprocated. I misted Country Apple body spray before he came over, read Margot's AIM chats with him she left open on the screen, looking only for references to me, never finding them. In my daydreams I let him do anything he wanted to me.

More than anything, Corrie said after a few steps, raising her hand to shield her eyes from the sun, which had just come out from behind a thin cloud, she thought they were joined by a mutual love of Leah as well as a fear of her, a sense of entrapment by her pregnancy and what it promised both of them. Maybe they both felt a desperate desire to be careless and cruel and selfish while they still could.

"But I don't know," she said, shaking her head. "Maybe that's the real reason why I've never told Leah. She'd ask me why, and I wouldn't have an answer, and she deserves an answer."

By March, Danny and Leah had started looking for apartments in Mead Valley. They planned to move out shortly before the babies were born—two girls, they now knew. They were due on June 16, but the doctors had told them to be prepared for an early arrival. Danny and Leah wanted to have their apartment set up and ready so they could come home from the hospital with the girls; they enjoyed thinking of the day they would bring the babies home, the first day they would be together as a family.

Mead Valley was near enough to Riverside they could visit often and use Corrie for babysitting as needed, but far enough that they wouldn't run into Danny's parents or anyone at school who had started calling Leah slut, trash, or ignoring her altogether. Even Rachel had stopped speaking to Leah. "Sorry, Leelee," Leah said to Corrie, mocking Rachel's high vocal drag, "I love you so much. It's my parents. It's like they think pregnancy is contagious or something. They're so fucking backwards." Danny's status, however, had not fallen, as far as Corrie could tell, though he had much further to fall than Leah, than any Tabor girl. When Corrie ventured to the upperclassman hallways between periods hoping to see him, making herself late for class, she'd find him walking with a group of boys who all looked like poor imitations of him, but who exuded more cockiness and wealth. She even saw girls talking to him, if anything, more than they had talked to him before. These girls were more beautiful than Corrie but no more beautiful than Leah, but they had what Leah didn't: designer jeans, rich hair, flat stomachs. Danny talked with them, laughed with them, standing close. They didn't know he was with Leah, much less that he was going to be a father—nobody knew, or nobody believed it. It filled Corrie with a rage that extended far beyond jealousy.

So she started hooking up with senior boys in the parking lot during lunch and free period and electives. She used her hand on them, rarely her mouth, sometimes letting them finger her. The boys each had their own taste and smell and texture, a way they used their tongue to draw hers from her mouth. Max Ahern was the first, and the one she saw the most. He had soft hands, and his flannel shirts smelled of sweet weed and natural deodorant, and sometimes, as she was going down on him in the backseat of his parents' Ford EcoSport parked at the far edge of the parking lot where they could see anyone approaching, their limbs at awkward angles, she imagined his mother washing the underwear that was around his knees, throwing it in with his flannels and white tube socks on a gentle cycle, trying to ignore the crusty stains.

Sanderson Hart and Jesse Kleiner and Derek Polanco were one-time-only hookups; she didn't like how they pushed her head down to their laps, and she didn't like how their tongues felt thick and sandy in her mouth, each tasting in their own way like corn chips. Nathan Lao was rough, but in a way Corrie didn't mind and sometimes enjoyed. She only hooked up with him a couple of times, until he told her he was dating Greta Ricci, and that she was starting to act suspicious. Nathan bit Corrie's lip and pulled at her hair as they made out and stroked each other over their pants, then under. His bites were playful, but sometimes too hard, and she'd find the taste of blood in her mouth for the rest of the day. He always insisted on making her come before she did anything for him. His hands knew what to do, and she was wet before he even reclined the seat and began to pull down her jeans and underwear. To come she always used the altered memory of seeing Danny and her sister together that afternoon in the summer, Danny from the back, wishing, she imagined, that he was fucking Corrie.

She never let the senior boys fuck her, not really. That she reserved for Danny alone; she feared he would be able to sense that someone else had been inside her, and that, more than anything to do with Leah and anything to do with the babies, would be what made him stop coming to the couch at night.

"You've been having this strange look about you," Leah said to Corrie one day as they were cooking dinner, tuna melts, open faced to stretch the last of the bread. Danny was out, at the library, maybe. He'd been coming to their house later and later, while Leah now always came straight home from school rather than going over to Rachel's or hanging out with her friends at Boba Tea House in the plaza. "Want to tell me his name?"

Corrie kept her eyes on the skillet, watching the cheddar bubble on the pan.

"What?" asked Corrie. "I don't know what you mean."

"I mean you have a strange look about you. Like you're hiding something and like that something is a boy."

Corrie looked at her sister then, who was leaning against the fridge. Her stomach was huge, stretching thin the magenta fabric of her maternity top Danny had bought her for Christmas several weeks before. Her face had filled in, it was more round than oval, and the effect had made her more beautiful than she had been before. Corrie found satisfaction in the pimples along her hairline.

Leah was smiling at Corrie, a knowing smile, but not a suspicious one.

"Okay, fine," said Corrie. "You know Max Ahern?"

"The dealer?"

Corrie shrugged.

"Max Ahern," Leah laughed. "You can do better than that."

This made Corrie angry with an anger she didn't understand. Max Ahern wasn't someone to be embarrassed about. He wasn't very bright, and he wasn't very wealthy, but he wasn't trash. He didn't hate women. He smoked weed and drank, yes, of course, but not nearly as much as the rest of his friends, and he only sold occasionally to save up for his own car. But Corrie didn't care about Max Ahern. If he never left another note in her locker asking her to come to his car at lunch, then she wouldn't care. She might even be relieved.

"He's fine," said Corrie. "It's not a thing anyway."

"I thought he was hooking up with Kendra Alvarez."

Leah took a butter knife from the drawer and scraped the cheddar from the skillet, blew on it and ate it off the blade.

"Maybe he is, I don't know."

This was the first Corrie had heard about Max and Kendra, and though she doubted it was true, the idea of it did make her feel a little hollow.

"I wish you'd have some more self-respect," said Leah, throwing the knife into the sink. "Danny said he saw you walking from the parking lot with Nathan Lao on Tuesday after lunch."

Corrie pressed the bread hard into the skillet. It was starting to burn. She hated the thought of Danny watching her when she didn't see him. She hated the thought of him talking to Leah about her. Danny never talked to Corrie about Leah. They never mentioned her name. They never talked about anything.

"Max is allowed to do what he wants, and so am I. It's not like we're married or something." She stopped, then hardened her voice. "I do have self-respect."

Leah gave Corrie the look she gave to show how much older, wiser, more mature she was than her younger sister. She was eighteen now; she no longer had to pretend to be an adult. It was a look that reminded Corrie of their mother.

"It's not like you and Danny are married either," said Corrie, then, gesturing to her sister's stomach, "And look at you. Talk about self-respect."

Leah's smug expression fell, and her face reddened. She looked close to tears.

"I'm sorry," said Corrie quickly. "I'm sorry. I didn't mean that. I really didn't," but Leah was already walking out of the room. She didn't emerge until Danny came home a few hours later, and she didn't look at Corrie when she did.

They were steely toward each other for days after, speaking only to talk over what to get at the store, what to make for dinner, to ask if the other had already dropped the rent check in the landlord's mailbox. Danny came to her once in that time, waking her with his tongue on her neck, and they pleasured each other with their mouths, moaning into the throw pillows. Corrie woke with his taste in her, a small victory over Leah. She didn't need self-respect; she had this instead.

Then Leah came home from school a few days later saying she had a headache and was going to lie down, as she often did. But this day she did not stir when Jenna and Bella came home from their after-school program. Corrie let Leah sleep until she heard whimpering coming from the bedroom. She found Leah in bed with the shades drawn, weeping from pain, saying that she could no longer see straight.

"Something's wrong," she said, running her hands through her knotted hair. "I'm underwater. I feel like I'm drowning. Something's wrong."

Corrie forgot her anger, pressed her hand to her sister's forehead, which felt hot and dewy. She called Danny and he was over in fifteen minutes. With hardly a word to Corrie, he helped Leah out of bed and drove her to the hospital while Corrie stayed home to watch the girls. She waited for their call. But the house phone didn't ring while she helped the girls with their homework, while she poured them Cheerios with sliced bananas, while she French braided their hair so it'd be crimpy in the morning. Their mother would do this when she felt guilty for leaving or wanted to win their favor over their father. All the girls loved the sensation of their scalp scraped by long fingernails too much to care what motivated it. This seemed the one thing the twins remembered and missed about her.

When they were asleep she stayed up on the couch, watching nothing on TV, then finally turned it off and lay awake in the dark. She was still awake when she heard the key in the door. She didn't pretend to be asleep. It was Danny, alone.

"Hey," he said.

"How is she?"

"She's okay. She had really high blood pressure, I guess. She'll have to stay there for a while."

"The babies?"

"They think they'll be okay. They don't know for sure but they think so."

Danny sat at the end of the couch, by her feet. Corrie didn't move to kiss him, though she desperately wanted to. Not as a secret lover, now, but as a friend, or a wife. Watching him slouched and drained, she had a strong vision of him as a middle-aged man, a tired father coming home from work. They sat in silence like that for a long time.

"We can't do that anymore," he said, finally looking at her, his face dark. "We never should have."

"Okay," she said. There wasn't anything else to say. She felt cold, childish, stupid. She sat up and pressed her hand to his arm over his sweater. He didn't flinch, but he touched her hand with his, then returned it to her.

"You sleep in the bed," he said. "I'll sleep here."

"I don't mind the couch."

"I don't want to sleep in the bed tonight," he said. "It's your bed, anyway."

"Okay." She stood and, fighting all her impulses, walked down the hall away from him.

That night was the first night she'd ever slept in a bed alone.

The twins were born on May second, Corrie continued, six weeks early, after a long labor that started during geometry class and ended up in an emergency C-section. Leah lost a lot of blood, and for some time there was worry that she might need a complete transfusion. The twins were taken away immediately after they were born to make sure they were breathing all right on their own, and those minutes were the most excruciating minutes of Leah's life: lying on the operating table with her stomach open, unable to move below her waist and unable to feel anything other than pullings and pushings of strangers' hands in her abdomen, the strangers dressed in blue and blurred behind the raised plastic sheet that separated the top half of her body from the bottom, smelling a nauseating combination of hospital and her own viscera, trying to listen above the din of machines and the strangers' frantic speech for the sound of two infants crying and not hearing two or even one.

When the babies were delivered back to her, after what felt like hours of unknowing, Leah held one in each arm and examined their raw, pink faces, their pruned fingers. It wasn't until then that she asked for Danny. They'd need to stay in the NICU for a while for some monitoring, a voice in blue told her, but in all likelihood they would be just fine.

Leah named the baby with the smaller upper lip Natalie, after Natalie Wood in *West Side Story*, and Danny named the other baby Graciela—the baby they both agreed looked more like him—after his beloved great-aunt, who had taken care of him in the Philippines when he was a baby and every summer when he returned as a child. The girls were too small for their names, and too small for all the onesies and caps Leah and Corrie had been collecting from Good Cents Thrift for the past several months. Nat and Grace were not identical, but they were difficult to tell apart—Nat refused nursing, and Grace refused sleeping, but they both seemed to love to be held and sung to, and they both calmed, a little, when Danny traced their eyebrows.

The lease for the apartment Danny and Leah had planned to move into in Mead Valley didn't start until June first, so when the twins came home from the NICU they came home to the Tabor apartment. The place transformed into something like a beehive, everyone working at all hours to keep one another fed and dry and alive. Corrie taught Jenna and Bella how to make simple meals on the stovetop, she told them they were no longer children, they were eleven now and could go to Albertson's and Chevron and the laundromat alone. They had to see what needed to be done and to do it without Corrie's prompting and no expectation of reward.

Corrie was back on the couch at nights then, sleeping less than she ever had before, listening to the twins crying and to Danny and Leah cooing and whispering, bickering. "No, do it like this," she'd hear Leah snap. "That's too loose." Now when she went into their room late at night it was to offer to help, but she was always told in impatient but apologetic tones to go back to the couch, there wasn't anything she could do. Leah's breasts were barely able to feed them both, and it seemed she now spent all day and night sitting up in bed in a half sleep with a baby latched onto her and the other crying in the crib, waiting her turn.

To protect the stitches from splitting, for several weeks Leah couldn't pick up the babies or anything else more than a couple pounds, so Danny and Corrie were the ones to lift them from Leah's breast and carry them from room to room, hoping the rhythm of their steps would calm their cries. They moved through the apartment, vertiginous in their own fatigue, whispering, *Shhh, shhh, it's all right, babe*, each only looking at the baby girl in their arms, careful to avoid coming too close to each other in the dark.

Corrie once stood in the doorframe late at night after hearing cries that sounded different than usual, about to offer help, when she saw that the twins were sleeping soundly and it was Leah who was crying. Danny was lying on his back as he had in the nights when Corrie would slip into the space next to him, passively touching Leah's back with one hand and massaging his temples with the other.

They never moved into the apartment in Mead Valley, or into any other apartment together. By the end of May, a few weeks before graduation, Danny told Leah that his parents, despite everything, had applied to USC on his behalf without telling him. They must've written his essays and filled out all the forms and forged his signature. And he'd been accepted. He said he was furious with them, and he wasn't going to go. He was going to stay with Leah in Riverside for at least a full year, until Leah could go back to high school and finish her credits and graduate and go to college, too—she only had to complete a few classes; it wouldn't take long. Then they'd be able to have an apartment in LA with the babies. That had been their plan, and it could still be their plan. And who would watch the girls when we were in class, Leah wanted to know, and Danny said someone would, he didn't know yet, they'd figure all that out when the time came, speaking the way Leah had come to realize was the vague optimism about everything working itself out in the near-distant future that came with having parents with money.

"So he and his parents have been talking?" Corrie asked as Leah told her about the conversation that had taken place the night before, as Corrie changed Nat's diaper and Leah nursed Grace. Danny was at graduation rehearsal at the high school.

"Apparently," said Leah. "And apparently they've been wanting to come see the girls, too. I don't know how long they've been talking. They've been paying for all this shit," she gestured to the diapers and wipes and baby powder, "that I thought Danny had bought on his own. They've been wanting to make up and meet their granddaughters. Or as long as Danny goes to USC they do."

After that, Leah told Danny that she wanted him to not sleep at their house so much, now that he had his parents' home to go to. Leah told him she slept better now without him, and the twins did too. Her stiches were out and she could carry the babies herself; Jenna kept the kitchen stocked; Bella kept the laundry clean; the babies at last took the bottle without much protest, so Corrie could feed them when Leah needed rest. They didn't need Danny like they did before. He agreed to sleep at his parents', if that's what she really wanted. He was there just once or twice a week at first, but soon it was more often than not, and Leah and Corrie no longer expected him.

June first came and passed, and the apartment in Mead Valley was never mentioned again.

On those nights when Danny stayed at Sierra Grove, Corrie returned to her space in the bed next to Leah and woke in the night and held the girls and touched Leah's back as she cried. She let Leah confess, but she no longer confessed herself. Leah told her how his parents had come by to meet the twins, when Corrie was at school, and they were kinder and warmer than Leah had expected. They were nervous around her, trying to impress her. They looked dressed for a business meeting and had made almond cookies and brought stuffed elephants for the girls, and this made it all the more painful for Leah. Her daughters would love these people, their only grandparents, as long as they were in their lives. Though after one visit to the Tabor house, they invited Leah to come to them instead. Leah didn't like going to their house—"it feels like an empty resort," she said—so most often Danny would take the twins himself to Sierra Grove for a few hours and then return them at night. They'd come home rested and calm, smelling like fresh talcum powder and lemon.

Danny started USC in the winter semester. Soon after, checks began arriving for Leah from his parents, five hundred dollars a month, that Leah did not cash out of pride for a few months but then did out of desperation, and a little out of spite. The money their father had left in the account had been enough for their needs before, just barely, but not enough for the needs of six girls. The formula alone, which Leah soon came to depend on when the babies' appetites surpassed what her tired breasts could produce, was so expensive that she had to stop buying meat to pay rent. Even if Leah and Corrie knew how to get in touch with their father, they wouldn't. If he had any more to give, which he likely did not, then they didn't want it.

Leah never asked Danny if he knew his parents were sending her money. She and Danny rarely talked by then, and when they did, it was only about the twins, never about each other. At some point in those days after the twins were born and before Danny went back to his parents, perhaps on the very day Danny told her about USC and she knew, even if he didn't, that he would go and leave them, whatever love that had kept them together this long had become a different sort of connection, still affectionate, but distant, almost professional.

It was clear what his life was and would be and what her life was and would be, and perhaps they'd been fools to ever believe it could have been any other way.

Corrie never told Leah or Danny or anyone else, besides listening strangers like myself in the years to come, that she had ever become pregnant. When her period didn't come after four weeks, then five, then six, Corrie assumed it was late again, as it often was, though by then it had been more consistent than in the spring and summer before. It was eight weeks late the night Danny sat far from her on the couch and said we can't do that anymore. Or maybe seven, or maybe nine. Another week passed, and her breasts seemed to have doubled in size and were sore every step she took and the waist of her pants were tight and she was so fatigued that she spent several class blocks a week sleeping in the nurse's office, complaining of migraines.

She never vomited. She didn't even feel nauseous, not like Leah. But she knew she was pregnant long before she took the bus to Planned Parenthood on Jenson Street above Taco Patio while Leah was watching Jenna and Bella, making the excuse that she thought she had a yeast infection and had to go to urgent care.

After Corrie peed in the plastic cup and waited alone in a small windowless room with brochures in English and Spanish of beautiful young women of various races about STIs and intimate partner violence, a woman who didn't look any older than Corrie said that the test came back positive, she was indeed pregnant. Corrie told the woman she didn't know if she'd keep it or not but she wanted to know what she could do if she didn't. The woman patiently recited to her from a clearly memorized script what Corrie's options were now, and what they would become as the pregnancy continued, and at what time she would no longer have any option but to continue until birth, at which point she could consider adoption.

"Do my parents need to know?" Corrie asked, "if I want to have an abortion?" and the woman smiled, she'd heard this question many times before, and she said, "No, they don't. Not in California."

But Corrie waited, and then she waited some more. It wasn't just the fantasy of the baby, or babies, if she were to have twins like Leah, and how the babies would be Danny's and this would tie him to her forever, their DNA would be inextricable from each other, nor was it the fantasy of growing as her sister had grown and feeling what her sister had felt inside her that kept her from going to the clinic for as long as she did. More than all of this, it was the vision of them all living together as family. She daydreamed a near future in which Danny, Leah, Corrie, and the three squirming babies all lived in an apartment that was just a little too small for them to fit, so they had to be always touching, always near one another. She couldn't imagine a home with more love.

The apartment—or small house, a bungalow, maybe, if they were all working—would be lighter and cleaner than their place in Riverside, it would have windows without yellow streetlights outside and sounds from the freeway and stomping from above. She imagined Danny cooking them all dinner, chicken parmesan or pasta with meatballs with a dishtowel thrown over his shoulder and the radio on, the way her mother had, on the rare occasions she decided to cook. She imagined Leah picking up painted wooden toys off the floor and placing them into bins as Corrie washed the children's little hands in the sink with gentle soap before they all sat to eat. She imagined weekend mornings on a king bed, the six of them, limbs entangled, hair tossed from sleep, letting the day go by.

She believed it was possible that Danny could and would love Corrie and Leah both entirely and equally and openly, and rather than jealousy and competition for his love tearing the sisters apart, it would bring them closer; they'd be joined by the knowledge of the love of the same man and the fact that this man was the father of their children. They would all be so entwined and dependent on one another that nobody could ever leave, there would be no option of abandonment, no empty rooms and no empty beds.

And so weeks passed, and Corrie kept her oversize peacoat on even when it was hot, and she wore her father's old flannels as Leah had to hide her expanding form, until, one day in the EcoSport with Max Ahern, as he ran his hands over her breasts and stomach, he said, "You knocked up or just putting on some pounds?" and he laughed, but he looked serious, and then, when she didn't laugh with him, terrified—for at that point, after Danny had stopped coming to the couch and she knew he would never return, she had sometimes let Max fuck her, though she always insisted on a condom and put it on herself. "Fuck you," she snapped, "and fuck off," and pushed his hand away. She left the car with her bra still unhooked. She never saw the inside of that car again, and she ignored Max's notes in her locker and his eyes in the hallway—and though she felt meaner to him than he deserved, she found it safer to be mean than to be truthful.

The next day she called Planned Parenthood and told them what she wanted to do and asked them where she needed to go.

Planned Parenthood was booked for the next three weeks, so they referred her to the clinic in the hospital, where the first available appointment was in two weeks. By then it was mid-April, the air already hotter and drier, the hills ready for fire, and Leah was seventeen days away from giving birth, though nobody knew that yet. After Corrie's calculus test in second period, she took the bus to UCR Medical

Center, a forty-five-minute ride with a transfer at Coronado and Beech, a ride that felt like an eternity. She listened to music on her headphones, but the sound from the streets and bickering in the seats behind her turned the music into noise. She tried to count all the red cars, all the red jackets, all the red lights, but she'd quickly lose track of the tallies and have to start again.

She was just over fifteen weeks pregnant, the nurse told her. Judging from her last menstrual period, that is, which was a date that Corrie had chosen practically at random. Time that spring had felt like an illusion; she had been missing deadlines at school and forgetting which day was which, convincing herself at times that she was living the same day over and over and over. The nurse gave Corrie two small white tablets to swallow, and told her to wait and to try to relax if she could, and then left Corrie lying on the chair like a dentist's chair, counting the pocks in the ceiling. Time passed, twenty minutes, or an hour, maybe more, until a pain bloomed from her gut, a tight, pulsing pain that she'd never experienced before that made it difficult for her to take a full breath and to stand up straight, and she thought she may vomit or pass out or have diarrhea, so she walked bent over into the hallway and found her pants soaked with blood, she called for the nurse and the nurse came quickly and said let's see if they can take you in now, you might not be dilated enough but we'll take a look, most women don't have this response, and soon Corrie was in another room with another nurse lying in another dentist's chair, clutching her cramping abdomen while a needle pierced the vein in the tender white of her inner elbow, and that was the last thing she remembered before waking up to bright lights and the knowledge that whatever they were going to do to her they had already done to her, and it was now something that had happened to her, no longer something that might or should or should not happen. It was done.

She rode the bus back home, transferring again at Coronado and Beech, uncomfortable in the stiff clinic-issued pads that stuck to her legs and the scrub pants she'd found next to her when she woke up, her bloodied jeans folded next to them as though freshly washed. On her way out she threw the jeans in the trash in the lobby. She didn't yet know how to explain the scrub pants to Leah, and she didn't yet know how she'd pay off her considerable debt to the hospital—that was all for the future, the hours and years to come.

Her cramps were muted but still strong through the extra-strength ibuprofen they gave her as she left. The ride was longer on the way back with rush hour traffic, the sky was pink and yellow and pale blue. She cramped and bled for days, she wept into the couch cushion late into the night, then, in time, her body returned to how it had been before: slim, simple, hollow.

Corrie stopped talking then, though I had said nothing, and the texture of her silence indicated that she was not planning on speaking again. We'd passed three tennis courts, busy with weekend matches, two playgrounds where children were all picking at the AstroTurf while their mothers or nannies or aunts scrolled through their phones. Thicker clouds had covered the sun and a cool wind had picked up. Corrie said nothing of being cold and didn't put on her long sleeve shirt tied around her waist. I was struck again by her extreme slightness, by how little there was of her.

We'd passed Briarcrest Drive several minutes ago, perhaps even half an hour ago, when she was describing in detail her nights of sex with Danny on the couch, and I hadn't pointed out that we were passing the street she was looking for, afraid to interrupt again and remind her that I was present and listening and retaining all that she had told me. But if one of us was leading the way through the streets of University Hills, it was Corrie, not me. It became obvious to me then, later than it should have, that she had also seen Briarcrest Drive when we passed it and had kept its location in mind. We'd been circling it by a radius of three to five blocks, never moving closer, until now, when she took a left on Vista Bonita which put us on a direct line toward the house where Leah and Nat and Grace were likely back from their tennis lesson and had been for some time and were now wondering where Corrie had gone off to and when she would be back. It seemed unlikely that Corrie had left a note.

"What happened after Danny left?" I asked. "Did you all stay in the house together?"

She nodded, and suddenly she seemed very tired.

"For a couple years," she said. "And then when the babies were two, Leah started dating this guy Tyler and they moved into his place. He was a good man, more or less. Divorced. He had a son the twins' age. They dated for five or six years, and then he moved to San Diego to start a restaurant with his brother, and he didn't want Leah and the girls to follow him. She was single for a long time after that. She worked as a manager of Tyler's old restaurant, and made decent money, but she still wanted to be a therapist. She talked a lot about getting her GED. She just needed those couple credits, and then she could go to college, then grad school. But it never came together."

Then, three years ago, after all those years single, she met Paul. Corrie didn't know what changed in Leah, why she decided to start dating again when she did, after so long alone. The sisters had long since stopped confessing to each other, though their relationship never became adversarial. After Leah and the twins moved to Tyler's, Corrie came over often, and after Tyler left, whenever Corrie was back in town she babysat the girls while Leah was at work and offered to watch them whenever Leah needed. She encouraged Leah to study, she'd watch the girls as long as it took her to study, until she could see that reminding Leah of her alternate future did not inspire her. It only caused her pain, it made her go quiet, then she'd change the topic to anything concerning the life she had before her: the new hostess at the restaurant was always late, Grace's frequent ear infections.

Paul was teaching at UCR for a year as a visiting professor when they met, and before he went back to Irvine he asked Leah to marry him and invited them all to come live with him here, in University Hills. And Leah said yes.

"I do love him," Leah said when she called to tell Corrie they were engaged, before she could respond. Corrie had only met Paul once, very briefly, and had not been able to form an opinion. "You might not understand it, and that's okay. This is the kind of love I want."

I asked Corrie where she had gone to, when she was not in town. She told me after high school she nannied full-time—her father had stopped putting money into the account the year before with no notice, no explanation—and Jenna and Bella worked for a catering company on weekends. They could support themselves, the three of them had found a new harmony together, until the girls graduated high school and left Riverside, Jenna for her boyfriend in Fontana and Bella for a full scholarship at Cal Arts. With all her sisters out of the house, Corrie found herself alone for the first time. And it was okay. She liked it, even. She became, quite suddenly, desperate to leave Riverside for a place with more silence and more space, the two things she'd been intent on avoiding thus far in her life. She wanted to go to the desert.

She drove to Joshua Tree with a car packed full of all the belongings she could fit, and she donated the rest. She'd never been there. The desert had seemed forbidden to her, it was her mother's place, where she had gone when she wanted to leave them, but there was some strong force inside her saying she must go there now.

Once she had reached the small strip of the town along Twenty-nine Palms Highway and drove through to the park's entrance, knowing that she had passed the place her mother had died but not knowing precisely when, the light was falling and the treeless hills of rubble were glowing brown and orange, she felt an instant and powerful sense of peace. She wondered if perhaps this was where her mother had spent her most restful days, not her most destructive. Perhaps this was the place that had kept her alive for as long as she lived.

Corrie quickly found a job working as a concierge at the Lost Horse Inn during the day and as a bartender at night at Rimrock Saloon, a restaurant with live music on weekend nights frequented by young tourists and mountain climbers from LA and Orange County. She camped in the park or slept on her coworker's couch until she could afford a small studio apartment in Yucca Valley, which she decorated tentatively with framed prints and wooden furniture from thrift stores, unsure how to fill her own space with her own things. Her most expensive purchase was a twin bed with a bedframe, new sheets and new pillows, and a real down comforter. In that bed, pressed against the wall under the window open to dry, clean air from the Mojave, she slept well and alone.

She lived there for a few years, and she was content, at times happy. Her mind and body had quieted, and the more time she spent alone, the more she enjoyed her solitude. She found some purpose and pleasure in her work, and came to love some friends she met there, but by the day's end, she only wanted to come home to the studio, to be with her things and with herself. It was harder to feel lonely in the desert, where everyone was alone, and everyone she met seemed to have both been the ones left behind, then the ones who left.

"That's where I met the guy," she said, and it was clear that she meant the man who had made her pregnant. At that moment I realized I'd forgotten she was currently pregnant, or at least that she had claimed to be pregnant. She fell quiet again. There wasn't anything more she was going to say about the man and how they'd met and why she was now here, without him.

We were at the corner of Briarcrest Drive. The street was silent, these houses were new, even newer than the other parts of University Hills, built just last spring. The windows were spotless, some still tagged with stickers for Pacific Construction.

"I don't remember which house it is," she said. "Paul has a little red Jetta, but I don't see one."

We walked down the street, looking at the windows and driveways, until Corrie stopped in front of one of the houses and said, "I'll find it from here, thanks. You don't have to walk with me anymore."

"It's okay, I don't mind," I said. I reached for my phone. "Do you want to call Leah?"

"No," she said, with some impatience. "I'll find it." She met my eyes then for the first time since she'd started telling her story and said, softer, "thanks, though."

We stood there for a moment, and then I said Okay, good luck, really, it was nice to meet you, and maybe I'll see you, I walk around here often. She smiled what seemed like a genuine smile and said Okay, yeah, maybe we'll see each other again—though we both knew we wouldn't, and, if we were to see each other in Trader Joe's or the streets of University Hills or in the plaza parking lot, especially when in the company of Isaac or Leah or Paul or Nat or Grace, we would most likely avert our eyes and walk the other way, out of something akin to respect.

I turned and made my way back down Briarcrest Drive, south toward graduate housing. I looked at my phone: nobody had texted or called or emailed in the time that had elapsed since I'd left the yoga studio (save a promotional email from Peet's), which both surprised and disappointed me, though it was a Saturday and it hadn't, actually, been very much time at all. I thought about calling Margot and confessing to her my foolish infatuation with Vince Balsamo, over fifteen years ago now. I'd tell her how I'd looked at him the way he looked at me only to hurt her, to enjoy a sense of power over her when I'd had none—always a pest and never a rival. And I'd tell her that though I fantasized about Vince, I wanted him badly, if he'd ever actually moved to touch me I would've retreated, terrified, and I never would've met his eyes again.

I quickly dismissed the idea; it would resolve nothing, and I was all but certain she'd never sensed the charge between us—that is, if Vince ever did really look at me in such a way, if it wasn't just a game I was playing alone. I thought of calling her and saying only that I'd been thinking of her, wondering how she was feeling—but I didn't want to make her regret telling me about her pregnancy so early by checking in with her too frequently. I'd do what we'd done for so long, I'd wait for her to call me, whenever that would be.

No, I thought. I'd text her after my next ultrasound, the anatomy scan in three weeks, and let her know if she was going to have a niece or nephew.

I put my phone away and looked back. Corrie was walking a few blocks behind me, now also heading south, near where we'd left each other. She must've seen me turn around. If she smiled and waved I didn't see it.

I kept walking away, through the park with the soccer field and grills and playground with mulch. Now there were more young families, babies strapped to their mother's chests and toddlers and school-aged kids playing tag. Some mothers looked at me as if they recognized me, with small smiles and nods, and some said hello, good afternoon. This was new, this recognition. My body was now visibly, decidedly pregnant, alerting itself to the kind of women who glance at ring fingers for rings and bellies for bumps, the kind of woman I was becoming. I smiled back and said hello, good afternoon, and kept walking.

A group of teenagers was sitting at a picnic table drinking sodas and laughing at their phones, lanky boys and pretty girls from a passing glance at a short distance, and I wondered if I'd recognize Nat and Grace if I saw them. I imagined them as beautiful, with long black hair, almond faces and ski-jump noses. One boy hung his arm around a girl's shoulder and she let him, and suddenly I desperately wanted to be back home with Isaac. He'd be on the couch now, reading, he was usually reading this time on Saturdays, and when I came home he'd set the book on the coffee table and kiss me and kiss my stomach. I wanted to lie in our bed with him and spread out our limbs. I was already rehearsing what I would and wouldn't tell him about Corrie, the ways in which I would embellish and alter the details of her story and infuse them with other stories I'd heard and read, both true and fictional.

Snake—missing my footstep by a breath, quick and brown and silent across the path and into the tall grass, it's skinny tail whipping behind it. I stopped and screamed, a young sound. A nearby couple looked up, confused. I smiled to them; I was okay. My hands were gripping my stomach hard and I was holding my breath. I didn't walk again for a little while, waiting for the beat of my heart to calm and my easy breath to return.

For the rest of the way back to my apartment I walked slowly with my eyes downcast, inspecting all sticks for movement and rattling tails. But they were all lifeless, fallen from branches above, waiting to be picked up by the children and used to draw lines in dirt, to be broken into bits and rescued from small wet mouths.

That night I dreamed of snakes, coiling up my legs and arms, licking my neck with forked tongues red as candied apples.

No Blue

I KNOW WHAT THEY MEAN NOW, when they say they lost the baby. They mean they don't know where the baby is.

.   .   .

"Oh, honey," my mother says over the phone. I call her from the hospital parking lot. She's never said it this way before. Honey like lead. You can hear her press her palm to her sternum; you can see her eyes fall to the earth; you can feel her remember.

"Oh, honey. Oh, poor baby."

.   .   .

———

FRIDAY JANUARY 4 2019

2:00 PM

UNIVERSITY OF CALIFORNIA IRVINE MEDICAL CENTER

ORANGE CALIFORNIA

"There is something wrong with the heart of this baby."

The OB's hair is blond, a white frame around her white face in a dark room.

"See the left ventricle. See the blue and the red. See how there is no blue in the left ventricle. There is white where there should be blue."

. . .

I don't know how to begin. This was never supposed to be part of this novel.

. . .

Isaac drives us home from the hospital under high sun. I have Google maps open on my phone and tell him which exit to take and when, which lane is best: farthest right, second to right. 5 South, 55 South, then 73 and by then we know the way.

When we're home we sit on the couch and watch *Avengers: Age of Ul-tron*; the sunlight from the window fades the screen. Isaac makes me toast with butter and cinnamon sugar and eats nothing himself. He provides me context for this movie within the greater context of the

Avenger's franchise and the Marvel Cinematic Universe. He explains Infinity Stones, Thanos, Ultron, how Samuel L. Jackson figures into all of it.

Then we watch *Thor: Ragnarok* and *Avengers: Infinity War*, and we both start to weep more than we've been weeping the whole afternoon after Thanos snaps his fingers and Black Panther and Groot and the Wakandan warriors and Elizabeth Olsen all turn to dust, and we really lose it when Tom Holland stumbles toward Robert Downey Jr. and says, "Mr. Stark, I don't feel so good, I don't know what's happening, I don't want to go, I don't want to go, sir, please, please, I don't want to go, I don't want to go, I'm sorry," and his face stills for an instant before it disintegrates like the others.

When the movie is over to feel anything else we start watching John Mulaney's Netflix Special *Kid Gorgeous at Radio City*, which Isaac had already seen parts of but I haven't seen any.

"How would that ever work?" Mulaney asks the audience, walking across the stage in his black tux. He is adorable and clever, and he reminds us of old friends we've been bad at keeping up with. "Years later I'd be in college about to go down on some rockin' twink and I'd be like, 'Wait a second, what would Leonard Bernstein do?'"

Once we laugh a couple of times we are too tired to watch anything anymore, so I take a long shower without washing my hair and brush my teeth and swallow my prenatal and go to bed.

All day and all night he kicks and kicks and kicks to no rhythm.

Shhh, baby, I think to him. *Shh, go to sleep, now is not the time to play.*

———

"Can you feel him?" I ask Isaac as we lie awake in bed. I press his hand on my stomach.

"Right there. Can you feel him?"

"No," he says.

. . .

Notice how in the first sentence of this section the subject is THEY, though it is also common for the subject to be SHE—as in THEY LOST THE BABY or SHE LOST THE BABY—but it is rarely heard THEY LOST THEIR BABY or SHE LOST HER BABY and more rarely heard I LOST MY BABY or even I LOST THE BABY.

The definite article is curious and it makes me recall how when Isaac and I were planning our wedding, we at some point without making a conscious choice began calling it THE WEDDING rather than OUR WEDDING though I had pointed out to him some time before that when couples say THE WEDDING it has always irked me more than makes sense and if I ever heard him refer to me as THE BRIDE or THE WIFE even ironically I would begin calling him MY FIRST HUSBAND or worse over THE FIRST HUSBAND.

Notice too how the word LOST is often the chosen word rather than some variation of DEAD or even PERISHED, or, as the case may be, KILLED. TERMINATED is the preferred term for some, MUR-DERED for others. Those who say TERMINATED would likely change the object to FETUS or EMBRYO or even PRODUCTS OF CONCEPTION rather than BABY or CHILD or UNBORN.

———

KILL: *cause the death of (a person, animal, or other living thing).*
MURDER: *the unlawful premeditated killing of one human being by another.*
TERMINATE: *bring to an end.*

LOST, too, implies a mistake, as in I LOST MY READING GLASSES or I LOST MY MIND, because of course intentional losing would not be losing at all, but hiding / concealing / obfuscating.

The passive voice could be appropriate in this context, as there is no one actor, in most cases, who caused the death of the baby, but THE BABY WAS LOST or THEIR/HER BABY WAS LOST both sound strange as euphemisms yet they work when used literally, as in THEIR BABY WAS LOST IN PENN STATION FOR FIVE HOURS BEFORE BEING FOUND BY CUSTODIAN UNDER THE SUSHI BAR.

I aim to use active sentences with no euphemisms or unnecessary definite articles when possible but it still feels wrong to write though it is factually true to say I KILLED MY BABY.

. . .

In the story Isaac will write about this a few months later, the wife, unnamed, is twenty-five weeks pregnant when she doesn't feel the baby's kicks for a couple of hours. She texts her husband, the baby's father, our narrator (also unnamed) and asks if she should be worried. He assures her that no, she shouldn't be worried, the baby is probably just sleeping.

———

When it has been ten hours—by now it is very early the following morning and neither of them has hardly slept at all—the wife and the husband drive to the hospital and the OB can't find a heartbeat on the doppler, then the ultrasound confirms the baby is dead. After an induction and long, painful labor the wife delivers the baby. Aside from the wife's heavy breath, the delivery room is silent.

The wife won't look at the baby, but the husband sees the baby's face— not on purpose, but not quite by accident. The baby looks just like the wife, the husband observes, but he doesn't describe what, precisely, is similar to her face. The baby is a boy and it was their first pregnancy.

"You made it a miscarriage," I say after reading it. "Why did you make it a miscarriage?"

"It's fiction," he says. "It's not our story. I don't know that I want to write our story."

"You don't like it," he adds. We're sitting next to each other on the couch. He is looking through the pages, pausing where I made a mark with my pencil.

"No," I say. "That's not what I'm saying at all. You made it better. It's the best thing you've ever written."

*   *   *

FRIDAY JANUARY 4 2019

2:00 PM

UNIVERSITY OF CALIFORNIA IRVINE MEDICAL CENTER

ORANGE CALIFORNIA

———

"Yes I see how there is no blue but what does that mean. What does no blue mean."

"No blue means there is no blood flowing into the left ventricle."

"Yes I know that but what does that mean. I mean is it a little bad or is it very bad."

"No blue means that when the baby is born he will not be able to breathe."

.   .   .

Though perhaps it is not at all factually true to say I KILLED MY BABY and it would be more factually true to say I SIGNED A FORM CONSENTING TO THE KILLING OF MY BABY, or I GAVE THE ORDER FOR MY BABY TO BE KILLED, the passive voice here because I do not know who, exactly, killed my baby. I didn't see their faces and I didn't learn their names. (Curiously, using the word SON rather than BABY feels disingenuous, even forbidden.) There were many people in the operating room, all cloaked in blue. One asked what kind of music I wanted to listen to as I went under.

"We have Bob Marley," she said. "Sarah McLachlan, Grateful Dead. Whatever you like."

I knew only the OB and the fellow's names that I will not share for their safety—let's call them Dr. Pak and Dr. Serrano, respectively— but I do not know if they were the ones to kill him, though I suspect it was the fellow, Dr. Serrano, as she was supervised by Dr. Pak, who cut the umbilical cord and waited twenty-five minutes for his heart to stop beating on its own before they proceeded further.

. . .

What did I write when the character I call Elizabeth tells Margot?

I LOST IT AT FOURTEEN WEEKS, she said, AND SAM FELL APART.

I HAD A MISCARRIAGE, is what she told her mother. Is how I imagine her telling her mother, I mean. I don't know how the real woman who inspired the character I call Elizabeth spoke to her mother about what happened, if she spoke to her at all.

I did not write a line like this for the character I call Corrie. The real woman who inspired the character I call Corrie did use the word ABORTION a few times, never TERMINATION, never a variation of LOST.

. . .

ROSEMARY'S BABY (1968)

Final scene.
131. INT. CASTEVET'S APARTMENT—(DUSK)

Rosemary stands in the entrance of the room, watching the gathering of the coven. She grips a knife. A black bassinet is on the other side of the room, covered in

black taffeta. The baby inside is hidden from view.
A crucifix of Jesus hangs upside down with black ribbon
tied around his ankles. Mr. Castevet, the leader of the
coven, sees Rosemary and the room quiets.

                    MR. CASTEVET
         Rosemary.

                         ROSEMARY
         Shut up.

                    MR. CASTEVET
         Before you look at—

                         ROSEMARY
         Shut up. You're in Dubrovnik. I don't
         hear you.

Rosemary approaches the bassinet and begins to pull away
the black veil to reveal the baby. As she sees the baby,
her expectant smile vanishes and she is horrified. She
begins to back away and looks frantically around the
room, holding the knife to her chest.

                         ROSEMARY
         What have you done to it? What have
         you done to its eyes?

                    MR. CASTEVET
         He has his Father's eyes.

ROSEMARY

What are you <u>talking</u> about? Guy's eyes
are <u>normal</u>! What have you <u>done</u> to him,
you maniacs?

MR. CASTEVET

Satan is His Father, not Guy. He came up
from Hell and begat a Son of mortal woman!

VOICES

Hail Adrian! Hail Satan! Hail Adrian!
Hail Satan!

[. . .]

GUY

I mean, suppose you'd had a baby and
lost it; wouldn't it be the same?

•   •   •

And how does Euripides phrase it?

CHORUS

Your children are dead, and by their
own mother's hand.

[. . .]

JASON

My children are dead.

[. . .]

MEDEA

The children are dead. I say this to
make you suffer.

Imagine Medea floating above the palace in a chariot
drawn by dragons, her handsome face framed by knotted
black hair. A cream tunic falls to her ankles and drapes
over her broad shoulders and hips and breasts. The dead
bodies of her young sons lay still across her arms,
their tunics, like hers, are blackened with blood, their
stab wounds still bleeding.

MEDEA

So now call me a monster, if you wish.

.   .   .

Let me write this another way.

Anna & Ruth

I SIT ON A CHAIR like a dentist's chair, still fully clothed, wearing a peplum maternity shirt gifted to me by Margot just a week ago—she has the same one in navy, she said, and she has worn it constantly and soon will again—and the black leggings that stretch over my stomach I've worn nearly every day since I grew out of my pre-pregnancy jeans.

Skinny bitch, I'd thought when I held up the pair of my high-waisted Levi's I'd found tucked in the back of my drawer a few days ago. *How dare she think herself a whale?*

The exam room I sit in now is familiar; I've been here before for other prenatal appointments. It's the one with the window overlooking the parking lot and three church steeples above the flat outlet mall roof. On the walls are the same posters as the other rooms on this floor, the rooms with westward views of the 55, the pink and beige diagram of the female reproductive system and the cross-section of a pregnant white woman, her baby head down in her pelvis, eyes closed.

I hadn't expected to be seen in this room, or in any of the rooms I'd been in before. But of course I would be—where else would they put me? They should have a designated Sad Room, with a more comfortable chair, dinner mints, lace curtains on the windows, aloe vera-infused tissues in ceramic dispensers, not the cardboard boxes with patterns like high school floor linoleum.

This room is familiar, but I haven't seen this woman before, who walks in now in a white coat and stylish thick-rimmed calico glasses. She introduces herself as the fellow, Dr. Serrano—"Pleased to meet you"—and she extends a ringless, delicate hand, still damp with sanitizer.

Dr. Serrano is young, perhaps younger than me, though I am not so young anymore, or at least not as young as I've been before. The obvious and perpetual truth of this has always brought me an odd sort of comfort, but today it adds to the churning panic in my gut. In addition to the baby I have lost—or the baby I am about to lose, the process of losing that will be set into irreversible motion in thirty minutes, or twenty, or ten?—I have lost time, wasted how many tens of thousands of fertile minutes immersed in nausea, anticipation, hope. To think of it as a waste of time suggests that the baby himself is a waste, trash, though nobody has dared to imply this other than myself when my mind goes to its darkest enclaves.

The enclaves where live the thoughts:

I'll be able to fit into those Levi's again sooner than I'd thought.
This will make my novel a better novel.
I hate all mothers of healthy babies.
I hate all healthy babies.

I don't deserve this.

I do deserve this.

The image, not for the first time today or even this hour, of my baby's tiny severed limbs in a trash bag on a curb filled with Stryofoam coffee cups and rotting deli meat, makes me want to wretch and weep and scream. But I do none of these. I am composed, a polite patient.

Dr. Serrano sits on a stool in front of the computer monitor and joggles the mouse until the screen shines blue, then quickly types her login.

"I'm so sorry," she says as the program loads, leaning forward, fixing her eyes on mine. "This must be so difficult. I'm sorry we have to meet under these circumstances."

Though her sympathetic affect has a studied quality to it, I appreciate the gesture. I'm glad they receive some training on matters like this.

"Me too," I say. "Thank you."

Dr. Serrano explains that today she and her attending, Dr. Pak, will begin the dilation for the termination surgery that will take place tomorrow morning, but first she has some questions she needs to ask. It shouldn't take long.

I verify my name (Anna Chase), date of birth (September 1, 1988), date of my last menstrual period (August 22, 2018), due date (May 28, 2019), and current age of gestation (20 weeks, 2 days). Dr. Serrano turns from the monitor to look at me as I answer the questions—*make eye contact when the patient speaks*—then faces the screen to type.

"Is this your first pregnancy?"

"Yes."

"How did you conceive this baby?"

"Naturally."

"And for how many menstrual cycles did you try to conceive?"

"One." I smile apologetically, almost ashamed at the ease of our conception. I wonder if Dr. Serrano has a baby, wants a baby, has lost a baby. She shows no reaction. She does not pity me, and for this I like her.

It wasn't so long ago, not at all, that Isaac and I first had sex with the intention of conceiving. The Denver Marriott hotel room the weekend of his younger brother Robbie's wedding. The pressured hour between the trip to Target for emergency steamers for the bridal party and the rehearsal dinner. The harsh hotel AC we couldn't turn down, the haze outside the window, tinted yellow from the wildfires that had burned all summer. The mental images I'd summoned that had so rarely failed to arouse me since adolescence, failing me then, not making me the least bit wet. Isaac going soft inside me for the first time, saying, I know I'm hurting you, and I don't want to hurt you. I asked him if he was sure he wanted to do this, and he said yes, yes, he wanted to make a baby with me as much as he could want anything. We'd looked up porn on my phone to help, which we'd never done before, asking each other, What do you like?, too shy to make the selection ourselves. How about this one, or this one? I don't care—you decide. We chose two white kids on a cabana, no older than twenty, long-limbed and shaven, slapping their flesh together and moaning like cats. We both came harder than we had in months.

I didn't become pregnant. I ovulated a week later, I realized after my period finally came; the dryness should've clued me that it was too early. I became pregnant the next month, when I disregarded my app's predictions and studied my toilet paper instead. I don't remember the sex we had that week. It was all at home, in our bed. For days before I allowed myself to take the test, my breasts ached with the knowledge.

"Well, two," I amend. "But the first time we didn't have sex at the right time. So, one with the timing correct. I don't know if that would count as one or two cycles."

Dr. Serrano just types, nods. *Nod to show active listening.*

"Any complications with this pregnancy?" she asks.

"No," I say, and it is true. I could carry him to term if I wanted. I still could. Though my pregnancy was perfect, and my risk factors for everything nil, I'd feared thoroughly, I'd thought, cataloguing all that could go wrong with myself and the baby and the fragile and intricate industry that connected us. But I had not feared what was happening now. Not this precise thing.

If only you had.

If only you'd had sex days after Robbie's wedding. Not days before.

If only it hadn't been with Isaac.

My phone vibrates in my bag on the floor. Just once: a text. Probably Margot again. I don't move to answer it.

"What is your understanding of this baby's condition?" asks Dr. Serrano.

"It's his heart."

She waits for me to elaborate, and when I do not, she takes an inhale as though she is about to explain it all in more detail, the particularities of the complication, as they all call it, what that means for his quality of life, should he live. I know it all already and I don't want to hear it again.

"Blood isn't flowing into the left ventricle," I say before she can begin. "So it's not developing as it should and it will only become less functional without blood flow. He'll probably die in the minutes after delivery from suffocation, or else soon after."

But there is a chance he could live beyond that.

But there is a chance he would want his life, such as it would be.

"Yes," she nods. "That's it, more or less. I can tell you about it in more detail, if you'd like? If you have any questions?"

My phone vibrates again. A reminder buzz, or another text. My mother would've told Margot that today is the dilation. I'd told my mother she could tell Margot everything I told her; I didn't see a point in hiding anything from her but I couldn't say it all more than once. Now Margot was the one texting me the same texts I'd sent her, not so long ago, *please let me know if there's anything I can do; just letting you know I'm thinking of you.* Hers went further than mine had, saying how she felt so sick over this and she'd fly down in a second if I wanted her here. I was sure my mother had asked her to offer to come, and it'd be so easy to offer, knowing I would never accept. I didn't want to see her. I didn't want to see anyone. When she called, I let it go to voice mail and didn't listen to the message. My text responses had been short, gracious enough, but I hadn't been able to talk to her on the phone. Whenever her name appeared on my screen, I imagined her in her Anchorage kitchen, feeding Alex cream of wheat, and her little bump with her little fetus inside, and I became filled with envy and anger, and then overpowering guilt about the envy and anger and I couldn't stop crying, and I was sick of crying.

She should've had the late loss and I should've had the early one.

She already has a baby.

Stupid girl, only fools believe in fair.

He kicks.

"He's kicking," I say. "He can't feel anything, right? He won't be able to feel anything?"

"No," says Dr. Serrano. "Don't worry. He won't be able to feel anything."

Her expression shifts, perhaps stifling a thought she does not want to share, an image of what awaits me. I notice now that below her glasses, she is pretty, quite pretty. The arrangement of her face is pleasingly simple, her makeup carefully applied. A subtle cat's eye, jet black, maybe a touch of blush, invisible concealer. She turns back to the screen.

"I see your mother had a baby with a congenital heart defect as well, is that correct?"

"Yes, that's right."

"Did she do genetic testing?"

"No, they didn't have it then. It was in the eighties."

"Right, sorry, of course. Unfortunately, with such limited information, it's hard to say if it's anything more than a coincidence. Are you planning on having genetic testing?"

"Yes."

"That may be able to tell us a little more about the chances of recurrence. But most often the results are normal."

"I know," I say, sounding more curt than I intended. "The genetics woman told us the same thing."

Her face shifts again; her mouth straightens. It occurs to me I could be one of the first late-term abortion patients she's interviewed on her own, without the attending supervising. Or I could be the tenth today.

This does not make you special.

You are more interesting now than you were before.

"Has anyone else in your family had a heart defect, besides your sister?"

"No, not that I know of." I tell her about Margot's healthy two-year-old son, her current pregnancy, her early miscarriage in the fall.

"The good news is that even if it does turn out to be hereditary, it's unlikely that this would happen to the baby she's pregnant with now. They will probably give her an extra anatomy scan just in case."

"Good, that's good."

I realize then that she meant my sister Jane, not my sister Margot. I hadn't ever thought of Jane as my sister. Jane is what my parents named the baby.

. . .

I'd called my mother two days after the ultrasound, four days before the surgery, as I walked around the apartment complex in the early evening, wearing a heavy sweater to conceal my shape from any passing mothers. I asked her about Jane—I said the genetics woman had called and had questions about her diagnosis that I couldn't answer. My mother told me what she remembered. Blockage of pulmonary artery. Chambers too large, chambers too small. She'd suffocate when she was born.

Jane was not a forbidden topic, but she was spoken of rarely, and only brought up by my mother. The story of Jane was not a story at all, but a series of facts: she was the baby who had been ill, who had died before she was born, whose death had allowed for my life. My mother had always called her grief for Jane a "closed grief," a grief that had a start date and an end date—so unlike the grief she felt and continues to feel years after the death of Granjan, or of her best friend from college. The grief began the day of the ultrasound and it ended the day I was born. Though it was clear from how my mother did and did not speak of Jane that the grief persisted, and it persists still. The grief just had a different texture now, now that Jane's death was not the end of the story of their family.

"I don't know if you want to hear the story," my mother said as I walked, crossing California Avenue into University Hills. "I don't know if it would be helpful for you now, or if it's the last story you want to hear. I'm remembering more."

"Yes," I said. "I want to hear it all."

"The story really starts," she said, "in the spring of 1983, when Alex started to itch."

They lived in Somerville then, in a tiny third-floor walkup between Davis and Porter, an apartment that always smelled like the muffins and scones baked at the café next door. They'd moved there two years before, and it was in that apartment that they went from boyfriend and girlfriend to fiancé and fiancée to husband and wife—a migration of status, my mother said, that seemed to have no effect on them at all. They were in love before, and they were in love after.

The year they were married was the year they both graduated law school, and they decided to stay in Boston; my father was offered a job at Hall & Neiman, a firm downtown that specialized in environmental law, and my mother advocated for tenants' rights in Southie. Though they had great affection for their Somerville apartment, they did not want to live there much longer. It was not where they envisioned having a family: there was no extra room for the nursery, no backyard, and my mother was sure that the paint chipping on all the windowsills was lead. They looked passively at the real estate listings in the *Globe*, circling potential candidates in the suburbs on the commuter rail—Brookline, Newton, some as far as Needham, but they didn't make any offers. They didn't even go to any open houses. They'd make a little more money first, establish themselves in their new jobs, and then, in the spring, they'd start to try for a baby and look for a house with extra rooms and a yard big enough to plant a small garden and have a kiddie pool, maybe a swing set.

In March my father began to itch. First his legs, then his feet and arms and hands. He started waking up with blood under his fingernails and blood on the sheets from itching in his sleep, and soon he was having night sweats and losing weight rapidly, and he didn't have much weight to lose. Every night for months, all spring and into the summer, he woke up shivering with his pajamas drenched in sweat and stained with blood from peeling off scabs from old scratches. Their bedroom reeked of a sour, sick smell, and no amount of washing and airing could cleanse it. It was in my father's pores, on his breath.

My mother began to worry it was HIV; so little was known of the disease at the time, and it was spreading rampantly and seemed to only be taking the brightest, kindest men, including a classmate of theirs from law school and one of my father's colleagues at the firm. My father had seen him in the office just weeks before he died, pale as snow, the color faded even from his irises.

My father's doctor was unconcerned. Told him to rest, buy hypoallergenic laundry detergent.

Then, one morning in early June, as my mother woke and turned to look at my father, she saw a lump the size of a ping-pong ball on his left shoulder. She let him sleep, studying his profile as her mind spun. She closed her eyes with the hope she would fall back asleep, and when she awoke it would be gone, it was just a trick of the angle or her tired eyes—it wasn't possible that such a thing had grown overnight and it wasn't possible she hadn't noticed it until now—but when she opened her eyes again, the mass remained. When he finally woke, she told him what she saw.

"Until that point," my mother told me, "I'd been the only one who was anxious. I'd been the one telling him to call the doctor, to get a second opinion, to insist on testing. Alex was sure it was nothing, and he didn't want to bother the doctors. The relaxed optimism that I'd always appreciated about him had turned into a passivity about his own health that drove me mad. But that morning, when he felt the lump and saw it in the bathroom mirror, his face fell, and I knew he was thinking about his father."

After weeks of appointments, tests, and waiting, waiting, waiting, they learned he had Hodgkin's Lymphoma, stage four. If my father didn't start chemo right away, in two weeks he would likely be dead.

The oncologist, Dr. Joan Raczkowski, told them all of this in a small exam room on the fifth floor of the Brigham, two floors below where Granjan would die, thirty years later, and one floor above where Margot and I would be born. Dr. R was older than my parents, but not by much, and she had taken, my mother liked to think, a special interest in treating my father. He was young and bright, quiet and polite, and his black hair and blue eyes still had their effects, even as the rest of him was gaunt and pallid. My mother tried to comprehend and absorb what Dr. R was saying, the particular ways in which my father's body was failing, and why, and what would happen if this, or if this, but she could only retain the fact that he was dying, what did the rest of it matter?, so she focused all her attention to willing Dr. R to fall in love with my father. If she were in love, she would do whatever she could to save him. That he may fall in love with Dr. R in return, and how could he not fall in love with the brilliant woman who saved his life?, was a risk that my mother would gladly take, knowing he would do the same for her.

At some point Dr. R stopped speaking. Then she asked my parents if they ever wanted to have biological children.

"Yes," they both said without looking at each other, though they hadn't thought about having a baby in weeks. To even imagine it—to imagine anything in their future—now seemed to tempt the fate they didn't believe in.

"If you ever wanted to have a chance of conceiving," said Dr. R, "you'll have to make a sperm donation by tomorrow morning, before we start the chemo. Once the chemo is in your system, you will be, in effect, infertile."

She told them the odds of conceiving one pregnancy with thawed sperm, especially with only one donation, were extremely slim. Most doctors didn't even tell their patients about this option, because it would only give them high hopes and then cause more grief when they couldn't become pregnant. The procedure had only been in practice for a couple of years, and the results were discouraging—though they were improving, slightly. The frozen sperm would only remain viable for one year, eighteen months at most, and it was very unlikely that any significant advancements would be made between now and then.

"But," said Dr. R, "it is ultimately your decision to make."

It was a hail Mary, they understood, but my parents didn't have to discuss it. They were not worried about their high hopes being shattered; they were more worried that they'd already lost their capacity to have high hopes at all. Early the following morning, as the nurses were setting up the chemo, they pulled the canvas curtain closed around my father's bed, gave him a plastic cup and an old Playboy procured from who knows where, and waited for him to let them know when he was done.

The chemo course was twelve months. My father's face was swollen, he felt terrible always, he vomited in the car on the way home from the clinic, sometimes he vomited on the way there in anticipation. But the treatment worked. The cancer started to wane, and by the end of the course it was gone. He gained some weight back, then more, until his body began to resemble the shape it had taken in health—still slim, he'd always been slim, but my mother could no longer see the bones in his chest and the ridge of his eye socket. He kept his hair, still thick and black, all but the hair on the back of his neck, which never regrew.

They ordered the frozen sperm while he was still on chemo, as soon as it seemed as though he was more likely to live than to die. The one donation had been divided into nine straws, as they called them: nine chances at conception. They'd been stored in a lab in New Orleans, costing two hundred dollars in rent for the year. A few days after my mother called to order one straw, a box arrived on their doorstep. It came in dry ice in what looked like a propane tank, for the grill, with a pamphlet of illustrated instructions on how to thaw and insert, a BBT thermometer, and an instrument, my mother said, that really did look just like a turkey baster.

On the day my mother ovulated, my father was in the hospital, dehydrated from vomiting, delirious with fatigue, and so she went to their bedroom, laid out all the supplies in a neat row and read the instructions over and over again, then she lay down over the covers with a pillow elevating her hips, and she did the insertion herself.

She knew she was pregnant, she told me, ten days later, when she woke up early with a need to go to the butcher she'd never been to before, buy five pounds of bone-in pork chops, sear them in butter and garlic and eat nothing else for days.

The luck of it terrified her as much as it thrilled her. She waited impatiently for death—the death of the embryo, or my father, or her own. She hadn't slept well since my father had started to itch, but now she woke constantly to nightmares of clotted blood soaking her thighs, or my father dying in his sleep beside her, riddled with tumors the size of cantaloupes. She tried to exhaust her mind by walking from Porter to Inman to Harvard and back, and she took on as many cases as her firm would allow, despite the vertigo that plagued her whenever she stopped for a moment to feel or think. But all was well with the baby, said her obstetrician, and all was well with my father, said Dr. R. They were in no position to offer certainties, of course, but they saw no evidence that my parents would lose what they had just gained.

My father was the one who, one morning, placed the newspaper on the kitchen table in front of my mother. It was open to the real estate page; three listings were circled in blue ink.

"There's an open house here on Saturday," he said, pointing to the three-bedroom in Medford. "Let's go. Just for fun."

A few weeks later, they bought the house on Myrtle Terrace in Winchester—a four-bedroom, "The House of Radical Hope," my father called it—for a price they could afford, if barely, a small fraction of what it'd be worth in the decades to come. It was a red colonial with a screened deck in back and a wide porch in front and natural light in the kitchen, a half-acre backyard with chestnut trees and silver maples, quiet neighbors. That house, of all the ones they'd seen, was the only one in which my mother could envision the children they did not yet have with a feeling of calm that was not immediately succeeded by pangs of anticipatory terror and grief.

"At the time we felt like the most fortunate people in the world," my mother said, "with a house, Alex well and me pregnant. We bought curtains and rugs and planted bulbs in the backyard, and Alex painted the porch. Though I was working full-time until the day I delivered, in my memory I spent the last twenty weeks of that pregnancy sitting in the living room in a leather chair, the old one of Granjan's that's in our den now, watching winter come outside the bay window and eating plain yogurt to ease the heartburn."

Margot was born on February 5, 1985, at thirty-eight weeks.

In August the cancer returned.

. . .

Dr. Serrano types for some time, longer than she's typed before, clicks and scrolls. She adjusts the screen, angles it away from me. I don't know how much time has passed and how much time remains. I know there is still time to stop this from happening. Right now I could grab my bag and run out to the waiting room, take Isaac by the hand and tell him we're getting the fuck out of here.

The doctors were mistaken.

The baby is well.

"What is the sex of your baby?" she asks.

"He's a boy."

"Right, sorry. I see that here. Boys are easier for genetic testing. With a girl it can be hard to tell if we're testing the mother's tissue by mistake."

"He's a boy," I say again. "My husband thought he'd be a girl."

She smiles—polite, but uninterested.

I have the strong urge to tell her more, to keep the time from moving, to say how Isaac could envision her clearly, our daughter—a tall, bookish girl with curly brown hair like mine. He was the one who had proposed Scout as our placeholder name, Scout from *To Kill a Mockingbird*, a name I agreed was cute but not too cute, after the character we both liked but who hadn't held any particular preexisting significance for either of us. I had visions of the baby, too, I want to tell Dr. Serrano, but always as a boy, looking precisely like Isaac as a child: round-faced and long-limbed. I didn't think my visions for a boy meant I had a preference for a boy; I wasn't the sort of woman who would prefer a son to a daughter. My image of a son was likely a result of having only a sister and always being curious about what a masculine manifestation of my genes may look like, which was perhaps also the logic behind why Isaac, who only has his brother Robbie, imagined a girl.

But as time went on, I want to say, and we came closer to learning the sex of the baby, I could no longer deny to myself that I was hoping for a boy, and hoping strongly—a thought I admitted to no one. I exclusively read lists of boy names online: *Top 50 Underrated Baby Boy Names, Baby Boy Names You'll Fall in Love With, 100 Unique Baby Boy Names You Won't Regret.* I read lengthy peer-reviewed articles detailing the risks and benefits of circumcision. I bought baby boy clothes at the Assistance League Thrift Store in secret, one-dollar onesies with polar bears and embroidered bow ties, planning to reason to Isaac, if he were to find them in my sock drawer, that the boy clothes were more versatile than the girl clothes, those dresses the color of Pepto Bismol and cheap cake frosting, costumes for dolls with heads of hollow plastic.

On a restless day alone, I washed the onesies in the laundry, and while they were still warm from the dryer I held them to my breasts like a talisman.

At our sixteen-week ultrasound, the ultrasound before the ultrasound that would be our last, when Dr. Mousavi brought us to the dark room a few doors down from where I sit now and she spread the warm gel on my stomach and Scout came into focus on the screen, and I could see the tiny nub between his kicking legs before she could even say, "Looks like you're having a boy," I was overwhelmed with relief. I saw, in a kind of cinematic flurry, all these images of this little boy, running through the grass of some abstract field, then brushing his teeth next to Isaac in matching plaid pajamas, standing only as tall as Isaac's hip, then a teenager, all limbs, growing so easily until he was taller even than Isaac, with big hands and a big smile, then a man, thicker in the neck and chest, moving through the world with grace and confidence and immunity. I felt certain he would be good and kind like his father, a man who would love women well and who would not see me as the picture of his inevitable decline, as a daughter would, but as his mother whom he loved without complication.

As soon as the relief came over me I covered my hands with my face, trying to hide my elation, fearing Dr. Mousavi's judgment. Isaac was laughing and saying, "Amazing! I was sure it was a girl!", sounding genuinely surprised but not at all disappointed, hitting precisely the right note. I said, "Oh, that's great," as flatly as I could manage. "Yeah, Isaac did think it would be a girl." I must've overcorrected my reaction so convincingly that as soon as Isaac and I were in the elevator Isaac asked, "Are you disappointed? It's okay if you're disappointed." "What?" I said. "About having a boy? No, I'm not disappointed. Not at all. Are you disappointed?" and he said no, he wasn't. He was thrilled about a boy just as he was thrilled about a girl, it would just take him some time to get used to the idea. And very soon, it seemed, he did.

Dr. Serrano is looking at me, her pretty face expectant, confused. She has asked me a question, perhaps some time ago.

"No," I say. "I mean—I'm sorry. What?"

"Would you like an ink print of the baby's footprints?"

"Oh. Yes, please."

She clicks once and pushes her glasses up on her nose.

"Could you tell me your understanding of your options with this pregnancy?"

"I can carry him to term, or I can terminate either by being induced and delivering him vaginally or having a D&E. I've decided to have a D&E."

She nods, types, and she does not say, *Well chosen! The dilation and evacuation procedure is indeed the morally superior option.* Instead she explains how today they will insert sticks of seaweed into my cervix, and as the sticks fill with my body's fluids over the next several hours, they will expand and dilate me a few centimeters. Then tomorrow morning at 7:00 a.m. I will have the surgery. I must be at the hospital by 6:00.

Cowards choose the D&E.

Strong women deliver their dead babies.

You will never see his face.

I have a sudden urge to laugh, then to close my eyes and cover them with my hands and pretend to be invisible.

"You'll be completely under for the surgery itself," she says. "You won't feel a thing."

I know all this. I'd woken up at 5:00 a.m. this morning to read through online forums I'd already read. The women's posts were specific and thorough, most were several paragraphs long with well-chosen scenic details. Some women had flown across state lines and bled in motel rooms alone. Others went bankrupt when they learned their insurance wouldn't cover the procedure. The same phrases appeared over and over: *Cried my eyes out for days. Physical pain was nothing compared to the heartache. Dilation was agony. Sad but relieved. Looking down from heaven.*

"Okay," I say. "That's good."

She types, clicks boxes, then she stands from her stool and walks to the other side of the room, and I fear the interview is over, it is time to begin—please, stop time, or skip time, flash cut to morning, waking up groggy and hollow—no: *One Year Later*—but she only walks as far as the cabinet above the sink. She pulls out a plastic bag with the hospital's logo on the front, hands it to me, and sits again on the stool. As she moves she explains that I will need to stop eating and drinking twelve hours before surgery, so it would be wise to have a sizeable dinner.

"Tonight you must shower and wash your body with the formula and loofa in this bag, and then wash and shower again tomorrow morning. Do not wash your hair after tonight. That's very important."

I nod, aware of my hair, the greasy knot it's made of itself at the nape of my neck. Her hair is clean and slick, blow-dried straight.

But wait—I want to say before she can move on. Now I want to tell you about something else, the mention of a shower just reminded me of a moment I don't want to forget, it's a moment that may not sound particularly poignant to you or to anyone else, and in fact I haven't thought about it much since it happened until now, and I'm afraid I'll forget it again if I don't recall it this instant. It took place in Crestline, in the San Bernardino mountains, where Isaac and I went for the long Thanksgiving weekend. I was about thirteen weeks pregnant. The day we drove there had been clear in Irvine and in Riverside, but as soon as we started driving up the mountains—Isaac was driving—a thick fog descended and we couldn't see more than ten feet ahead of us until we reached the top of the ridge. From there, all the lights and clutter of LA and the Inland Empire below were totally obfuscated by cumulus clouds, giving the illusion of a fjord in the sky. On Thanksgiving day we drove the windy roads of the town and around Lake Gregory, looking for any open restaurant, and eventually we found a free community dinner provided by the Rotary Club in a multipurpose event center on the lake. We ate deep fried turkey, canned beans, canned corn heavy with salt, gravy, mashed potatoes, and apple pie; my appetite was finally returning at this point. Isaac gave a thirty-dollar donation, and we walked around the lake until we got too cold, then went back to the Airbnb, where we watched *The Americans* and fell asleep early. Even though it was just the two of us, it felt to me like it was our first Thanksgiving as a family.

Once we returned to the Airbnb, before we watched *The Americans*,

I decided to take a shower to warm up. The shower was huge, one of the biggest I've ever been in; it could easily have fit five or six adults. The floor was a mosaic of stones that massaged your feet, and the showerhead was detachable, the water pressure incredible. The walls were all clear glass, and if you faced the bedroom you'd see a full-length mirror so you could watch yourself shower; in fact, it was nearly impossible *not* to watch yourself shower, and my eye kept catching the moving figure in the reflection by accident, before I decided to look at it with intent. I watched my naked body in the mirror, turning pink from the heat.

A few months before, if I'd seen my reflection like this, even though I would've been slimmer all over, I would've turned my back to it. I would've tried to convince myself that the mirror's reflection was warped and so was my self-image, and it was the two warped perceptions laid over each other that had created an image of my body that offended me and it was not true to reality. I would've tried to focus instead on the feeling of the hot water on my back and the stones on my feet and the smell of the shea butter body wash, and to think of anything other than my body and how it looked and how sick I was of feeling this way toward my reflection, and sick of the guilt that followed, knowing that my body is able, healthy, relatively young, free of chronic pain and discomfort, and even beautiful to some and most importantly to Isaac.

That night in the shower in the Airbnb in Crestline, my breasts were swollen, mammalian. The left breast was a little bigger and lower than the right in a way I'd never noticed before. My thighs were thick and soft, and my stomach was undeniably starting to bulge into a perfectly smooth, round orb, bisected by the slightest hint of a linea negra. I washed each part of my body slowly, moving my hands over my skin, even the crevices between my toes.

I don't know if it was because I'd never felt so attuned to my body in pregnancy, or that I'd never felt so alien from my body in pregnancy, that enabled me to see it in this way as I never had before. I felt, suddenly and acutely, a heightened appreciation of all the microscopic favors my body had done for me from the moment I'd been conceived until now, favors descended from generations and generations and generations and generations, the cellular wisdom always imperceptibly improving. Then came the knowledge that I was a part of it, my role in our evolution was just as significant as anyone else's—and yet the knowledge of my insignificance in our evolution was also a comfort, in a way, because if I were to die in that instant in that shower, these processes occurring in my body would still be occurring in billions of other bodies. What I mean is, I saw my body as not only my body, but rather as a single reiteration of the female human body. So to call my body ugly and weak as I have so often called it would be to call all female human bodies ugly and weak, to call ugly and weak Virginia Woolf and Alice Munro and Adrienne Rich and Frida Khalo and my mother and Doris Lessing and Emily Dickinson and Toni Morrison and Margot and Mia Farrow and Serena Williams and Sylvia Plath and Sharon Olds and Michelle Obama and Elizabeth Bishop and Elizabeth Taylor and Lady Gaga and June Jordan and Audre Lorde and Mavis Gallant and Joan Didion and Judy Garland and Sappho and Colette and Elena Ferrante and Beyoncé and I could go on and on but I'm sure you get my point.

As I tell you this now, I realize I'd thought this cascade of thoughts before, many times, and the moment in the shower of the Airbnb in Crestline was not an epiphany at all, but rather a recurrence of an epiphany that I experience just infrequently enough that it continues to have an epiphanic effect. For a short time, anyway.

After I rinsed and toweled, I lay naked in bed next to Isaac, who was grading composition papers on his laptop. The acuity of the feeling of love and perspective about my body had by then already faded and I was thinking of other things, but I felt a heavy sense of calm and contentment as I lay there, drying in the unfamiliar bed with the fog and pines in the window. Soon after we started *The Americans*, I fell into a deep sleep that lasted until late the following morning.

. . .

In those months after the cancer returned, my mother told me, in the fall of 1985, all she could remember with any clarity was walking Margot in her carrier for hours and hours through wooden paths in the Fells. There were miles of trails in the park, and once she started walking for more than ten minutes, she could almost believe she was in a wilderness rather than a reservation in the city, and she pretended to be walking in the woods behind Granjan's house in Vermont, in North Pomfret, where she had spent the best afternoons of her childhood exploring and making forts with her brothers and friends from school. On days she wasn't at the firm—she was working part-time then, writing briefs from home as often as she could—she'd take Margot on a walk as soon as they woke in the morning, then another in the afternoon, and another in the evening, so she was spending as much time walking as she did dressing and undressing herself and Margot for the walk and loading and unloading Margot into the carrier.

She took long baths with Epsom salt in the evenings to ease the aching in her back and shoulders from the pull of the carrier, though Margot hardly weighed anything. She was tiny. She had been born at a normal weight, just over six pounds, but she did not grow, and soon she fell to the second percentile and stayed there until she was in the third grade.

"She stopped growing as soon as Alex became sick again," my mother told me. "Alex and I weren't eating much either. It was the first time in my life that I truly forgot to eat entire meals, and it wouldn't be until late at night, when I woke up nauseous with hunger that I'd realized I hadn't eaten since some toast and jam for breakfast. I was losing weight quickly, between all the walking and forgetting meals and perhaps most of all the relentless anxiety. I tried to breastfeed Margot constantly but she wouldn't latch or she'd take just a little, then shake her head in an adult gesture, as if to say, *it's not quite to my liking*. My milk started to dry up, and she wouldn't take formula either. I wanted to scream at her for not eating as much as she was supposed to. I wanted to forbid her from causing me any worry until Alex was either cured or dead."

Granjan came to visit from Vermont often during that time, sometimes staying for over a week, watching Margot when my father had chemo and when he was resting and my mother had to work. She slept in the guestroom that later became my room, and she always brought a small suitcase for clothes and a large suitcase for books. By the time my parents came home from the hospital, Granjan would have already gone to the grocery store and made pecan cookies that my mother devoured, and a whole chicken with crispy flour skin would be roasting in the oven. She'd make rice pudding for Margot on the stovetop with a stick of cinnamon. Margot would eat a full bowl of it without complaint, spreading it all over her face and arms, the only food she ate during that time. Granjan would say as she fed her, "This is cinnamon, this is sugar, this is rice, and this is milk."

One day after my parents came home from treatment, my father was feeling sicker and more depressed then he'd been in some time. My mother helped him into bed, took off his shoes and socks, covered him with blankets to help with the shivers. The bedroom and the whole house felt stuffy and sick, it was starting to smell like the hospital, and it was too cold to open the windows. My mother went downstairs and saw Granjan at the kitchen table, feeding Margot rice pudding and she said, "Let's go out, let's go get Alex something. I can't stand to be in this house anymore."

"Okay," said Granjan; then, to Margot, "Let's get the hell out of here," and the three of them loaded into the Taurus.

"I didn't know where to go so I just started driving north on 93," my mother told me. "It was in the middle of the afternoon and the traffic was lighter than usual, and when we'd only been driving about fifteen minutes I thought if I kept driving for much longer I'd keep driving into New Hampshire and into Canada and who knows after that. I would stop for gas before the border and when Granjan and Margot were out of the car I'd drive away and leave them there and keep going north on my own and leave Alex to die hating me rather than loving me, it would be easier for him to die that way, then Margot could be raised by Granjan in Vermont, eating rice pudding and crispy chicken and having the woods to explore herself, she would be happy there, it would be good for her and Granjan both, and I would begin again in some small nothing town. I wasn't even thirty.

"So I said, against all my impulses, 'We have to go back.' I said something about how I couldn't leave Alex alone at home, I hated the thought of him waking up and having us all gone. I hadn't even left a note. 'Pull over, Ruth,' Granjan said. 'Just stop the car. Pull over at the next gas station.' I took the next exit and pulled into the first gas station I saw even though the tank was three-quarters full. We sat in the car in front of the Cumberland Farms and I cried and Margot cried and Granjan waited for us to finish. 'I'll drive,' she said when it was time, and we got out and switched seats. As she was about to turn back onto the road I saw an animal shelter across the street. I suggested we all just go take a look, maybe seeing the puppies and kittens would make us feel a little better, and if it made us more depressed we'd leave immediately.

"That was the day we adopted Vivi," she said. "Do you remember Vivi?"

Vivi wasn't a kitten. She was ragged, with knotted gray fur and pewter-gray eyes, bent whiskers. She lay calmly the whole time they were at the shelter, as other cats whined for their affection. The cat and Margot stared at each other for a long time, neither one breaking eye contact, a stare that spelled Margot into an instant, deep sleep, right in my mother's arms. The cat has all her shots, the woman working there told them, and she's been there for several months; the older cats have a much harder time finding a home than the kittens.

"This lady is a sweet one," the woman continued, "but if she gets a chance to escape outside you can be sure that you will never see her again."

The cat was free. They bought a green carrying cage that cost thirty dollars and a bag of dry food, forgetting the box and litter. Her name wasn't Vivi yet; the shelter had named her Princess, maybe, or Duchess. As they drove back, with the cat in the carrier in the back seat, strapped in and silent, they discussed what to name her.

Granjan said, "You know, my mother used to say, nobody even named a cat after me."

My mother had heard this before, and until that moment it had always struck her as more comical than tragic. Her name had been Genevieve, a name my mother had always liked and had thought vaguely of using for a future daughter. Genevieve; Vivi. Genevieve had died when my mother was seven, but my mother had vague memories or reconstructions of memories of sitting on her lap in a warm kitchen and feeling calm there, a calm not dissimilar to the calm inspired by this cat. And right then my mother didn't think she'd have another daughter to name.

When they returned home my mother brought Vivi upstairs in her arms and she didn't struggle, and she didn't try to bury into her chest, either. She lay Vivi down next to my father while he was somewhere between asleep and awake; he didn't seem to notice that they'd gone. My mother didn't know if he liked cats. He hadn't grown up with them, and he'd never expressed a desire to have one. She didn't even like cats herself—she still doesn't—but she loved Vivi. When my father opened his eyes, my mother said, "We brought you a cat, we thought you might like her, but don't worry, she was free and she's returnable. We can take her back right now if you don't like her." My mother thought, if he doesn't love her, if he doesn't even like her, then I'll carry her downstairs and let her out and none of us will ever speak of it again.

"But he took to Vivi immediately, as we all had," my mother told me. "She slept by his side that fall, and that winter, and then for nine more years until the day she whined and pawed at the door, begging to be let out in a way she'd never begged before, and while the rest of the family was elsewhere, you, maybe seven years old then, opened the back door and let Vivi walk away, across the driveway and into the tall grass and out of sight."

It was that day, watching my father sleeping with Vivi, when my mother decided with certainty that she was going to try to get pregnant again whether or not my father would live to see the baby, or even its conception.

A few days later they ordered another straw from the lab in New Orleans, and she didn't get pregnant. So they ordered another the next month and she didn't get pregnant, and another the month after that and she didn't get pregnant. By then they only had three straws left. Margot had been a lucky fluke, and perhaps they were fools to expect to get pregnant again, to even attempt it. And the sperm would be unviable by now, anyway, Dr. R had warned. Spoiled.

My mother said to my father, "Let's try one more, and if it doesn't work, then it doesn't work."

They ordered one more straw, and that month she became pregnant.

"Only two moments of that pregnancy have survived in my memory," she said. "The first moment was near the end of my first trimester, in March, and there had been a heavy snowfall the night before, the last of the season. I woke up and looked outside and saw Alex, bundled in all of his winter clothes—that blue down parka from L.L. Bean he still wears when he does yardwork—and he was shoveling a path from the front door to the driveway. He was moving slowly, and I could see it was straining him, but it was the first kind of physical labor he'd done in nearly a year. He had finished his second round of chemo then, and the doctors were saying it had worked, it had worked much better than any of them thought it would. I was weeping, watching him just walk to the garage and pour salt on the stairs and the path, looking like a normal, well man.

"The second moment was when I was twenty-three weeks, twenty-three weeks to the day. Alex and I had been planning a vacation to Yosemite, where he had gone as a child and loved it, and I'd never been. Margot was two, just old enough, we thought, to be able to tolerate a trip and maybe even enjoy it. We'd go for ten days; I'd be twenty-five weeks along, still able to go on some easy hikes. I hadn't had an ultrasound with Margot—they weren't routine then, but the OB said maybe we should do one before I go to California. Just in case there's something to be concerned about, we should know before I take a long trip with some distance from a hospital.

"The appointment was a Wednesday afternoon at the Brigham. The room was small, and when the lights turned off you could only see the monitor. We watched her—but we didn't know it was a her yet—moving on the screen. I could feel her kicks inside me a split moment before I could see them. We listened to her heart, the fast *whoosh*s, and it sounded strong. We watched her like that for some time, waiting for her to move into a good position, and though I could tell the tech was growing impatient, I could've watched the baby move like that for hours. When the baby finally settled down and fell asleep on her side, the tech started measuring the limbs, the brain, the spine, telling us each part she was measuring as she did so.

"When she reached the heart she paused for longer than she had paused anywhere else. She zoomed in, and out, measuring the same spots over and over. My blood fell cold, watching the tech's face watching the screen, though I didn't yet have the thought, *it is not right, the baby is not right.* I felt it before I thought it. The tech was silent as she measured. Then she left to get the OB, and after what felt like a very long time, the OB came in and measured all the same spots. Then she said, 'There is something wrong with this baby's heart.'"

.   .   .

"Ms. Chase?"

Dr. Serrano looks equal parts concerned and irritated.

"Yes. I'm sorry. What?"

"Have you ever had anesthesia before?"

"Only my wisdom teeth when I was eighteen. I think I tolerated it well. I don't remember being in pain until I was back home in bed."

Any other surgeries? Allergic to any medications? Taking any medications besides the prenatal?

No and no and no.

"All the instructions are written out in the pamphlet in the bag in case you forget anything we talked about today," she says. "I need to tell you that there is a risk of cervical laceration, uterine perforation, hemorrhage, infection, and retained fetal tissue. There's also a chance you won't respond well to the anesthesia. But that happens very rarely."

"Okay."

She types, and time moves.

"What is your relationship with the baby's father?"

"He is my husband."

"Is he pressuring you to terminate this pregnancy?"

"No."

"Is anyone pressuring you to terminate this pregnancy?"

"No."

"Is anyone pressuring you to carry this pregnancy to term?"

"No."

"Do you ever feel afraid of your husband?"

"No, never."

Except for a few moments when we were new, when he'd pick me up and toss me on the bed, the mattress on the floor in his stuffy third-floor Northampton apartment, in a playful fit of lust, and I feared my neck would snap—

"I'm sorry about these questions. I have to ask them."

"I know, it's okay. I understand."

"Do you and your husband plan on trying to conceive another baby after this termination?"

"I don't know. We haven't talked about it."

"What form of birth control will you use after the procedure?"

"Condoms, I guess. Maybe I'll get another IUD. But not right away."

"Do you have a history of depression?"

"Yes."

"Have you ever contemplated suicide?"

"Yes."

"Have you ever attempted suicide?"

"No."

But that depends what you mean by suicide, really, if you mean killing myself in only the literal way, stopping my own heart with a knife, pills, gas, rope, or if you also mean killing myself as in killing the self I have become, destroying all that makes Anna "Anna," whatever that means, all except my heart. There were all those years of failed starvation that began as soon as I recognized my body as a woman's body, a tiresome performance of my own annihilation that only yielded—

"Have you been contemplating suicide lately?"

"I couldn't do that to Isaac. Not now."

"In the folder in the bag there are some names of therapists who specialize in pregnancy loss in case you feel it could be helpful to talk to someone after—"

"Thank you. I plan to."

She keeps typing, clicking, then scrolls up on the screen.

"Okay, that's all the questions I have. Thank you for your patience. I'm going to step out now while you get ready. Please remove your pants and socks and underwear, but you can keep on everything from the waist up. Dr. Pak and I will be back in a few minutes and then we'll start the dilation."

"Wait."

I don't know what to say next. She looks at me, expectant. There is still time to stop this from happening, and it is now.

"Yes?"

I could tell her the story of how Isaac and I met, in Northampton that summer after college, at the party in the tilted Victorian off Cherry Street. Or the story of how when we shared our writing with each other for the first time I felt far more naked than I did the first time we had sex, or the first time I had sex with anyone, and how we each applied to MFA programs, knowing that if we were both fortunate enough to be accepted somewhere we would live several states apart for three years if the distance didn't break us before then, and how on the day we were both accepted to Irvine, I feared, just underneath the joy and disbelief, that we had just spent all the luck of both our lifetimes. And how I still fear it. Or the story of how we came to decide to have a baby together, a decision that was hardly a decision at all, but late-night discussions of when and where, even though we both agreed to have a baby now, on this planet at this time, was totally unjustifiable and perhaps morally reprehensible. Or the series of moments over the past several years I realized I loved Isaac more than I'd ever loved anyone, and that I believed I could possibly love anyone, and the series of moments over the past few weeks I realized I already loved this baby more.

But I can't recall any of these moments clearly, not now.

"Can my husband be in the room with me?"

"If you'd like him to be, of course. I can get him from the waiting room."

She stands, pushes the stool, and I want to grab her by the hand and scream, convulse and speak in tongues, see how she reacts.

"Wait."

She stops at the door.

"How much does it hurt?"

"It's different for everyone," she says. "But it will hurt. I wish I could tell you it won't hurt. Most women say the dilation is the worst part, and it doesn't last too long."

"Okay," I say, and she pauses, keeping her hand on the door handle.

I don't want to stop this from happening anymore. I want this to be over.

"Thank you," I say. "That's all. I'll get ready."

She smiles, says she'll be back soon, and then she is gone and I am alone.

. . .

"I was induced five days later," my mother told me. "I wasn't offered a D&E or that's what I would've done; they didn't perform them then. Induction and delivery was the only option. I don't remember much about the birth other than it hurt, it hurt as much as labor with Margot, only it was harder to breathe and push because of how much I was crying, and it was harder to push through the pain knowing that the baby didn't want to come out. They'd injected some poison into my stomach before the induction; she was dead already. I had strong memories as I was pushing of delivering Margot, and for a few seconds at a time I became filled with excitement and hope despite my pain that I was again having a healthy baby, before I remembered that this time was different.

"When I finally birthed her, the room was silent. The nurses cleaned her up without urgency, and then gave her to me. They said I could hold her for as long as we wanted, and then they left us alone. We didn't know it was a girl until then. She looked like Margot, like a tiny Margot. Once I had you I realized that it was you who she really looked like. Something about her mouth, her chin, was just like yours.

"I said to Alex, 'I think we have to name her.' He asked if I was sure, and I said I was sure. I couldn't let her go without a name. We'd discussed the name Jane when I was pregnant with Margot; I'd wanted to name a daughter after Granjan, but I didn't love the name Janet. I did love the name Jane, though. It hadn't felt right to name Margot Jane, I'm not sure why, but this baby could be Jane. I'd had a child-hood friend with that name, Jane Wainwright, and I loved her. We used to play hide-and-seek in the woods behind the house in Vermont, though we were much too young to be left alone. I would call her name over and over again, 'Jane! Jane! Jane!', and I liked how it sounded. Now, as I think about it, maybe the name Jane came to me then be-cause it was the name of a girl I loved but I associated with loss, a girl who I could never easily find in the woods, who moved away with her family to Phoenix the summer after sixth grade and I never heard from again.

"Alex and I spent some time with Jane alone in the delivery room. Down the hall we could hear women screaming and babies screaming. I'm not sure how much time we stayed there, staring at her, and once we named her I'm not sure we said anything at all. When we were ready, Alex pushed the call button and a nurse we'd never seen before came in and wrapped Jane in a white terry-cloth blanket and carried her away."

When they came home from the hospital that day, my mother went upstairs to her bedroom and slept in a deep, dreamless sleep for a long time. When she finally woke up, at some odd hour the next afternoon, her stomach was flat and her breasts were already starting to ache with milk. She came downstairs in her nightgown and saw my father and

Margot—she doesn't remember who had been watching her, where Granjan was—eating oatmeal at the kitchen table. Vivi was curled up in a patch of light on the floor. My mother held Margot for as long as she'd let her though holding her hurt her breasts and Margot was already resistant to hugs and laps.

While she'd been sleeping, my father had picked up all of the objects in sight related to the baby—the yellow and white knit socks Granjan had mailed the week before, the stuffed koala they'd bought at a craft fair, and some of Margot's baby things they'd taken out to examine if they'd hold up for another use. He put them all in plastic bins and stored them in the deep closet by the front door, behind the snow boots.

"I didn't know if it was something I should wait for you to do," he said, "or if you wanted to do it alone, but I couldn't wait any longer to do it."

Then he said, "I was just about to cancel the tickets."

My mother didn't know what he was talking about.

"I'll cancel the hotels, too," he added. "I don't know if we'll get any money back at this point but I want to cancel them anyway. I hate the idea of an empty room."

Yosemite. She had completely forgotten.

"Today's Thursday?" she asked him.

"Friday."

"Are we supposed to leave Sunday?"

"Saturday. Saturday as in tomorrow."

"Let's go," she said without thinking.

"What?" He laughed. "Really?"

"I mean it," she said, and when she gave it a second of thought, she knew that she wanted to go, she needed to go, the only thing she felt she could do was to get on a plane and leave this place and she didn't care where they went. So they packed that night and left early the following morning. They flew from Logan to San Francisco and stayed at the Hyatt near the Embarcadero. While my mother was standing in the lobby, waiting for their room to be ready, she felt a sudden wetness and a sensation akin to relief and looked down and saw that her shirt was soaked with milk.

"We drove to Yosemite in a rented Buick. I didn't feel up for hiking and my breasts were so engorged it hurt to even sit still, and Margot was growing too heavy to carry for long but she couldn't walk much herself, either, so we mostly drove and looked out the window. I don't know that we took any pictures. It was stunning, even from the car, and the expanse of the cliffs and the valley made me forget, for a short while, what had happened. Alex said he wanted to do something in honor of Jane before we left. He wanted to stop in a beautiful place and have a few moments for her, is how he put it. But we didn't stop, either he wasn't thinking about it or no place seemed like the right place, the most scenic spots were too crowded. He didn't mention it again until the last day, when we were driving on our way out of the park. After an hour or two of windy roads through dense forest, we came to a wide clearing where the river joined with other, smaller rivers. Tuolumne Meadows, it was called. I loved the name. Alex said, 'This is the place,' and I knew what he meant."

My father pulled over and they walked just a little bit away from the road. Margot was asleep in the car seat and she stayed asleep as he picked her up and carried her into the meadow. A few other cars were parked along the side of the road, but for several minutes they didn't see or hear anyone but themselves. It was a cold day, and there were high, white clouds over the mountains, and the river reflected the white. The doctors hadn't given them the option of keeping Jane's body or her ashes, and they probably wouldn't have taken them even if they had, but for that moment my mother regretted that she had nothing to leave here or to keep. My parents stood in the meadow next to each other in silence for a long time.

When Margot woke, she wanted to stand on her own, and so they let her wander, but as soon as the grass became wet near the river's edge she came back to them. The whole trip she'd insisted on wearing the same Dodger's sweatshirt, a gift from Uncle Frank, and by that day the front and sleeves were caked in mysterious stains. They hadn't made her bathe or wash her hair in days. She looked feral, and she looked happy. She was arranging pebbles on the ground into some sort of arrangement that was never quite right—she was very precise, my mother said, even then—and when my father saw her bring a stone to her mouth he rushed to her and intercepted.

"Mmm, snack," Margot said, mimicking their feeding prompts. She brought her dirty fingers to her lips and kissed them and said, "*Delish!*" sending herself into a fit of laughter. Soon she was cold and wanted to leave, but my mother didn't want to leave yet, even though she was cold, too, and the milk in her bra was making her colder. When Margot asked again, "Home now," my father looked at my mother and asked if she was ready to go, she nodded and they walked back to the rental car.

Before they left, my mother saw my father glance at the stone he'd saved from Margot's mouth, still in his palm, small and white, and drop it in his pocket.

That night my mother lay awake in the hotel bed in Manteca where they'd stopped to break up the drive, drifting in and out of feverish dreams, not awake and not asleep. In that state she had visions of Jane being cut up during the autopsy with a cleaver knife, still alive, and she held her severed head to her breast and nursed her. She had visions of the nurse who had taken Jane away in the white terry-cloth blanket saying they had made a mistake and Jane was okay, that after they took her away they did the autopsy and her heart was perfect, they were terribly sorry for the error. In her vision my mother rose from the hospital bed that was her bedroom bed and walked past the nurse, out into the hospital hallway, opened the window that didn't open and lifted one leg out and then the other, looking down to the moving traffic and construction and bodies below, small from the great height, and then, as if moved more by magnet than by will, she let herself fall.

. . .

I lie on my back and wait. I notice new features of the room: one light panel on the ceiling is covered with a scene of hummingbirds drinking from daisies, and there are no latches to open the window. Isaac is sitting next to me on a metal folding chair, close enough that I could hold his hand if I asked for it.

"You were in there for a long time," he says. "Is everything okay?"

"Everything's okay."

"They were playing *Parks & Rec* in the waiting room. I watched a whole episode."

"Which one?"

"The one where Jerry retires."

"I don't think I've seen that one."

"Do you want to watch it? I can try to find it on my phone."

"No," I say. "That's okay. They won't be long."

He kisses my temple.

"Tell me what you need."

"Just you."

Isaac had brought his students' stories and offers to read from them to distract both of us but I ask him to tell me a story of his own.

"There once was a frog," he says.

"A frog? What's his name?"

"Her name is Brenda."

"What does Brenda want?"

"Brenda wants to go to Prague."

"Brenda the frog wants to go to Prague."

"Yes, very much. Only there's one big problem."

"What's that?"

"She can't afford it! She's barely making rent from her job as a trainer at the bog's gym and she's way behind on her student loan payments."

There's commotion in the hallway. Dr. Serrano should be back in the room by now, and Dr. Pak. There's trouble with the patient in the room next door. I can't hear what they're saying but it is clear from the tones and quick steps and the wait that something has not gone the way it was supposed to go.

Kicks. He kicks again and again, to the left of my navel.

"He's kicking," I tell Isaac. "Do you want to feel?"

He stands and leans over me, and I press his hand to my stomach.

"Right there. Did you feel it?"

"No." He waits, closes his eyes in concentration. "I wish I could but I don't feel him at all."

There's a knock on the door, and Dr. Serrano and Dr. Pak come in. Dr. Serrano looks different than before—her hair is now tied back in a high knot, and she seems smaller, aware that she is now being observed. Dr. Pak is notably tall, and when she introduces herself she has a low, velvety voice. She says she's so sorry. This must be so difficult. She's sorry we have to meet under these circumstances.

"Do you have any questions?" she asks, directing her question at both of us.

"No," I say.

"I don't think so," says Isaac.

"Are you ready to get started?"

"Yes."

She sits on the stool that Dr. Serrano sat on earlier and wheels it to foot of the reclining chair, leans down between my legs, moving quickly.

"If you could just move a little closer to me, just a little closer, until you feel the ledge of the table underneath you—yes, that's perfect. Now just let your knees fall open and relax as much as you can."

The speculum isn't cold but it feels like it's pulling my labia and going to tear it, but soon it is all the way inside me and opens wide.

"You've clenched up," says Dr. Pak. She guides my knees apart gently with her hand and tells me to try to breathe. "I'm going to give you the anesthesia now, okay?"

"Okay."

"Here comes a pinch."

A shot like a hot poker hits deeper inside me than anything has ever been before, into my gut, and I hold my hand on my stomach. Kicks under my index finger. Dr. Serrano is standing over Dr. Pak's shoulder, observing.

"Why don't you do the next one," says Dr. Pak, and they switch places.

"Two o'clock?" asks Dr. Serrano.

"I'd say closer to four. Yes, right there."

"Here comes a pinch," says Dr. Serrano.

The shot hits, deeper than the first.

"Try to breathe," says Dr. Pak. "I know it's uncomfortable. The anesthesia should take effect soon. Try to count your breaths."

She's standing over me now and offers her hand and I take it, and Isaac holds my other.

"I'll distract you," says Dr. Pak. "I'm the Master Distractor. What do you do for work?"

"I'm an MFA student. In writing, at UCI."

"Wonderful! What do you write?"

"I don't really know. Fiction. I'm bad at answering that question. Ow, *ow*. Fuck."

"Tell me where it hurts."

"I don't know how to describe where."

She takes a step away and looks over Dr. Serrano's shoulder.

"It's the vaginal wall," says Dr. Pak. "It's caught in the speculum."

"Is that better?" asks Dr. Serrano.

"A little better."

"Here comes a big cramp," says Dr. Serrano.

They are no longer two women to me, but one woman with needles and four hands. Isaac squeezes my hand and his other is in my hair.

The big cramp comes. It doesn't stop coming. He kicks and kicks and I try to breathe one breathe two breathe three and the time to stop this is gone.

"I love to read," says Dr. Pak. She's standing over me again. "I just wish I had more time. I try to listen to Audible on my commute but it's hard for me to concentrate, and I so often can't *stand* the reader's voice. What do you like to read?"

"It's still cramping. Really hard. It's hard to breathe. I don't know if it's supposed to hurt like this."

"It's supposed to hurt," she says. "I can't promise when it will stop hurting but I can promise it won't be forever. Please try to breathe. It'll all be easier for you if you breathe."

Then time melts.

I sweat with pain for the rest of the day. He kicks and kicks and kicks to no rhythm. I sleep in a red dream for a long time in the afternoon before it falls dark. Isaac draws the curtains and pulls in a chair from the kitchen and sits in the corner of the room reading by the desk light.

"Time for Tylenol," Isaac says.

Time passes.

"Time for ibuprofen."

"Time for toast."

Time passes.

"Time for a shower."

I shower with the orange liquid soap and loofa and Isaac sits on the covered toilet and reads me the instructions from the pamphlet. I tell him it hurts and I feel like I'm going to pass out.

"Why don't you sit down," he says.

He holds my arm to help me sit on the bathtub floor and lathers the loofa with the orange soap. He asks if I want to do it or if I'd rather he do it. I say I'd rather do it. He hands it to me and I rub it over my skin and it smells good, like hand soap at an airport bathroom.

"Don't you want to know why Brenda the frog wants to go to Prague?"

"Why does she want to go to Prague?"

"Prague has the most beautiful frog gym in the world. The finest frog athletes from every continent go to Prague to train. Brenda has big dreams of competing in the Leap-A-Thon at the World Championships."

"The Leap-A-Thon?" I tease. "That's the best you can come up with?"

"*I* didn't come up with it. This is a one hundred percent true story."

When I'm done washing I ask him to turn off the water. He steps into the shower and helps me stand, slowly, letting my blood move with me. I wet his shirt with my wet body and my tears and spit as he wraps me in a towel and hugs me for a long time.

"You have never looked so pale," he says, pulling away to look at my face. "You don't look well at all."

"I wish he were dead," I say. "I wish he'd never existed."

Isaac doesn't respond. I press my cheek back against his chest.

"We have to tell people soon," I say.

"We don't need to think about that now."

"What are we going to tell people?"

"The truth, I guess."

"I have to email Carol and tell her I can teach in the spring after all. What if they've already given away my section? I should email her right now."

"It's late—you can email her tomorrow."

"I'll just go on maternity leave anyway. I'll stuff pillows under my shirts. Or get one of those fake pregnant bellies they made us wear in Health. I bet you can order those; they can't be that expensive. Got to be cheaper than a car seat."

"Worth a shot," he says, but does not laugh.

The towel is starting to cool, and my muscles tighten and ache.

"I need more Tylenol."

"You're not supposed to have more Tylenol."

"I need to lie down."

"Your mom keeps calling. I talked to her for a little while. I told her you were in a lot of pain but you were okay. She said to tell you to call her if you wanted to talk to her but only if you wanted to. Do you want to call her? I can get your phone for you. And I don't know if I should tell you this now but Margot has been calling you too. She texted me and said she understands if you can't talk to her now but she wants you to know she loves you very much. She sent us a gift certificate for Postmates so we can order delivery tomorrow."

"I can't talk to her. Can you text her I love her too."

"Of course."

"I need to lie down."

. . .

"We ordered another straw soon after Jane's due date had passed," my mother told me. "And you know the rest. After you were born there was one straw left, still in the lab in New Orleans, and though we knew we didn't want to have another baby, we couldn't quite let go of it. We kept it for another eight years, and then we stopped paying rent and let it thaw.

"One summer, when I think Margot was around eleven so you must've been seven, we were on Martha's Vineyard eating soft serve on some benches outside in Chilmark near my brother Frank's place. Down the street, I saw a woman who I could've sworn was Dr. R, Alex's oncologist the first time he got sick in Boston, walking toward us with a man I assumed was her husband. The man looked like Alex, slim with black hair, and it made me wonder if she did have a crush on him after all, if somehow that had helped to save him. She'd moved away soon after Alex finished the first course of treatment, to somewhere in Connecticut, I think, and we hadn't stayed in touch. Over the years, I'd thought a few times of looking her up and writing to tell her that Alex had survived, that I was pregnant, that we'd had children. I wanted to thank her. But I never did. I never seemed to have time to write to her just then, when I thought of it, and so the thought would pass and years would go by before it returned.

"When I pointed to her and said to Alex, 'Doesn't that woman look just like Dr. R?', he agreed it did look a lot like her, though his memory of that time was less clear than mine. He didn't want me to call out even if it was her. He said he didn't want to bother her, and there was no way she'd remember us. I called her name anyway, and she recognized us right away. 'Nobody has called me Dr. R in ten years!' she said. 'Not since I got married. You just sent me back in time.' We talked for just a few minutes, and she introduced us to her husband, who looked less like Alex up close but there was still a slight resemblance. They were on the Vineyard for her niece's wedding, and they had to run, they were late for the rehearsal dinner. She couldn't believe how well Alex looked.

"'Meet my daughters,' I said to her before she left. And you both waved with your free hands and said, 'Nice to meet you.'"

.　.　.

Time passes and then I wake when it is still dark. Isaac is dressed and smells like coffee and toothpaste and his face is close over mine.

. . .

"Anna, it's time to wake up now."

"Anna, you have to get up now. We have to go soon."

"You have to take your shower."

I bathe again with the orange liquid soap and the loofa, standing this time, keeping my hair out of the water. Isaac sits on the covered toilet and talks to me to keep me awake. I stare at my stomach; it eclipses my toes. The pain is gone.

I dry and dress and Isaac says, "We really should get going."

"Do you think I can brush my teeth?"

"I don't know. I don't think so. There's nothing in the pamphlet about that."

"I'm so thirsty."

"I know, baby. You'll be able to drink soon."

"Did you sleep?"

"No. Did you?"

I nod. I slept better than I have in weeks.

My mouth tastes stale but my skin is clean from the orange soap. No kicks. He hasn't kicked since last night but he is still alive. He sleeps. Isaac has already packed a grocery bag with crackers and cookies and apple sauce and one of my sweaters and a scarf.

"Ready?" he asks.

"No," I laugh, and we walk to the car.

The road is quiet; the sun lights the sky just in the corners.

"I want to try again," I say.

Isaac doesn't say anything right away.

"We don't have to decide that now," he says.

Kicks—two light taps against my palm.

Shhh, baby. Shhh, my love. Please please please go back to sleep. It'll be better if you are asleep.

"I want to try again too," he says to my silence, turning to look at me. "Just not for a little while. Is that okay? I think it'll take me a little while."

I nod, but he can't see me. I'm looking out the window, at the tired faces of the drivers we pass, at the sky turning white and pink and peach, and at the gray of the pavement shifting from slate to ash.

Marisol

THE RIMROCK SALOON, on Twentynine Palms Highway in Joshua Tree, was dimly lit by market lights woven through the ceiling's exposed beams and decorated with paintings of wild horses on plains that looked more like Wyoming than California. The tables were crowded with beautiful young tourists from LA, where else, in vintage velvets and lace and bold lipsticks, and a few young families clad in lightweight hiking attire. On the black-painted stage across the dining room, a young woman with strawberry-blond hair was singing Joni Mitchell, *to say I love you right out loud, dreams and schemes and circus crowds.*

It was a Saturday night in late May, the week my baby may have been born if he had been born, and I had come to the desert alone.

I'd seated myself at the bar, a cushioned stool at the far end;

everyone else at the bar seemed to be alone as well, except for an older couple who were paying as I sat down. I ordered a glass of chardonnay and a basket of sweet potato fries for dinner.

A woman was sitting next to me; she'd been sitting there when I sat down, and we'd smiled briefly, acknowledging each other's solitude, but we had not spoken. She was in her midforties, Latina, I guessed, drinking a beer, black in the dark bar. I sensed that she had been here for some time before I arrived, and that she was accustomed to drinking in bars alone; she had that unselfconscious presence, no fidgeting with her phone or eyes flitting around the room. She drank her beer; she watched the singer sing. The white man on the other side of me was in his fifties or so, he glanced up from his phone when I sat down, and seeing my driving clothes, no makeup, nodded once and returned to his screen.

If Isaac had been texting me and calling me, asking if I could just let him know I made it here safe and I was doing okay, then I didn't know it. I'd intentionally left my phone at the inn, charging on the bedside table, and I felt itchy for it now, regretting the challenge to myself to see if I could go without it for a short while, to be alone in this way, too. But what was there to prove, and who was there to prove it to? I was alone enough already.

"I think I need to go to the desert that weekend," I'd told Isaac several weeks before, in bed late at night.

"That's a good idea," he said. "I've been wanting to do something that weekend, too. I've been trying to think of what to do. Nothing seems quite right."

When I told him I thought I needed to go to the desert alone, he didn't press. I'd never traveled alone before, never fallen asleep in a hotel room alone, and I felt I needed to do it now. Since the surgery, Isaac and I had more difficulty being apart than we ever had before, and I knew our grief-infused unity had started to curdle into codependence. He walked me to class on days he didn't teach, spent the hour in the humanities library, reading nothing, then walked me back. We showered together more often than not, and on days we didn't, I'd sit on the covered toilet seat and talk to him while he showered, or sort through expired antihistamines until he was done, then help him choose a shirt.

I wanted the due date to come and go in a place I didn't know and that didn't know me and I may never see again. I thought I might dissolve if left without a witness.

Tears came, right there at the bar. It was the brief thought of going to the park tomorrow morning, when the date would at last be behind me, or it was just the wine hitting my blood, I didn't know for sure. Crying spells still came on like this, though less and less often, sudden and strong, they didn't always care to explain themselves. Isaac and I laughed at them. "Hey there, Miss Waterworks," he'd say, kissing them off my cheeks, "to what do I owe the pleasure?" I'd given up trying to resist the tears, it gave me a terrible headache, and I let them come now, grateful for the dark of the room. I blotted my eyes with the napkin and ate my fries, soggy with grease and perfect.

There was a warmth on my forearm. The woman next to me had laid her hand there, and she didn't take it away, and the tears came on stronger, as though she'd granted them permission with her touch.

"Do you want some water?" she asked.

The woman was broad in her shoulders and had a blanket of black hair that fell to her waist, over her full breasts, and green eyes traced with charcoal and framed by crow's feet. Her lips were what I was drawn to, painted eggplant, her upper lip heavier than her lower. She took her hand away and my skin cooled.

"No, thanks, I have some." I said. "Sorry."

"No reason to be sorry," she said, more corrective than comforting.

I took a long drink of water, then more wine, and blotted my face again.

"You're okay?" she asked.

"Not really, no," I said, smiling. "But I'm fine. I didn't mean to bother you."

It was true, but I regretted the words as they left my mouth, afraid she would interpret this to mean I didn't want her to talk to me, touch me, see me.

"I'm Anna," I said, to keep her with me.

"Marisol."

Tears came again, and this time I tried to resist them but they kept coming, my nose was running and I dried my face with my napkin, the thin paper already wet and tearing. I kept my face hidden in my napkin, waiting for the surge to pass, it never took long. I didn't want to be invisible, but I would've rather been invisible than ugly.

"I'm sorry," I laughed. "This just happens."

She looked at me warmly, or merely puzzled.

"I thought I was going to have a baby," I said.

"Ah, I see."

I wanted her to touch my forearm again, or to press her palm against my wet cheek, as my mother used to do, but she just held her pint glass. On her ring finger she wore a single gold band.

"You're young," she said plainly. "You'll have one if you want one. Life is long."

I didn't like that she'd said that. I wasn't so young, not in this way. And she didn't know what would and would not happen to me any more than I did.

"Thanks," I said, choosing to be kind. "I know. It's just hard to remember."

I drank my wine as Marisol drank her beer, and when the bartender passed I ordered another glass. "I'll have another as well," she said, then finished the remaining few inches of her pint in one swallow. I felt small next to her—I wasn't used to the feeling, even though I'd been able to fit into my high-waisted Levi's and pre-pregnancy bras for the past couple months. I watched her lips open wider to let the black beer down her throat.

She turned to me and said, "I saw you earlier, you know. At the Lost Horse Inn."

"You're staying there too?" I asked.

She nodded. "Just for tonight."

I'd checked into the inn earlier that day, but I hadn't seen her, or any other guests. The place had been eerily empty. It made me uneasy that she'd seen me without my seeing her, but I liked that she'd noticed and remembered me.

"Me too. Just for tonight."

But I didn't want to go back to our apartment in Irvine, not tomorrow, and not the next day. I just wanted to be here, in the loud comfort of the bar, next to a stranger with a warm hand, wet with wine. Marisol was explaining how she'd been visiting old friends in LA, and the woman she was going to stay with tonight had to go to Sacramento: her mother had a fall and she had to take care of the dogs. Marisol thought she'd rather come here than stay in her friend's apartment alone, and she was glad she had.

We thanked the bartender as he set our drinks before us. He was handsome, boyish, though probably at least in his midthirties. He moved without apprehension behind the bar, pouring quickly and gracefully. He'd been working here for a long time. I wondered if he knew Corrie. I'd forgotten the name of the restaurant she worked in, but I remembered it was in Joshua Tree—it took little effort to determine it was Rimrock Saloon, the only one with live music on weekends—and I remembered she'd been happy in this town, she'd slept well alone, she thought this was where her mother might have found some peace. It seemed to be a place that altered you, if just a little, if you asked it to.

Marisol was looking back to the room, now, in the direction of the stage—the singer was between songs, sipping water through a straw— and the pause between us became a silence. This was a natural ending to an exchange between two single patrons at a bar, if we were quiet any longer I would again be alone.

"Do you have children?" I asked.

Marisol drank from her beer, her eyes on mine now, appraising me with something like amusement. I didn't know that she'd answer. It was a rude question to ask a woman over thirty with a wedding ring alone at a bar in the desert, invasive and charged, and she knew this, by the way she was looking at me. I might as well have asked her age, her pant size, how much she had in savings. It felt good to ask it. She simply didn't have them, I guessed, and didn't want them. Or she did have children, and they were estranged, they lived with their father in another state; she appeared too young to have children old enough to be elsewhere without some story of loss or betrayal or failure of love.

I needed stories like this now. I needed them like I needed water and salt, to tell me what was possible in the course of a life after the life you'd planned dies inside you. I searched for these stories everywhere, in novels and memoirs, movies and TV shows and YouTube testimonials, always left wanting. I needed them to tell me how to remain intact.

I resisted the urge to apologize; I wasn't sorry. I was sick of saying sorry when I wasn't sorry and I was sick of making myself small.

Marisol took a long sip of her beer and set her glass down.

"My father loved Stevie Nicks," she said. "He would never say so. But he was always listening to her."

I didn't understand. I looked at her, confused, and she gestured to the singer, who had just stepped back to the mic. *Dare my wild heart, dare my wild heart.*

"He used to take me and my brothers to Cheyenne Mountain when we were kids," she said. "We'd listen to this album on the way up, and when we drove back, too."

It was as if she didn't hear my question, but she did hear it—I'd seen her take it in. The song was familiar to me, too, it was playing on the radio on the way home from the surgery. Isaac and I were so tired. I wasn't in pain. He knew all the lyrics and he couldn't explain how, and we'd talked a little about memory, scents and songs. That was all I remembered from that day. That and the blood in the toilet water, the shock and beauty of it, the tendrils falling slowly in pink and red and black.

The more I listened, the less convinced I was that this was the song that had played that day, it could've been another one of hers, or Fleetwood Mac. I didn't know this song.

"That was where he took his life," Marisol continued. "Soon after I left for college. Some young hikers found him, not far from where we used to camp, in the 1953 Ford pickup he'd been repairing all summer. He had his father's rifle in his lap and a hole from his chin to his skull."

I nodded, conveying my sympathies as best as I could, but I wasn't sure I wanted to be there any longer. I thought of going back to the inn and taking a long shower and watching a movie on the TV, or an old sitcom with a family always in their living room, something with a laugh track. I ate some fries.

"I'm giving you the long answer," she said, seeing my attention fade.

"Oh," I said, embarrassed at my transparency. "I'm sorry. I shouldn't have asked. You don't have to answer."

"I know," she said, and I resisted another apology.

I watched her think, her fingers idly playing with her bracelets, jade stones and hammered brass.

"After he died," she went on, "I vowed I would never go back home again."

Home was a town called Prosperity, she went on to say, a gas station and liquor store town in the high plains off Route 36 an hour west of Denver. She'd left Prosperity the week she graduated from high school, and at forty-four, the closest she'd been to the split-level in which she grew up since then was a rushed layover at DIA a few years ago on her way from her home in Mexico City to Calgary for a ten-week artists' residency. She'd looked out the window as the plane descended, though she was in the middle seat and facing west, toward the mountains and the city's silhouette—the suburbs had spread considerably in the years she'd been gone, and the skyline was taller and broader against the Rockies—and when she glanced out the window across the aisle, mostly obscured by the shaggy hair of a young boy, she saw the flat brown land under the flat blue sky, both unchanged since she'd seen them last, and she did not feel the desire to look any closer.

On both merit and need-based scholarships that combined covered most of her tuition, she attended the Cabot Institute, a small studio arts college in a Boston suburb that had since been usurped by another, larger school nearby and lost its name. A week before her first semester was over, her mother called for the first time since Marisol had left home and said, "Your father is dead."

His death wasn't unexpected, not really. He had smoked cigarettes since he was twelve and drank Southern Comfort without ice every night after he came home from the plant, and he disparaged doctors and anyone who was quick to call on them—Marisol had never expected him to live past sixty, and he didn't—but the particular nature of his death did surprise her, as did the grief that accompanied it.

He'd been sober at the time, her mother said on the phone. He hadn't had a drink in six months, not since Marisol had left. Marisol had trouble believing this, though her father had never hidden his drinking and her mother had many faults, but she was not a liar. Her father was a sentimental and sleepy drunk—not angry, not violent, not impulsive. This was unlike him, though perhaps it was more aligned with his character than she knew; she clearly did not know him so well. The demons of his youth, whatever happened in Vietnam, whatever he witnessed—he never once spoke of it—must've haunted him more than she'd ever imagined.

Her mother was the one who, without a sip of alcohol, would leave Marisol's arms and neck purple with bruises when she gave any lip. Her mother was the one whose rages broke glasses, and, once, Marisol's wrist, and she was the one who, with one twitch of her lip, could send Marisol running up to her room where she'd stay for the rest of the day and night. Marisol would spend those hours sitting crosslegged on the floor as her legs numbed, drawing portraits of the dolls she never played with and imagined landscapes where she'd one day live in peace.

Then there were the debts. Those, too, were not a complete surprise, though they were much deeper than Marisol could have imagined. The family went bankrupt, and Marisol could not attend Cabot for another year; the amount of her tuition and living costs that remained hers to pay was still too much.

"We never should've let you go there in the first place," her mother said before Marisol hung up. "Look what happened when you left. You have his blood on your hands, girl. You need to come back here right now and help the only family you have left."

Marisol began frantically looking for work, any work, and by March she'd started working at Wild Oats, a health food store in Framingham, promising to herself that by the time she got kicked out of the Cabot dorms in June, she'd have some money and a plan that was anything other than going back home.

Marisol saw the ad for the studio assistant to an artist in Faraday Falls, Maine, on the bulletin board she frequently scoured outside the ceramics studio a few weeks before the semester's end. The flier was printed on white copy paper and mostly obscured by brighter, newer ads for summer internships and residencies whose application deadlines had all passed. It had several tack holes in the top and the paper was limp: it'd been hanging up for a long time, but her eyes had always skipped over it, rendering it obsolete before she could judge it herself.

Marisol had never been to Maine and she had little concept of it, and she'd never heard of Faraday Falls. Faraday Falls—she liked the sound of it; it sounded like a place nobody who had ever known her would have ever been, or would ever come looking. It sounded cold and green and quiet. The flier advertised fifteen dollars an hour to assist painter George Bradbury—she'd never heard of him either—on his "new work." *Private Cabin on Property Included—Free Rent*. She took down the flier, anxious that the position may be suddenly coveted by the students still looking for summer work, and she called the phone number at the bottom later from her dorm when her roommate was out.

A man answered after several rings.

"Oh yes," he said, following a thinking pause. "The assistantship is still available. Why don't you come by next week, and we can talk it over. You're at MECA? Or Bates?"

She told him no, that she was a student at Cabot, but she was going to Maine for the weekend anyway and Faraday Falls wasn't too far out of the way.

"Cabot," he said. "So Jenkins finally put up my flier. I sent it to him last spring. Nothing moves slower than an academic."

Marisol laughed, though she didn't quite get the joke, and she didn't tell him the flier had probably been up for a year. She didn't know who Jenkins was.

"So," he said. "When would you want to come by?"

They made an arrangement to meet the following Friday; he'd give her a tour of the studio and the cabin, and they'd talk over the position and see if it may still be of interest to her, as he assessed her fitness, in turn—but this last part was not spoken explicitly. When Marisol hung up she stared at the phone, unsure to what she had just committed herself. She hadn't looked on the map; she didn't know how far north Faraday Falls was, or how she'd get there, but this didn't concern her. The conversation was over in less than four minutes, and in that time, the anxiety about what she would do next, the anxiety that had been edging on panic over the past few weeks, had subsided greatly, and a restless optimism had taken its place.

Though she still had one month to live in the dorms and she knew she had not yet been hired and may not be, early on Friday morning she was on a Peter Pan bus moving north on 95 to the station in Lewiston, with a suitcase holding everything she owned and all her Wild

Oats earnings wrapped in a rubber band and tucked into a single sock in her backpack.

She called George from the pay phone at the bus stop when she arrived, as he'd instructed her to. Nobody answered. She didn't leave a voice mail. For what felt like a long time she sat in the bus station lobby, an enclosed room with metal benches and a mounted TV showing the same pictures she'd already seen over and over: Timothy McVeigh, the wreckage, the fireman holding the dead toddler. She looked away from the screen and watched two buses unload and one bus depart, the lobby filled and emptied, and she felt as though, but she could not say for sure, some of the passengers looked at her questioningly as they passed, even accusatorily. Her skin was paler than it'd ever been before, but it was still darker than most of—no, not most, but darker than every single person in the bus station. This was the whitest place she'd ever been.

She began to feel small and young. She pulled her hair back into a ponytail and put on her down coat, too hot for the day but too large to fit in the suitcase, and she waited, averting eyes, staring again at the recycled images on the TV, now Ted Kaczynski in his orange jumpsuit, and after some more time passed she bought a bag of pretzels from the vending machine even though she had some granola bars in her backpack. She ate them slowly, savoring the salt.

No George.

She called him again and there was no answer, and she didn't leave a voice mail. What would she do next, she began to think. Where would she sleep and where would she eat and what would she do the following day and the day after that. Her plan had been to ask George where to go if he hadn't offered for her to stay with him. Suddenly this plan, if she could call it that, felt totally foolish, childish, too trusting of the world. This man was a stranger and this place was not meant for her.

He lived alone, for all she knew. She quickly sifted through the limited research she'd done on him in the library the week before, and she could recall no mention of a wife or girlfriend, no mention of any woman. So she had called a man she knew nothing about and asked him to take her to his house in the woods of central Maine. Nobody knew where she was; she'd told her roommate and her new friends she was moving out early because of some ailing aunt back in Colorado. A half-baked lie that convinced no one. She didn't tell them she wouldn't be back in the fall.

The schedule informed her that the last bus to Boston had already departed hours before, and there wouldn't be another one until the following morning. She didn't need to pull out the sock to know she had $532 in cash, enough for a hotel room, dinner, a few days of time, but no more than that.

She was about to ask anyone with a nametag to call her a cab, she didn't yet even know to where, when she saw a white man with a white beard walk into the lobby. The man was much older than the man pictured in George's profile in a 1982 edition of *Art & Artists Magazine*; he looked to be about sixty, maybe a little younger, her father's age. But it was George Bradbury: he had the same square face, high forehead, light eyes. He wore jeans and a thick canvas coat, work boots, and a faded Red Sox hat. He smiled when he saw her. Upon recognizing him and seeing that he had identified her, Marisol was filled at once with relief and dread. The time to escape had passed.

"Marisol?" he asked, and she nodded instinctively. "I hoped to beat you here. I didn't want you to have to wait. But you've been waiting, I see. I'm sorry about that. C'mon, I left the truck running."

In his blue pickup he drove them out of the station parking lot and through the outskirts of Lewiston, which looked like only a few old mill buildings, some steeples and a wide river, and soon they were

driving on a long straight road with farm fields on either side that reminded her of the plains of Prosperity. She began to feel claustropho-
bic, stifled by the smell of the truck's musk and the exhaust coming in
through the open the window. But it was green here. This was the
east, not the west. The fields were green, the trees filling the low hills
in the distance were green. The trees grew taller, cutting into the
clouded sky.

"I should've brought you something to eat," said George. "I hope
you're not too hungry. I think there are some peanuts in the back."

"I'm not hungry," she said, but she was desperate with thirst from
the pretzel salt. "Thanks though."

"Just say the word if you change your mind."

"I will."

"It's not far."

George asked her a few questions about where she was from, and
how she liked Cabot and what she was studying. She answered hon-
estly, if vaguely, that she was from outside Denver and she'd spent a
year at Cabot and she'd only taken a few survey courses but her favorite had been figure drawing. Marisol didn't know what to ask him in
turn, and she was afraid of betraying anything she'd read about him
already. She knew, mostly from the *Art & Artists* profile, that he was
originally from a Mormon family in Idaho, that he'd dropped out of
high school and he'd lived on a remote island in British Columbia to
avoid the Vietnam draft—(Marisol unwillingly imagined her father's
face upon learning his only daughter was going to work with a draft-
dodger)—and it was on that island that he began to paint. He'd been a
professor at several colleges around the country, most recently at
Bates, but was now retired. George filled the silences, commenting
every so often on whose farm was whose, which road led to the lake.
He pointed out the town's main street and said, "Welcome to Faraday

Falls!" with genuine or ironic enthusiasm, she couldn't tell. The three-block strip had a hardware store, diner, library, gas station, and Shaw's. A few minutes later they turned onto a gravel road and pulled up in front of a large cornflower house. A woman in a wide sunhat was bent over, pulling weeds along the stone path leading to the front door. She raised her hand when she saw them and then quickly returned her attention to her task.

"That's Ellen, my girlfriend," he said, and Marisol felt a tightness inside her loosen, but only a little. A woman lived here, but she couldn't see her face.

George walked Marisol to the cabin, which was no more than a room the size of her childhood bedroom. All that was inside was a twin bed, a bench with wool blankets folded on top, a space heater, a mini-fridge and a hotplate and a microwave, and shelves above the sink holding a few mugs and dishes. There was no running water, he explained, so she'd use the water from the Poland Springs cooler on the counter, and the attached wooden outhouse as a toilet. "But our house is always open," he said, "for a shower or a bath, or if you ever just want a real bathroom." He then showed her the studio, a small barn, surprisingly barren inside, with two folding tables holding jars of paints and brushes in empty bean cans. Several pieces of unstretched canvas and empty frames were piled in one corner. She loved the smell inside, wood and acrylic and badger hair brushes.

When the short tour was over, George led her to the open acres behind the studio and gestured to the garden ("Ellen's latest enterprise") and to the trail in the woods that eventually led to the Hundred-Mile Wilderness. As they stood on the lawn, he said the position was hers if she wanted it, and she said yes, she'd love it, and she was able to start as soon as he'd like her to. "I can even start tomorrow," she added, laughing, and he smiled but he didn't laugh back. By then, she understood that he understood that she was not coming up to Maine for the weekend anyway, and that she had nowhere else to go. He might have realized it as soon as he saw her at the bus station, sitting alone with her bags and down coat; he might have watched her there for some time before deciding whether or not to approach. And he was regretting now that he had. But the way he was looking at her, with something between pity and intrigue, made her think that probably wasn't so.

"Start tomorrow," he said. "If you really mean that, if you want to. You can stay in the cabin tonight. Unless you already have plans to stay elsewhere."

"Thank you," she said. He invited her to join him and Ellen for dinner, they were probably going to have a roast chicken—but Marisol declined. She was too tired from the ride, she said, and it was true, and she still had the granola bars at the bottom of her backpack to eat. And, mostly, she was uncertain if she could accept more of his kindness and if she wanted to enter the cornflower house and meet the faceless woman in the sunhat who had pulled weeds so exactingly and who hadn't come out to introduce herself.

George didn't push the invitation further, and soon he disappeared into the house and returned with a set of linens and new sponges for the cabin, and they agreed that whenever she woke tomorrow she would come to the studio and they would begin.

Throughout the summer, Marisol woke early. The cabin, set at the edge of the property against a row of skinny pines, had translucent cream curtains that made it hard to stay asleep after the sun rose, but Marisol, for the first time in her life, enjoyed waking up early. After only a few days, it was already difficult to believe she was the same person on this property in Maine as she had been in the two places she'd lived previously; the physical distance from her past began to feel more temporal, and all her memories, when she had them, felt more like retained images from movies or dreams than anything she'd lived herself. She thought briefly of trying to go by another name now, something whiter, a Maine name, maybe Melissa or Meredith or Mary. But she had always liked her name, it was one of the few gifts her mother had given her, and she feared that if she were to change her name now then in a short time she would forget who she was entirely. And if she forgot this, if she forgot where she was from and why she had left, she may be more susceptible to returning.

If nothing else, she was named Marisol there and she was named Marisol here.

Here, after Marisol woke, she stretched her legs and straightened her sheets, then sat on the folding camping chair outside the cabin door and drew. She drew rough sketches in pencil of whatever she saw in front of her, the grape vines and blueberry bushes covered with black plastic netting that did nothing to protect against the deer and crows, the slate paths connecting the cabin to the studio and the studio to the cornflower house, her own toes. Her morning practice became ritual, and she soon found satisfaction in seeing how the disparity between what she saw and what she drew collapsed, little by little, as her eye and her hand became more attuned.

She'd spend the meat of the days helping George in his studio, mostly outlining in thick black oil paint what he'd sketched in pencil the day before or filling in different segments with the colors he instructed and set out for her—a giant paint-by-number, as he'd described it. George's hands shook easily; he could no longer draw a straight line and stay within the boundaries with consistency, so he relied on her for this. He said he was never very good at staying in the lines, anyway. Marisol spent the hours bent over the worktable until her lower back ached, and her vision blurred when she'd look up to rest her eyes and massage her cramping palms.

They worked almost entirely in silence. He listened to his Discman and hummed along—she could make out the chorus to "You're So Vain" and "I Feel the Earth Move" more than a few times every week—and he spoke to her only when necessary, and rarely in complete sentences. "Here," was sometimes the most he'd say for several hours, as he handed her the brush or pencil sharpener she'd been looking for. Or, "That's perfect, but a little thicker there." George only gave her sections of the work at a time, no bigger than eight by ten inches of stretched canvas, so she had trouble imagining the work as a whole; but from what she could tell from the sketches he'd taped along the walls, he was making a mosaic of canvases, maybe into a mural as big as the studio floor, with some shapes that resembled maple leaves, others coral, perhaps some were women's breasts and collarbones. Most shapes she could not identify as mimicking the shapes of anything in particular. It was nothing like the realist landscapes of his earlier work—"Land Studies," as he called them in the *Art & Artists* profile—that had been shown in a few galleries in midsize American cities.

She quickly abandoned her hypotheses of what form she was coloring and what sort of project she was helping him to create and began to focus only on what was before her as she outlined and painted with more shades of purple and blue than she'd thought possible, and, toward the summer's end, oranges and yellows.

Marisol hardly left the property that summer. As soon as the sky started to darken, George would stop his work and offer her a ride to town if he was going in, or ask if she needed anything at Shaw's, and he repeated that the truck was always hers to borrow if she needed it for any reason. She rarely accompanied him, only to buy items like deodorant and tampons and whatever else she wanted to pick herself, and it was on these outings she was reminded of where she was, a land of sharp looks from white faces that made her feel small and young and afraid and angry. George didn't look at her this way; he hardly looked at her at all, but he was aware of her isolation. "There are students your age at Bates now," he said more than once. "A lot of them stay over the summer. Nice kids." Marisol expressed interest at meeting them, and she almost meant it. But the thought of meeting someone else her age felt somehow impossible and forbidden. She imagined girls her age, those she knew and those she didn't, were forever together, eating at gastropubs and dancing on sugary wine and kissing boys they didn't want to love.

That life would be there, she thought, waiting for her when she wanted to rejoin the world of youth; she would be young for many more years to come—but this, what she had here on this property in Maine, a realm apart from all else, she knew would only exist now and never again.

George continued to invite her for dinner, and after declining several offers in a row, one night her third week there he asked that she join them with a new insistence.

"Ellen's been asking about you," he said. "Please, come tonight. She'd really like to meet you." The way he said it implied that to decline anymore would be taken as more of an insult than shy politeness.

"I'd love to come," she said. And so after her studio work was done for the day she went back to the cabin, washed her hands and face from the water cooler, changed into a button-down blouse she hadn't worn since she'd left Cabot, still wrinkled and musty from the suitcase, and walked over to the cornflower house, aware her hands were empty of anything to offer.

George answered the door and led her back to the kitchen, which Marisol had only seen a sliver of before as she walked to the stairs to shower. It went farther back than she'd thought, revealing a long row of cabinets and a kitchen island, over which hung a rack crowded with hanging copper-bottomed pots and pans. The room had a weathered, rustic look, but all the surfaces were clean and the appliances shiny. Ellen was stirring at the stovetop something smelling of soy sauce and garlic and sugar.

She turned to them and said, "Wonderful for you to come, Marisol!"

Ellen was tall and thin-limbed, though heavier across the waist, and she wore her blond-and-white hair in a ropy braid down her back. The hours in the garden had given her pale skin a pink tint in her cheeks and nose. She was younger than Marisol's own mother, yes, no older than forty-five, younger than she had imagined her to be, and considerably younger than George.

Marisol extended her hand, but Ellen hugged her, quickly and tightly, and said, "I was starting to wonder if you were a figment of George's beautiful imagination."

Marisol had hardly seen Ellen since she'd arrived, even from afar, though she knew of her presence through the truck in the driveway and sometimes the cooking smells that reached the cabin. She was careful to time her showers when the truck was out of the driveway, to avoid encounters in her towel and to allow herself to admire all the wooden furniture and art books and framed paintings along the staircase. At times, Marisol had been curious what Ellen and George talked about at dinner and how they spent their evenings in the cornflower house, and what Ellen thought of Marisol, or what was likely her idea of Marisol—who was this young Mexican girl, she'd wonder, with apparently nowhere better to be than here, living rent-free on her property and spending all day alone with her husband?

Ellen must have been aware of Marisol's presence, too, through the humidity in the bathroom after she came home from wherever she went, the lights in the cabin. She well knew that Marisol wasn't a figment. She might have even watched her walk to and from the studio from the kitchen window, appraising from afar.

"Would you like a glass of wine?" Ellen asked. "I've already broken into this delicious sauvignon blanc, but we have others, too. I can open anything."

"Yes, please," said Marisol. "I'd love to try that one."

"What kind of dressing do you like?" asked George. "I can make a vinaigrette, or Russian if you'd prefer something creamy."

"George's vinaigrette is inspired," said Ellen. "He uses white pepper. You must have it."

"Vinaigrette, then," said Marisol, grateful for the direction.

Upon seeing Ellen close up, inside, without a sunhat and sunglasses, Marisol realized she had conjured an image of Ellen, despite hardly thinking of her, that had been far from accurate. Ellen did not exude a submissive kindness like George. She had a hard stare, though the hardness seemed undermined by her loose skin over her jaw and eyelids. This was not the stare of the white people in the bus station: it was not angry, but knowing and penetrating, as though she could read Marisol's thoughts and she liked them.

They sat to eat, a chicken stir fry with wild rice and a tomato cucumber salad from Ellen's garden, all of which was more delicious than Marisol could adequately express. They drank the sauvignon blanc out of tall-stemmed, adult glasses.

"George has told me nothing about you," said Ellen. "Other than that you have excellent fine motor skills."

Marisol wasn't sure if this was a joke or a compliment, or neither.

"I'm from Colorado," she said. "I went to Cabot."

She didn't know what else to say. When Ellen looked at Marisol, her eyes were on her the entire night, Marisol became aware of her own appearance for the first time in months. Her jeans and blouse were not as fitted as they were meant to be; she'd lost weight since the spring, eating only oatmeal and microwave meals and too distracted by her drawing and the studio work to acknowledge hunger if she felt it. Her nails were unclipped and jagged and black with paint stains. She hadn't worn any makeup in ages, she'd hardly even brushed her hair, now well past her shoulders and fraying at the ends. Her mother would have taken the fabric scissors to it long ago; she would've cut it in Marisol's sleep if she'd put up any resistance, a threat she made good on more than once when Marisol was a young girl.

Ellen wasn't wearing any makeup either, from what Marisol could tell, and her nails were bitten and rough. But still Marisol felt plain and young. She did not know how to interpret Ellen's straight mouth.

Marisol gave her short answers that were truthful, if not complete. When Ellen asked what she was majoring in at Cabot, Marisol said she wasn't returning in the fall, "for financial reasons." When asked what her parents did for work, Marisol answered that her mother worked at a law office, without specifying that she was a paralegal, not a lawyer, which her mother always said just meant that she did twice as much work for one tenth the pay. She said her father had been a technician at a power plant.

"He died this winter," she said, and she did not say how. Ellen and George both looked at her then with overt sympathy. They said nothing, and the nature of the silence seemed to invite Marisol to go on, if she wanted to, and tell them more. Marisol did not want to say more, and she regretted having told them even this. She wanted to be someone who kept her own secrets.

So Marisol said, too quickly, "I love that painting," looking to the one hanging on the wall behind Ellen. She had complimented it before really seeing it, but as she looked at it now, avoiding their pitying gazes, it was quite striking, even though it was a scene she'd seen rendered before. A nude woman, an older woman, contoured with grays and beiges and pinks, sat on the edge of a clawfoot tub with her feet in the water. The wallpaper behind her was ornate and floral, which somehow made the woman seem discontent by contrast, though the strokes of paint on her face were wide and abstract, obscuring her expression. Ellen and George turned to look at it as well, as if to remind themselves what was there. Marisol felt relief with their eyes elsewhere.

"Is it one of yours?" Marisol asked George.

He shook his head.

"I love it, too," he said. "It's Ellen's."

"From a long time ago," said Ellen. "The light is all wrong. But I couldn't bring myself to sell it."

Marisol didn't agree. The light was subtle but perfect, brightening the woman's arched back and the side of the tub as if from a small window just outside the painting's frame.

"Do you still paint?" Marisol asked her.

"Not so much anymore."

Ellen and George exchanged a quick look then, the temperature and significance of which Marisol couldn't gauge, and then Ellen filled Marisol's wineglass without asking if she'd like some more, then filled George's and, lastly, her own.

"You have to come eat with us again," Ellen said as Marisol stood to leave, after they had finished their dinner and each had a bowl of rum raisin ice cream and the wine bottle was empty. "Please, George and I are so sick of each other," she laughed, and George said, "Yes, it's true." "I will," promised Marisol. When George invited her again a few nights later, she accepted, and she accepted a few nights after that, and soon the three of them were sharing a meal together two or three times a week at the oak dining table in the cornflower house. As the meals became reheated leftovers or fried eggs with buttered toast more often than roast chickens and lasagnas—though there was always a side of fresh vegetables from Ellen's garden with George's vinaigrette—the conversation became easier and Ellen's gaze and mouth grew softer until Marisol nearly forgot her shyness completely.

Marisol came to learn, mostly from Ellen over desserts and second and third glasses of wine, that Ellen and George had met at MassArt in Boston when she was a sophomore and he was teaching her still life class. While they had an evident fondness for each other at that time, neither of them thought of their connection then as romantic. George would never touch a student, and besides, Ellen had an adorable boyfriend she loved and George was in a content marriage at the time. Their romance came much later, nearly twenty years later, when Ellen was working at The Gallery on 4th in Portland, which showed his work soon after he'd started teaching at Bates. Ellen had expected him at the opening, but she did not expect him to recognize her; to Ellen's surprise, as soon as he saw her, he said her name without Ellen's prompting, even though in the time that had passed she had gained weight in her hips and lost weight in her breasts and no longer wore lipstick or eye shadow.

"But he," Ellen said, appraising George sitting next to her, "looked exactly as I remembered him. He was even wearing the same loafers."

Ellen had already married and divorced by then—"not to the adorable boyfriend, unfortunately," she clarified—and George had been divorced from his first wife for several years. Ellen and George dated only for a few months before Ellen moved out of her Portland apartment in Munjoy Hill and into George's home, a small colonial in Lewiston owned by the college, and Ellen opened a shop on Canal Street that sold antiques and some locally-made goods like soy candles, ceramics, quilts, and sometimes her own sketches and water colors. Five years ago they'd moved here, to Faraday Falls, "to continue living in sin," as Ellen put it.

Neither of them said what prompted the move five years ago—George was teaching up until last fall—and Marisol didn't ask. She never felt as though they were deliberately withholding from her, in fact their forthcoming storytelling about their lives before each other and how they met was striking in contrast to her parents, who spoke so little about their pasts that Marisol had almost become convinced they didn't have them. Even so, she still sometimes felt as though there were long corridors within Ellen and George's story that were for them alone, that she would never be permitted to enter.

And that was all right. It was wise for her to remember that this couple had been together for years before her arrival and they would continue to be together for years after she left. The three of them were not a family, not even close, and they never would be.

By late August, when the elderly maples had already started to turn and the air in the early morning was cool and smelled like mud and must, a restlessness started to stir in Marisol. She still couldn't say with confidence if the new restlessness began after Ellen started gardening in her view in the mornings, or if the restlessness preceded seeing Ellen, as if it had somehow summoned her.

It wouldn't be until later, after Marisol had left Maine and moved into her cramped walk-up in East Village, when she tried to understand what had happened that fall and the year that followed and at what point abstract ideas had become irreversible decisions, the full repercussions of which she would choose to never know. By that point, the story she crafted of the time in Maine was just that, a story—not a memory—and she could not reliably say when things changed, and why, and what she might have done differently.

Before, Ellen had been tending to the summer crops in the south garden, largely obscured from Marisol's cabin view by the studio; but in the late summer, her work had shifted to the plots between the cabin and the cornflower house, the one with trellises for tomatoes and peas and rows of corn and crops with leafy green tops that Marisol had drawn in various stages for the past few months. Ellen gardened early in the morning, soon after the sun had risen. Often by the time Marisol came out of the cabin to draw, Ellen was already outside. Ellen would look up at the sound of the cabin door shutting, and they'd wave to each other, call good morning, just too far away to speak without shouting. Then they'd return to their work and not speak until the next time Marisol went over for dinner, which was never more than a day or two away.

Marisol started to draw Ellen in the garden. She hadn't drawn a human form since her figure drawing class in the fall at Cabot, which felt much more than a year in the past; her instructor had been critical of her proportions, but Marisol had liked figure drawing. She liked the feeling of manipulating and analyzing another's body without having to touch them. Her instructor was correct, her proportions were not accurate, but Marisol had altered them with intention and the outcomes often pleased her. Ellen had offered herself as an ideal subject. She stayed in the same positions for long periods of time, kneeling on the ground with a green pad protecting her knees. Her back arched and her hands dug the earth, neck straight and gaze down. She always wore the same outfit, a navy baseball cap and an oversize canvas shirt, one of George's, Marisol assumed, and baggy cargos and hiking boots.

At times, she would lay back on the grass and stay there for several minutes, perhaps asleep.

She was too far away to make out the details of her face, so Marisol studied Ellen at dinners to inform the portraits, and she recognized the slope of her nose in the women in George's earlier paintings, even those who did not resemble Ellen in any other way. She wondered if the breasts and collarbones she'd been coloring milky blues and coppers—if that's actually what they were—had also been modeled after Ellen.

The act of looking at Ellen, she thought in retrospect, so closely, over and over, even from a distance, and the repeated attempts to contain her on the thick cardstock of her sketchbook, none of which were at all successful, at some point started to feel like the act of loving.

Marisol finished her beer and held the glass, watching the last of the foam fall and pool at the bottom. I drank my wine, three gulps in a row. It was too sweet and ached my jaw. I couldn't remember what I'd ordered, but I didn't think this was the same wine I'd had the glass before. I tried not to look at her in the short silence that had fallen between us. The beautiful vintage people had multiplied and grown louder as Marisol told her story, and the hiking families had left, back to their hotels.

The strawberry-blond singer's eyes were closed, now singing Bonnie Raitt, her voice stronger and throatier than it'd been with the other songs, *I will lay down my heart and I'll feel the power, but you won't, no you won't*; an hourglass waitress fed the bartender a maraschino cherry; the man across the bar kissed the hand of the man next to him. The saloon became charged with a sexual energy. I felt an arousal I hadn't felt in several months, aware of the bodies around me and the pleasure they were capable of inspiring in one another and in themselves. The whole room felt it. The beautiful vintage people stood to dance, arms found the smalls of backs, eyes rested on eyes, lips spoke close together, and hips angled toward each other, moving closer.

Even in the weeks I bled after the surgery, even in the days I padded my bra with iced peas and cabbage leaves to stop the milk, when the thought of having anyone or anything inside me revolted me, I dreamed of sex and woke sweating and tried to make myself come as Isaac slept next to me. My hormones frayed, spiked, and plummeted. When Isaac was teaching on campus, on days I didn't walk with him—work was the only time we were separated for more than an hour—I'd touch myself until I climaxed, right on the couch. The thrill of him coming home early and catching me as if in an act of infidelity only heightened my arousal. Pleasure was a gift I wanted to give myself alone.

But now, at the bar, watching the touches and near-touches around me, I desired attention, attraction, someone to touch me.

"What happened with her?" I asked, turning to Marisol. She was already looking at me, watching me watch the room, with a stare that made me look back to my drink. "With Ellen, I mean."

"I fell in love with her, of course," she said. "And she loved me, too. It was a different kind of love for her, but she did love me. None of it would've happened if she didn't love me. She wasn't that sort of person. That's what I thought for a long time, anyway."

She laughed and brought her drink to her painted lips, but did not taste it.

"It occurred to me recently that I'm the age now she was then," she said, "and as I grow older I see it all differently. I think she was more selfish than I ever gave her credit for. Manipulative, even. And I was so doe-eyed and trusting, she couldn't help herself. I worry it's made me too callous, what happened between us, my inclination is still to be

228

suspicious of great kindnesses. It would be unfair to blame that entirely on her, though Ellen was the one who taught me how intricately engineered a trap can be, how well hidden the metal teeth can be under the forest floor, when someone wants a thing badly enough."

After several weeks of drawing Ellen in the garden in the mornings, Marisol had developed an infatuation that kept her up late at night. Her thoughts were loud in the quiet of the cabin and the night and the deep pine forest around it. She hadn't ever felt this way before. As a girl in Colorado she'd had crushes, she supposed one could call them, on friends of her brothers; but she'd only felt any affection for these boys after they had expressed their lust for her, usually by grabbing her ass or kissing her when she wasn't expecting it. In high school she'd had sex with some of them, and she came to sometimes enjoy it—or, at least, she enjoyed how they wanted her and how much it would infuriate her parents and brothers if they knew what she was doing and who she was doing it to. But she had never felt before what she felt now for Ellen.

It wasn't a pleasant feeling. It ached and bloomed in her stomach, it confused and frustrated her, and she wanted more of it. It was clear to Marisol that her solitude had started to resemble loneliness; what else could account for these sleeping and waking fantasies of Ellen, Ellen who had to be at least twenty years older than her, who was a woman, a woman partnered to her employer, who had shown Marisol no indication that she thought of her as anything other than another one of George's students who he'd never come to love as he'd come to love her.

Still, Marisol wondered sleeplessly in the dark: what did Ellen think about, when she lay on the ground facing the sky? Were her eyes closed or open? Did she think about Marisol, what did she think about when she thought about Marisol, did she watch Marisol walk to and from the studio from the kitchen window, did she ask George about her, and what would he say? What had Ellen meant that night at dinner when she said, "I can tell you're a girl from the West"? Did Ellen notice that Marisol couldn't look at her directly across the dinner table for more than a moment, and did she know what it meant?

What Marisol wanted to know more than anything was the charge of Ellen's gaze, the gaze that always seemed to be waiting to meet Marisol's eyes when she raised them and was never the one to look away.

When she felt ridiculous, and fatigued from her ruminations, Marisol would sometimes briefly entertain the idea of driving the truck into town and meeting the Bates students George mentioned. By now they'd all be back on campus; she could go to a bar or café and see if anyone caught her attention—she could even audit an art class. She'd always dismiss the idea soon after it entered her mind, already unsure what to say to them and what it was she wanted from them. She felt both as though she were far older and more weathered than her peers, yet also far less equipped for the world. Here was where she felt safe and understood and wanted.

The nights went on like this until one evening in November, an evening Marisol had not planned to come to dinner, there was a knock on the cabin door. When she opened it, after a brief moment of horrifying conviction that it was her mother who had somehow found her and driven all the way here and would pull Marisol back to Prosperity by her earlobes, Marisol saw Ellen standing in the doorway, wrapped in a tartan scarf.

"George isn't feeling well," she said. "He's already gone up to bed, hardly ate a thing. But I've made dinner, if you want some. Just pancakes. I wanted to use the last of the blueberries. I was just sitting down to eat and saw your light through the window and thought, it's silly for us to both be alone. Are you hungry?"

Marisol had already eaten some canned lentil soup warmed on the hot plate, but she said of course, she'd join her, and they walked along the slate path together to the cornflower house in the falling dark, close enough for Marisol to catch Ellen's hand. George didn't do well in winter, Ellen explained as they walked, it'd always been this way for him. He never got used to the cold up here, but in the past few years it's taken a greater toll on him. "He just sort of—lessens," she said. "And then spring comes and he blooms again." Marisol had noticed that George had been moving more slowly and less exactingly in the studio, going inside earlier and earlier, thinning in the cheeks.

"Let me just heat up the maple syrup," Ellen said as they entered the warm house. "You can grab the pancakes—they're in the oven."

They sat at the table in the same seats they always sat in, Ellen in front of her painting of the woman in the bathtub and Marisol across from her, eating the thick buckwheat pancakes generously lathered in butter and hot blueberries that dissolved on her tongue. As they ate, talking about winter—how winter in Maine was not like winter in Colorado, here the cold clung to you even after you came inside—Marisol felt Ellen's gaze on her as she so often did. Though this one did not feel like it had the first few dinners, where she had sensed Ellen's judgment, or at least an appraisal of her appearance, her demeanor. This look was different—just as intense, but tonight it betrayed a clear affection that Marisol enjoyed, though it inspired its own sort of discomfort.

"I'm so glad you're here," said Ellen after a pause. "I feel like we don't tell you that enough. You've been such a gift to us."

Marisol smiled. They hadn't ever told her that, not so explicitly.

"What do you think you'll do next?" Ellen asked as she passed her the maple syrup. "After here?"

"I don't know," said Marisol. Ellen hadn't asked her this question in some time; she knew Marisol wasn't returning to Cabot and hadn't come up with an alternative, and she hadn't probed further. Marisol hadn't had an answer then, either. Now a season had passed, and she still didn't want to think of a next place to put herself; she couldn't even think of a lie.

"I'll definitely stay until the project is done," she said. "Or for as long as George wants my help with it."

"That could be forever," Ellen laughed. "Or until he's in the ground, anyway. He's only been working at a larger scale and a slower pace as he's gotten older. I don't think he even knows quite what he has in mind for this one."

She served Marisol another pancake before her plate was empty and passed the butter.

"You know," said Ellen, "he only started working on it when you called about the position. He'd been in a bad rut before then. He'd started saying he'd made everything he was going to make, and he hadn't been satisfied with any of it. He went out to the studio the day you called for the first time in months."

Marisol was surprised to hear this, but she tried not to show it. She remembered the barrenness of the studio when she first arrived; it was now busy with drying canvas and sketches tacked into the walls.

"I think it's his most interesting work so far," Marisol said. "Whatever it is."

Ellen smiled as if she disagreed and she knew that Marisol wasn't sure she really meant it, either.

"I just don't want you to feel as though we're keeping you hostage," said Ellen after a pause. "I want you to know you don't have to stay here any longer than you want to."

"If you and George want me to leave—"

"No," said Ellen curtly. "No, of course not. That's not at all what I'm saying. We love having you here, truly. I don't want you to leave. I just don't want you to forget that you can."

"I don't want to leave, either. I want to be here, with you."

Marisol hadn't meant to say it like that, I want to be here *with you*, and as much as she wanted to retract it from Ellen's memory, she wanted to see how it settled in her, and how she would respond. But Ellen was just quiet, and her straight mouth returned. She lay down her fork, took a deep sip of her wine, and for the first time that Marisol could detect since meeting her, she looked uncomfortable, averted her eyes, as she chose her next words.

"Marisol," she said at last. Ellen rarely said her name, and it sounded round and pleasing on her tongue. "I've been wanting to ask you something. It's ridiculous, I know. But I can't stop thinking about it."

Marisol waited, suddenly hot and tense.

"I'd given up on this idea," she continued. "I thought I had, any-way. And then you came here and it felt like—I don't know," she shook her head and smiled, looking to Marisol, perhaps, to infer what she was trying to say and to save her from having to say it, but Marisol was at a loss. She tried not to move any muscles in her face.

"I was wondering if you would consider donating your eggs to us. To me."

Marisol repeated the sentence in her head, trying to make sense of it. She held her wineglass by the stem and looked into the red liquid but didn't drink from it—she'd only had a sip, but her head felt heavy and wet.

"I know," said Ellen, laughing. "I know it's absurd. George didn't want me to say anything to you. He will hardly even discuss it with me. He says it's too much of an imposition to even broach the topic with you. He adores you, you know. And he says you're incredibly talented. But he thinks of you as younger than you are."

"I'm nineteen," was all Marisol could think to say. The heat stayed, tight around her throat, rising to her face. But something else inside her had cooled, fallen.

"You're an old nineteen. Not like me. I was a child when I was nineteen. I was nineteen when I met George, and I thought I knew everything. I had no idea how much I didn't know."

"My eggs," said Marisol. "I'm not sure I understand."

Over their cooling pancakes, Ellen explained how several years ago, George noticed that his hands were unable to hold his brushes and pencils in a steady grip without discomfort. He could no longer draw so fine a line, they slipped and worried over the pages; the spaces between the visions in his mind and the images on the canvas were widening by the day. But his eyes were unaffected: he could see the disparity perfectly, and it troubled and depressed him. He began to lose his appetite and spent hours in bed, thinking he had just fallen ill. The rest only made him feel worse, and soon he was often stiff all over and could no longer control his knees and hips.

Rheumatoid arthritis, his doctor told him. There was no cure, and it would become worse in time, though there was a medication that could slow the progression and ease some pain. The doctor listed the risks and side effects quickly. All George heard was possible infertility.

"That's unlikely," the doctor said with a look almost like amusement when George asked him about the chances that he would not be able to father children. "But it is a possibility. To be honest, there isn't much research on it. By the time most people need this med, those days are long behind them."

Ellen and George had only been dating for a few months by the time George had this appointment, and they hadn't yet talked about having children together. When George asked her if she thought he should freeze some sperm before he started the medication, just in case, Ellen gave him an unequivocal yes.

George had always wanted children, he told her, but he'd given up on the idea because his first wife Diana had always been adamantly opposed, she thought of it as the ultimate narcissistic act, and he thought he loved her enough to give up his paternal fantasies. And for many years, he did. He focused on his work, and his career was going better than he had ever imagined, and he had come to accept that in his art he would find fulfillment and a sense of immortality and contribution. Then Diana left him on a weekday afternoon when he was teaching, with no warning and only a note on the kitchen table saying she was sick of loving a man who loved his work more than he loved her. He hadn't seen it coming, though in retrospect, she'd been telling him for years that she was unsatisfied in their marriage. He'd so wanted to believe that she was enjoying his success as much as he was, the success which required him to often be away from her, in body or in mind, that he did not recognize her unhappiness.

In the years after Diana left, he half-heartedly dated the few single female professors at SUNY New Paltz, where he was teaching at the time, and women who approached him after his lectures and openings. At times he could almost envision a contented future with the woman across from him, if only she were a little different and he were a little different, yet the idea of fatherhood seemed even further away than it had during his marriage.

He fell into a deep depression, not the first of his life, in small part inspired by his present loneliness with no future relief, and in large part inspired by the growing realization that his early successes were not showing themselves to be foreshadows of bigger successes. He would be remembered as an art teacher more than he'd be remembered as an artist. So much for immortality and contribution. He'd been so thrilled to be shown in local galleries and college museums in Omaha or Cincinnati or St. Louis when he thought they were predecessors to MOMA or the Getty, but they hadn't been. He hadn't been accepted anywhere in New York or LA, even Chicago, and if he hadn't been able to live solely on the profits of his work yet then there was nothing to indicate that he ever would. Now he could see his work and his talents objectively, and he was mortified by what he'd displayed to the world, and with such pride; he was furious with the fools who had encouraged him. He no longer wanted to try to become the caliber of artist he was not going to become. Now he wanted only to live in a beautiful place, where he knew nobody, to be left alone in his defeat, unwitnessed.

It was in the midst of this depression that he left New Paltz and took the position at Bates, and soon after this, his work was shown at The Gallery on 4th in Portland, where he saw Ellen.

By that night at The Gallery on 4th, Ellen, for her part, was also feeling ready for a change. Two years had passed since her divorce: one year of intentional celibacy and one year of disappointing dates followed by more disappointing sex. She and her ex-husband, Landon, had both always known they'd wanted children, at least three, and they'd started trying as soon as they married. But for the four years of their marriage, she hadn't been able to get pregnant.

"Landon loved me less because of it," Ellen said to Marisol across the kitchen table, "though he never said it aloud. I know that he did. And I could hardly blame him. I loved myself less because of it."

They talked about other ways they could have a family, because there were other ways—they could still be parents to children they would love and who would love them in return. Yet something vital had already died between them. They agreed they wouldn't be able to weather whatever lay before them, with children or without. It was a quick and amicable divorce: no shared assets, no lawyers, no custody disputes. "Count yourselves lucky," her lawyer had said. "Kids make divorce a living hell." Within the year, Landon remarried their recently-widowed friend, and soon he fathered a daughter, then another.

During their marriage, Ellen and Landon had both undergone several rounds of tests and exams. Landon's sperm count was a little low, but otherwise they were fine, viable. It was her. She'd always known it was her. The birth of Landon's first child felt more like a validation than an insult. Though nothing was ever conclusive, the doctors told her that her uterus, hormones, and menstruation cycles all seemed to be functioning well. The most likely culprit for their—her—infertility was the quality of her eggs.

Ellen, unlike George, had never abandoned the idea of having children. She didn't think it was something she should ever have to abandon, and certainly not before she was even forty. In the months preceding meeting, or re-meeting, George in The Gallery on 4th, Ellen had been thinking more and more concretely about mothering a child alone, either by egg donation or adoption—but she didn't want to adopt; she so badly wanted to know what it would feel like to be pregnant, to give birth, to have her baby drain milk from her breast. When Ellen told George about this, after he'd asked if he should freeze his sperm, the week before he started his arthritis medication, he seemed only relieved. He told her, in the flavor of a promise, that as soon as he was able, they would move out of the little house in Lewiston and into a bigger house in the country, and there they would have a child.

"He said, 'We just need an egg,'" said Ellen. "I remember him saying it like that, like, we get eggs from Shaw's all the time. Even though George was fifty-five and I was thirty-nine, I felt as though we were both twenty years younger that night, and however much time it would take to have a baby, we had it to spare."

That was five years ago. As soon as George was able to move a little better and his depression had loosened its hold, they bought the cornflower house in the summer for an extraordinarily low price (it'd been on the market for twelve years), and they settled into their new home. He'd started antidepressants along with the arthritis medication, at Ellen's encouragement, and the combination had helped to return him to his more confident, creative self. He started working again, spending long hours in the studio, experimenting with new forms and mediums that were more forgiving of his unsteady hand and the restricted movement of his wrists, elbows, shoulders. Ellen tasked herself with making a garden, a long-deferred dream of hers. She sliced up sod with a spade, nourished the soil with fallen leaves from the woods and manure from neighboring farms, and at night she read gardening books she'd checked out from the library.

They spent as much time in their new home on their new endeavors as they did sitting at the kitchen table on the phone, inquiring with the hospitals and private egg donation agencies about what would be entailed, meanwhile trying on their own and having not so much as a late period. Not one month passed when the sight of the blood didn't make Ellen want to scream with impatience and fury.

"I could hardly do anything on those days," said Ellen, cutting into her pancake, but not taking a bite. "And my cramps have always been terrible, and they seemed to only be getting worse as I got older. I'd take four ibuprofen and a hot water bottle, lie in bed, wishing away time, trying to believe I wasn't being punished for some sin I couldn't remember committing."

Somehow fall passed, then winter, and just as Ellen was starting to feel ready to settle on a donor, George began to retreat from the effort. It took several prompts by Ellen, who knew something had changed, before he voiced his reservations. He hadn't realized how expensive it was, for starters. They couldn't afford it, and even if they could, they wouldn't have enough left to responsibly raise a child. The procedure was invasive and risky and it could take years to have a successful implantation, and the odds would never be in their favor. The fact that George's sperm were fifty-plus years old and had been frozen decreased their chances even further. None of the donor profiles compelled him; the only pictures of the women were from when they were children, school photos, mostly, virtually indistinguishable from one another in their jumpers and plastic hair clips in front of pastel backdrops. He wanted, and he felt he was right to want, a donor that felt like a real human woman to him, someone with intelligence and creativity and drive, a woman like Ellen, who can at the very least write a personal statement he didn't instantly forget.

He had the good sense to not bring up Ellen's age, but they both knew it didn't make it any easier. Ellen was over forty by then, an age which seemed to irritate the doctors more than inspire their compassion. ("Even with the egg of a twenty-five-year-old," one particularly thorny OB told her, "we're still dealing with a geriatric uterus.") Ellen had a retort for each of George's points: "I have all that money in my trust; I don't know what I'm saving it for if not for this;" "It's no riskier than IVF and it's my risk to take;" "They are all real human women, you're imposing unrealistic expectations on these profiles—you haven't even read the new ones I've flagged yet," etc., but George only became more detached and demoralized.

"Maybe we should just put the idea behind us," he said. "I've done it before and I can do it again." He said they should focus instead on the love they had between them and the life together they could still design.

"It soon came to the point," Ellen said, as she refilled her own wineglass—Marisol hadn't touched hers—"that we could no longer discuss it at all without one or both of us in tears, and all other discussions felt forced or vapid. I thought a lot about whether or not I could stay with him. He had led me on, I felt, even though I knew he hadn't meant to—and I was disturbed by how easily he gave up on what he wanted, maybe even more than the idea that we wouldn't have children together. I didn't know if I could be with someone like that, so quick to resignation on something he seemed to want so badly. I took long weekends away by myself, I spent nights in a small inn in Belfast, right on the water, and visited old friends in Portland, wondering if I could just return to the life I was living before I'd met him. But I always missed him when I was gone; I always wanted to come home. I loved our life here together, even if it was just the two of us. And I realized that though not having children would be a great loss in my life, losing George would be even greater."

Ellen's eyes rested on her wine as her fingers absently climbed up and down the long stem. Then she stared across the table at Marisol, as if taking in her face, committing it to memory. She smiled.

"Then you came. I saw you and George together, I heard how he talked about you, how much your presence here enlivened him. I know he still wants to be a father. It just hurts him to want it. I've started to think of you as family, too. I thought, maybe, possibly, this could work after all, with you. Since the idea came to me, really as soon as I met you, that first night you came to dinner, I haven't been able to come up with a good enough reason to not at least ask you. You're so beautiful," she said, softening her face, "and of course that doesn't hurt."

Marisol tried to temper her smile. Nobody had ever called her beautiful before.

"And if you agreed to it," said Ellen, "then George might come around. I think he would."

Ellen leaned back in her chair, exhaled a laugh and shrugged her shoulders. "And now I think, even if he doesn't come around, I'm still going to try. I need to at least try."

The bartender passed, and Marisol signaled for another beer before the last swallow had left her throat. I'd finished my second glass of wine and was on my way through my third, feeling warm and cozy in my stomach, light in my head.

The saloon had grown louder as even more of the beautiful vintage people came and joined those already here and they all ordered more drinks. A young couple had entered some time ago to great applause and had been at the center of the commotion since. The woman wore a flower crown and a tight white dress on her curvy figure, all lace with a high collar, and the man wore a cobalt velvet tux: bride and groom. A new band was now on the black-painted stage, all teenagers, by the look of them, dressed in torn jeans with pins and patches. I didn't recognize the songs they played. The strawberry-blond singer sat at the far end of the bar with a female friend, or maybe a lover, drinking an amber cocktail.

The din had brought me and Marisol closer. We leaned into each other, her to be heard and me to hear, and now I could smell the oil on her skin, the scent of shops that sold crystals and sage, and, when she laughed, the beer on her breath.

Marisol's eyes followed the bartender, who had stopped on his way to the rack of drafts to talk to the strawberry-blond singer and the girl next to her. He leaned on the bar with his elbows, his face close to theirs. The singer extended a hand to his face and tucked a fallen lock of hair behind his ear. No, he was the one she was sleeping with, and they would be sleeping together tonight.

"What did you do?" I asked Marisol, pulling her attention.

"I did it," she said, and her eyes settled back to mine. "I don't remember even deliberating, to tell you the truth. I couldn't think of a reason not to. I didn't think I ever wanted to have children, anyway, the idea had only ever sounded terrifying to me when I thought of it, which I hardly ever did. I felt selfish keeping all my eggs to myself when Ellen wanted them so badly, and she deserved them.

"When I told her I was sure I would do it, she told George our plan; she thought it was best she tell him alone, and I thought she was probably right. He was furious, as she'd suspected he would be. He was insulted that he'd been excluded until now, and he was protective of me. They didn't speak for several days, and I didn't go to their house for dinner. He didn't even come out to the studio. But after some time he invited me over for dinner and told us that he'd been thinking a lot about it and he knew he couldn't control what we did. He wanted Ellen to be happy, more than anything. And he would sign whatever he needed to sign to let us use his frozen sample, if we still wanted it."

The bartender passed; she caught his eye and again signaled for another.

"Did they pay you?"

"I told them I'd do it for free. They wouldn't hear of it. They insisted they pay me two thousand dollars a cycle, even if it didn't work. I thought it was so much money at the time, and it was, I suppose, for someone in my position. But now I see that it wasn't actually all that substantial, for what I did and what they likely could afford. Most donors make five times that. They would have known that, after looking into it. I couldn't see at the time how much power they had, and perhaps they didn't think of it as power, but they should have known that's what it was—they were so much older, they knew how the world operated better than I did, they were white, they were educated, they had each other and a house, they had money. I think Ellen had more money from her family than she ever let on, maybe even to George. It wasn't money she was proud to have, I don't think. Still, I felt uncomfortable taking it—I still felt as though I was in their debt. I'd never even brought anything for dinner."

The bartender swiftly placed Marisol's beer in front of her, and she nodded thanks.

"I'm glad I took everything they offered me," she said after a long sip. "I don't know what I would've done if I hadn't had that money."

Ellen ordered the hormone kits, one for Marisol to stimulate more eggs when she ovulated, and one for Ellen to sync her menstrual cycle to Marisol's. The three of them now ate dinner together nearly every night, but the tenor of the evenings was different than before, at once more intimate and more tepid, and after the meal was done and plates cleared, the women injected their stomachs with shots in the living room side by side. When Ellen laid the supplies on the coffee table, George, clearly uncomfortable watching the ritual, would go upstairs to read or rest.

"I'll leave you to it," he'd say, averting his eyes from the needles. "All right then, good night."

Marisol hated the shots. She'd always hated shots, and these were particularly painful. They left blisters of liquid under her skin and a constellation of bruises that hurt whenever she buttoned her pants, leaned over, lay down. She couldn't inject herself without holding her breath and tensing all her muscles, so Ellen did it for both of them. She'd pinch Marisol's arm right before she shot her, hard, then rub the spot tenderly. Then she'd inject herself, holding the conversation as she did so, betraying no discomfort, not even the quick wince of her eye. Whatever potion was now in Marisol's body made her tearful and irritable, bloated and tired. Though she didn't like these sensations, she liked that they were shared with Ellen. Their bodies were already connecting to each other in the most intimate way she could imagine: a part of Marisol that had been inside her for her entire life would soon be moving through untouched channels of Ellen, take root in the deepest part of her and grow.

After their injections, they'd sit next to each other on the couch, close enough that their arms would occasionally touch, inspecting the new marks on their skin and the mounds of the oil beneath. Ellen's stomach was paper white and soft with a thin layer of fat; Marisol's was darker and firmer. Ellen pressed her hand to the skin around Marisol's navel, gently, giving her chills all over, noting how her own marks were pink and Marisol's were purple. They'd watch *ER* on Thursdays and whatever else on the other nights. Ellen preferred Anthony Edwards to George Clooney—"Don't ask me why"—and, once, she said of Julianna Margulies, when her character had been left at the altar, "She's way too hot for Tag anyway—good riddance!" When they no longer felt the memory of the needle and Ellen's eyes were closed for longer than they were open, it was time for Marisol to go back to the cabin.

"Good night," Ellen would say as she hugged Marisol at the door, holding her close in a way that made Marisol want to melt into her. "See you tomorrow."

On those nights, sitting close, Marisol remembered Ellen saying what she'd said that night over pancakes and the way she said it and how she looked at her when she did. *You're so beautiful.* She'd turn the words over in her mind, and, for the first time since she'd started drawing Ellen in the garden, she found sleep with ease.

Every few days, Ellen would drive Marisol in the truck to Maine Medical Center in Portland for an ultrasound to see how the eggs were developing and to predict when she'd be ovulating. Her blood was drawn, urine collected, weight and blood pressure noted by nurses not much older than she. Marisol's ovaries were gorgeous, one tech assured her during an ultrasound, and the follicles were promising. Ellen sat in the dark room in the foldout chair next to the bed, holding Marisol's hand, sometimes caressing it with her thumb in a way she'd never done with George, at least not in Marisol's presence. Once, George came, too, and he stood on the other side of the bed, transfixed by the monochrome screen showing one ovary, and the other, the buds of eggs.

"Amazing," he kept saying. "Absolutely amazing."

After the appointments, Ellen would drive Marisol downtown, past her old Munjoy Hill apartment, the chipping pink paint unchanged since she'd lived there, and treat Marisol to lunch at the Appalachian Tavern: a tuna melt and ginger ale for Marisol and the turkey club or the day's soup and a decaf coffee for Ellen. Throughout the lunches and the drives to Portland and back, Marisol came to know more about Ellen's life before she'd met George, though many years remained willfully oblique in her stories. She shared that she was from a very wealthy family in Rye, New York. Her mother was an heiress of some oil magnate and her father was a financial consultant, and she had several sisters who all still spoke to one another but not to her. She'd attended an elite boarding school in New Jersey, which she hated, except that the grounds were expansive and beautiful and she could smoke weed in the woods behind the playing fields with the lacrosse boys without ever getting caught.

"I don't think my father would've even believed I knew what pot was," she laughed. "Not one of the Geller girls. He was a very smart man, but a real idiot."

Marisol noticed that Ellen never mentioned having a job that lasted more than a couple years, at most. There was The Gallery on 4th, the local goods shop in Lewiston, various assistantships and internships that may or may not have been paid. She never mentioned a desire to have had a career, even as an artist. Art for her was a pastime, it seemed, not an imperative like it was for George and Marisol. All her interests seemed passive and temporary; all her attentions shifted with the seasons. All, perhaps, except her desire to become a mother.

Marisol came to understand that Ellen was someone who did not need to think too far into the future. She had never come to a dead end with no prospects, no money, no idea what to do next—she had a trust in life working for her, as it had always done, a trust made possible by the riches of her family. As one phase of her life was coming to a close, the next phase had already come to her without her even looking— George walking into her gallery; Marisol moving into her cabin. As Ellen spoke, Marisol had flashes of envy and anger that she herself had not been able to take securities for granted the way Ellen had, but the feelings were not directed at Ellen and the intricate, immutable systems that allowed and assured for these disparities, but at her own parents. Though her parents had always been employed and able to pay their expenses, there was an ever-present, anxious sense that the life they had built could be ripped away at any moment and leave them raw. Marisol found it easier, at the time, to imagine her parents' tenuous station in life was entirely their own fault. Ellen's was a detached yet present way of being that Marisol planned to adopt for herself, no matter her nonexistent inheritance, at some time in the opaque future, if she were to ever find herself elsewhere and alone.

In response to Ellen's stories about her family, Marisol would sometimes talk about her own father, though she found that she was already having trouble remembering him. She couldn't remember her mother well, either, or her brothers—she couldn't visualize the details of their faces and how they spoke to her and how they moved their lanky bodies around the house. They'd all look different now. Freddie would be twenty-eight and Kevin twenty-five, maybe twenty-six. Jason twenty-three. No, not yet. Not so much time had passed; she'd seen them all less than eighteen months ago, which felt impossible. What story had she become to them? She was the one who left for college in the east because she thought she was too good for everyone and drove her father to suicide and was too cowardly to return. That was all right. Maybe it wasn't even a lie. Maybe they hadn't heard anything about her at all, her presence had been redacted from the family's story, her face scraped out of all photographs.

These thoughts sometimes moved quickly through Marisol's mind as she sat with Ellen in the booth at the Tavern, her stomach tender from the shots and cool from the ultrasound gel, and they didn't upset her. She was going to be an inextricable part of Ellen's narrative, and George's. She already was. She was going to gift them a baby. Her value to them would be as undeniable as their value already was to her.

This, she thought, looking at Ellen looking back at her, is a better kind of love.

On the day of Marisol's ovulation—"the retrieval"—as the doctors called it, Ellen waited with Marisol as the anesthesia dripped into her veins, lying in a robin's egg gown in a windowless room, and when Marisol awoke, sore and foggy, Ellen was already by her side with a smile and red eyes. "It's over?" Marisol asked, and Ellen said yes, it was. Now they just had to wait.

None of her eggs fertilized that month. So they did it again. More shots after dinner, more ultrasounds, more blood draws and tuna melts at the Tavern. When Marisol woke from the anesthesia the second time, Ellen was there again, looking as grateful and hopeful as she had the first time. It wasn't until the third round that her face had hardened, and when those eggs didn't fertilize like those before them, she insisted that Marisol stop if she wanted to. She'd done more than enough already. Her stomach was purple all over, her once-clear skin was pocked with zits, and she became tearful at the slightest sentiment.

"If it's not going to work," Ellen said to Marisol after getting off the phone with the doctor one night, spine slackened and mouth unsteady, "it's not going to work. There are other ways to have a baby."

"I want to do one more," said Marisol, "just one more," though she knew she would do another one after that, and then another, until George's samples were out, and she'd keep doing it after that for as many cycles as it would take with the sperm of a stranger.

Marisol was warming hot chocolate with milk at their kitchen stove after dinner when the doctor called for the fourth time in as many months. Ellen ran into the kitchen and stood next to Marisol, followed closely by George. She put the phone on speaker before she answered. The three of them gathered by the stove, leaning in to hear that the eggs had been fertilized—three of them, in fact.

"Nothing is guaranteed, of course," the doctor said, an older man with a kind voice. "The egg still needs to implant. But this is good." Now Ellen just needed to come in for her exam and the transfer when she was ovulating.

"Let me get my calendar," Ellen said, laughing through her tears, "just one second," and two weeks later she was pregnant.

Ellen's pregnancy was uncomfortable but uncomplicated, and the weeks moved slowly from spring to summer to fall. Marisol worked more hours than ever before in the studio with George, who seemed to have been infused with more energy and agility, as if draining these resources from Ellen, who was now perpetually either waking up from a nap or putting herself down for a nap, or else in bed for the night by nine o'clock. If she went to work in the garden, it was for no more than an hour, most of which she spent lying down with her hat covering her eyes. The plots bled into the lawn; crabgrass and wild cane choked the trellises; cherry tomatoes split and rotted on their vines. But George's project was taking form, Marisol could see it even if he couldn't, into a kind of mosaic of organic matter, manipulated from reality with odd proportions and colors. She noticed more bulbous shapes resembling breasts and bellies. After George insisted several times that Marisol use the studio space and materials for her own work, too, she took him up on the offer, and she began redrawing the sketches she'd made over the summer with different materials and techniques—charcoal and ink, oil paint and acrylic—though she made sure to leave all the sketches of Ellen in her cabin, under her bed, out of view. At times she showed her work to George, and he'd speak about the pieces as if they were real art by a real artist, with both praise and critiques, commenting on themes and patterns she hadn't been aware of until he noted them.

"I didn't know it then," Marisol told me, "but I was building my portfolio. These were the first drafts of the pieces that ultimately gave me my career as I know it. It was like we were all gestating at once, is how George thought of it. He loved thinking of it like that. All three of us were creating something apart from ourselves, from inside ourselves, and none of us knew what it would look like in the end—and if it would survive in the world without us."

Marisol cooked for the three of them most nights during those months, simple recipes she didn't know she remembered from her childhood: cheddar cheese quesadillas when Ellen was queasy, beef lasagna when she was ravenous, three bean chili when she needed to "make a move," as she put it, even if it gave her terrible heartburn.

George made quick breads and blueberry muffins that Ellen ate during the day with thick slabs of butter. Ellen, too, had been drawing when she felt up to it, on the back porch when it was warm enough and at the kitchen table when she had the house to herself. Though she never showed her work or spoke of it in detail, Marisol sometimes caught incomplete glimpses of the topmost paper as Ellen cleared them from the table before dinner. The drawings were always of female faces, never shown directly, like in the painting of the woman in the bathtub.

"Who is that?" Marisol once asked as Ellen gathered the papers, and Ellen shot her a harsh look that Marisol hadn't seen before. Her mother, she thought. No, an old lover. She immediately regretted asking.

"Just an exercise," said Ellen. "Just trying to get my hand back. Nobody real."

Ellen and George no longer asked Marisol what she planned to do after she left, and Marisol hardly thought of it herself. Leaving there felt more impossible now than ever. She wouldn't parent this baby, no, she still didn't want children of her own, but she would care for it—for her, as it turned out—and she'd cook and clean and do their laundry, vacuum and dust. The baby should have the clean, quiet space that Marisol had craved when she was a child.

After George went upstairs to read once he was done with the dishes, Marisol and Ellen would watch *ER* on the couch as they had done after the shots. Now Ellen pulled Marisol's hand to her belly when the baby was moving and they felt her together. Marisol loved the feeling of Ellen's skin and the mound below it, the softness of her palm over her hand and the new firmness of her belly, and the faint knocks that came from within.

"She loves you already," Ellen would say. "She told me earlier."

Though Marisol still felt the urge to kiss her, and to move her hand from her belly to touch more of her, she always resisted, even when she could swear Ellen was looking at her with a love that was more sexual and romantic than maternal or sororal. *You're so beautiful,* she'd said. *Of course that doesn't hurt.* This wasn't their time, Marisol knew. It didn't need to be spoken. It may not be their time for a little while, but it would come, it had to come, when Ellen's body was her own again, when the baby was weaned, when George was dead. Every time Ellen touched her hand, moved a hair from her face, called her honey or love or dear, she was promising her that they would be together in the way they wanted to be together, at a time just out of view.

"They named her Mary," said Marisol after a pause. "Mary Bradbury Geller."

"Mary like Marisol?" I asked.

"Mary like Mary. After George's mother."

She'd been holding the glass of black beer for some time but had only taken a sip since it arrived.

"When was the last time you saw her?"

"When she was two months old."

I waited for her to go on. Marisol was twenty by the time Mary was born, or nearly twenty. Forty-four now. I was closer to Mary's age, then, but I'd drank enough wine that I couldn't calculate by how much. I needed water; I needed food. I needed to lie down. Marisol pivoted on the stool and stood, settled herself against the bar and pressed her hand into my shoulder and her lips to my ear.

"I'm going to the bathroom. I'll be right back—don't go any-where."

I watched her walk down the narrow hallway to the bathroom, protective of the empty stool she'd left beside me. I took a sip of her beer to taste what she'd been tasting and found the flavor was as dense as it looked, like molasses. I drank some more. The strawberry-blond singer was alone now, too, waiting for the bartender to get cut, I supposed, and the bride and groom were dancing in front of the new band and singing along. This song I knew, and I loved: *and I scream from the top of my lungs, what's going on?* Her flower crown had fallen off somewhere, and her hair was now in a high messy bun, the groom's blazer was off and his collar unbuttoned. Their friends sang and danced around them, as if in slow motion, spinning around with loose arms. They all looked flush and hot, and I was hot, too. It was too hot. All I could smell was sweat and breath and perfume.

Marisol came back and didn't sit down. She leaned over the bar and asked the passing bartender, an older woman I hadn't noticed until then, to close out.

"I'll get hers, too," Marisol said, not turning to me.

"Oh, you don't have to do that, I'll pay for my own—"

"When someone wants to buy your drinks," she said curtly, "just let them buy your drinks."

"Okay," I said. "Thank you."

She signed the receipt, pulled cash from her purse and left it on the bar, uncounted.

"Please tell me you drove," she said.

I drove as slowly as I could, blinking to try to stop the blending of the headlights and streetlights into the black air, scanning for the inn's sign on the left. Marisol had pulled out her phone for the first time all night and was texting, murmuring quick Spanish I didn't understand, and when she looked up she said, "You missed it." I made a U-turn when there was a break in traffic and drove back, so slowly cars were lining up behind me, until I saw the Lost Horse Inn. I pulled into the spot I'd parked in earlier. Above us the sky was darker than I'd ever seen it before, and the air was thin and cold, blowing west from the Mojave Desert, drying my sweat with one breath.

We walked together to her room, a few doors down from mine. I wasn't consciously choosing to follow her, but I wasn't able to detach from her, either, and I didn't want to. She turned on the small lamp on the bedside table, keeping the overhead light off, which made the wooden walls look warm. Her room was the same as mine, but oriented in reverse—queen bed with a heavy red comforter, microwave and minifridge, small TV. On every wall were monochrome photographs of arthritic Joshua trees and boulder outcrops, jumping chollas backlit by a low sun. The hotel was known for being the site of the death of a folk singer whose name and face I didn't recognize. The lobby and breakfast area were decorated with his tour posters from the sixties and seventies with the Byrds and Emmylou Harris, and in the rock garden by the pool was a small memorial to him: a stone statue of a guitar, candles, charred sage, an unopened bottle of Patron. Some flowers were fresh. He'd overdosed on tequila and morphine in one of the rooms, but I didn't know which one.

I wondered if Corrie ever lay on this bed for a rest when the front desk was slow, if she ever slept here when she knew it was empty for the night. I wondered if she knew the strawberry-blond singer, and if she had slept with the bartender and if he was the one who had made her pregnant. Their child would be good-looking, I thought, though at the moment I couldn't recall anything other than her slim shoulders and waist, the declivity above her collarbone.

She'd still be pregnant now, if she were ever really pregnant at all, and if what had happened to me hadn't happened to her.

I unwillingly imagined then, as I'd been imaging all week, a cascade of scenes in graphic precision of what might be happening to me now if I'd carried the baby to term: I'd be screaming into a hospital pillow, or an epidural would be piercing my spine, or I'd be holding him now, seeing his face, he'd be breathing fine, we'd learn that all the scans had been wrong and he was fine, or he'd be dead, or dying, drowning in air, taken away.

I felt dizzy and tired, far away from myself. Marisol filled the two plastic cups on top of the microwave with water from the sink and brought me one. It was lukewarm, but it felt good on my tongue. I lay down on top of the comforter with my feet still on the ground and closed my eyes. I wasn't sure how I'd arrived here—in California, in the desert, in this room with this woman, this stranger. What would Isaac say, seeing me here, like this? I didn't know what time it was, but he was probably asleep by now, lying on his back with his arms folded across his chest, all the muscles in his face at rest. For a brief moment I wished I were next to him there, trying to sync my breath to his, following him into sleep.

I'd left him alone. We should be together this night, of all nights. He'd wanted to be together. I was selfish and cruel, claiming the loss as mine alone, insisting I mourn unwitnessed. I could walk to my room and call him now, tell him I love him and I'm sorry, tell him I made it here alive and I'll be back soon. But I couldn't move from the bed; I didn't want to move from the bed. Here felt like the only possible place.

I heard the water in Marisol's throat and the empty cup touch the table. The mattress shifted; she was laying on the bed, too, and we were close. Maybe she was looking at me with my eyes closed, but I didn't think she was thinking about me.

"Do you think about her?" I asked.

"Mary? Sometimes. More often lately."

"Where is she?"

"Colorado," she laughed. "Of all places. Last time I looked her up, anyway. Nowhere near Prosperity, though, thank goodness."

I slipped off my shoes and opened my eyes, sat up. Marisol was laying down in an undershirt, white with thin ribbed fabric, showing her black bra underneath and the soft creases on her chest, a cluster of freckles above her left breast. Her eyes were closed and she didn't open them when I lay down, alongside her now, my nose close to her shoulder.

As soon as the baby was born, Marisol told me as we lay together, she realized what a fool she'd been. It took her that long to see that Ellen wasn't in love with her the way Marisol thought she was. Ellen was in love with George; they had a love Marisol had been unwilling or unable to recognize as valid and true, and now Ellen loved the baby more than both of them.

That was the family: Ellen, George, Mary.

It was all so clear the instant Marisol walked into the delivery room after Mary had been born and saw the three of them clutching one another, all flushed and weeping. The love between them was palpable and unmalleable, not like their love for Marisol. Marisol had been a dear friend to them, and a dear employee, student, confidant, donor, audience. This scene would not be possible without her, but she was not a part of it. Of course she wouldn't be. What had she expected? Ellen hadn't mislead her. Ellen had never promised her anything in return but money, and Marisol had taken it. Marisol didn't want to be this baby's mother, and she didn't want to be Ellen and George's daughter. None of that had changed.

But still, watching the three of them together, not noticing her at the foot of the hospital bed, she felt the breaking of a promise she could not articulate even to herself.

They didn't ask her to leave; they didn't have to. Marisol knew she no longer belonged there. The space she'd once occupied in their lives had become all but obsolete, and she now felt like an object in their way they couldn't quite bring themselves to donate, like an extra end table. The dinner times had become erratic, and when they did manage to cook a passable meal and sit down together, they were all focused completely on feeding and burping the baby. Often when Marisol went to the house to see if they needed help, if they wanted her to make them some food, they were already upstairs putting the baby to sleep. When she heard George reading *good night comb, good night brush,* or Ellen singing "Moon River," humming the instrumental interlude, Marisol would let herself out of the house without announcement, walk back to the cabin and heat canned soup on the hot plate and enjoy a renewed appreciation of the room's silence.

When Marisol told them she was leaving one night several weeks after the birth, as the baby breastfed and George spooned Ellen bites of fried rice off her plate, they were visibly saddened, but not upset. They didn't question her and they didn't put up any resistance. They'd expected this, perhaps hoped for it, perhaps were relieved it was coming sooner than later.

"We're going to miss you terribly," said Ellen. "You know that, right? We'll all be empty when you leave."

When George asked where she was going to go, Marisol said New York City. That was the easiest answer. New York was where people went when they didn't know where else to go, and not people she knew. She wouldn't belong there, either, but she figured she'd belong there better than anywhere else, and she'd belong anywhere else better than Maine. She'd saved nearly all the money from the studio work, and she had the thousands they'd given her for her donation. The checks were uncashed, next to the sketch books she hadn't opened in weeks. That money would buy her time, quite a lot if she was careful. George didn't say anything about the work in the studio, which was not complete—he hadn't been out there himself since the baby was born, and on the two occasions when Marisol had asked if there was anything she could do on the project without him, he'd seemed pulled from a pleasant reverie and could think of nothing.

"You'll stay here until you have a place to go," George said. "As long as that takes."

But he moved quickly to help her, and Marisol was appreciative of his efforts. Once she had told them she was leaving, she felt a strong desire to leave as soon as she could. By the end of the week George had put her in touch with an old friend of his, an installation artist in Williamsburg who owned a craft supply store. This friend didn't have any work for Marisol himself, but he had an ex-boyfriend named Harrison who was looking for an attendant for his new gallery in East Village, and Harrison's sister had just been abruptly left by her live-in boyfriend and was looking for a roommate for her walkup not far from the gallery. And so Marisol's new life took form.

The morning they said goodbye, Ellen handed her a thin cardboard box, reused from an old shipment, bent to fit its new contents and sealed with packing tape. It was the painting of the woman in the bathtub, she said, still in the frame.

"We certainly won't forget you," she said, kissing the baby on the top of her head. "I want you to have this so you won't forget us."

She smiled, but she seemed serious, at least in part. Marisol didn't resist the gift as she might have done not long before; she accepted it, grateful, and promised to hang it up in her new apartment as soon as she arrived. She thought briefly then of giving Ellen one of the many sketches she'd drawn of her in the garden the summer before. They were all in a folder in the backpack she carried right now. But she didn't want to give anything else of herself away, not to Ellen, not just then. She hugged her instead, noting all the places their bodies touched, and the absence of the desire that had been so strong, not long ago.

She kissed the baby's cheeky face. Already, Mary looked more like George than any of them—her high forehead, and her fair hair and skin, translucent enough by her temples you could see the blue branching veins. She could pass as their baby, for a while anyway, and for a while longer from a distance; she did not look like a Mexican changling, and that was a relief to all of them, it must have been, though nobody ever dared to say it. Ellen had put an envelope of some pictures of Mary in the package, too, in case Marisol didn't have any of her own.

"Whenever you want to see her again," Ellen said as they parted with a second, longer embrace, "you just say the word and we will come to you. I want her to know who you are."

George drove Marisol to the bus station in Lewison where he'd picked her up less than two years before. At her feet was the same suitcase filled with the same clothes; out the window were the same pines and the same pastures. Ellen's painting lay flat on her lap, and though that day Marisol had every intention to hang it in her new apartment, she never did, and she never opened the envelope of pictures of Mary, either. The package lay unopened on her desk, then in her bottom bureau drawer, then in her closet, pressed against the wall behind off-season boots and her sparse collection of formal heels for openings at the gallery. She noted it on the rare occasions she saw it, and she noted its migration, remembered the general image of the painting and her long-ago curiosity about its subject and what this woman had meant to Ellen, if she had meant anything at all, if she was a real woman. But otherwise, she did not think of it for many months at a time.

In East Village, Marisol drew in the mornings and worked at

Harrison's gallery in the afternoons and bartended weekend nights for a few years, until she started submitting her work and winning small grants, then short residencies—then the small grants became bigger grants and the short residencies became longer residencies across the country, and some in Canada and western Europe. Her art started to resemble itself, as she found a way of approaching the canvas that felt more often like dreaming, or breathing, on her most fruitful days, and less like chiseling in stubborn concrete. She learned how to retroactively package her own work, using phrasing in her artist statements like "interrogation of a Chicana existence" when her subject was some manipulated rendering of herself or Ellen or Mary or her mother, and "depictions of colonialism's scar on the modern landscape" for what became of her morning drawings, whatever it was she saw outside her window.

When she could call herself an artist and believe it, she broke her lease and sold most of her furniture to the woman taking her room and stored her few valuables, Ellen's unopened painting included, in Harrison's basement after he moved with his husband to the Berkshires.

More often than not, Marisol wasn't ready to leave the strange new place when the residency was over; she had found a local lover, or she liked the colors in the land or the rhythm of the city, or she simply had nowhere else to go, and she'd rent an apartment there, finish the project she had started, sell it and use the money to move on.

And in this way two decades passed.

"Then I met my husband," she said, "when I was in Mexico City for a fellowship at Casa Cuadrado, and I've lived there since."

I'd forgotten about her ring.

"Does he know?" I asked. "About Mary?"

"I've told him about Ellen and George. I told him they had a baby."

"He doesn't know she's your daughter."

"She's not my daughter," she said plainly, without bite.

"I'm sorry," I said.

She didn't respond.

"What's he like, your husband?"

His name was Tomás. He had come to see the public show at the end of the residency and had intelligently complimented her work. His flawless English had surprised her; her poor Spanish had surprised him. His mother had been from Illinois, and he'd spent the years after his parents' divorce in his childhood shuttling between Chicago and Mexico City, where his father lived. After he graduated from high school, turned eighteen and was no longer subject to any custody orders, he moved to Mexico with no intention of ever moving back. Now he practiced intellectual property law and was very successful, though he was generous with his wealth, and much of it went to the care of his aging father. He had a son, a precocious seven-year-old boy named Rafael, who looked exactly like him.

"When he mentioned he had a son the night we met," said Marisol, "the instantaneous attraction I'd felt for him subsided a little. But we kept talking, and I enjoyed talking with him. By the time the gallery was closing I didn't want to say good-bye. I asked him if he'd ever like to have dinner with me, and he said, 'Are you hungry now?'"

That night they went for a late dinner of steaks and wine at a white tablecloth restaurant in La Codesa, and Tomás told Marisol that his first wife had died quickly of a rare blood disorder when Rafael was a baby. Tomás still loved his wife, her name was Bianca and she was a singer, and he was unable to stop loving her after she died. He didn't see why he should try.

"She was a loss for the world," he said. "When she sang, there was nothing else. Her voice became the only true thing."

On their fourth date in almost as many days, he told her he'd been looking for another love for years, and he hadn't felt anything close to what he felt for Bianca until he met Marisol. Marisol loved Tomás quickly in return; she loved his honesty and his earnestness, his clear intentions, how easily he was moved to tears and how he never apologized for them. She had nothing to give him but her company, and that was all he wanted. Besides, she'd started to fatigue of traveling, sleeping in stiff beds with strangers and waking to new noises and not knowing where she would be next. And she loved Mexico City, the dark stone buildings unsettled by centuries of earthquakes, the crowded markets and the murals of revolution and laboring men with bent backs. She even came to love hearing Spanish all around her, the language she'd only ever associated with her mother's anger, and she enjoyed when she could retrieve a word she didn't know she knew. They married within the year.

Marisol loved Rafael, too, and Rafael was quick to warm to her. "I am glad you live with us now," he said one night at dinner. "It's better when you're here." She helped him with his English homework, though Tomás was more than capable, and she took him to museums and lunches around the city when Tomás was working weekends. His favorite was the Palacio de Bellas Artes; he would stand transfixed in front of *Man at the Crossroads* for twenty minutes, always finding new details. Marisol didn't know how to speak to children—she hadn't spent any memorable amount of time with anyone under thirty in the past several years—so she treated Rafael as an adult peer, and was often surprised by his wit and astute observations. He saw the world in a pure, unreceived way; he thought for himself. When she asked him what he thought of a painting, he would pause to think, he would not answer simply, "I like it," or "I don't like it," but he would observe the colors, the faces, guess what the subjects were thinking.

"This man looks serious and upset at the same time," he once said, looking quite serious himself. "Like he realizes he's been very wrong about something very important."

Though Rafael never called Marisol mother and she didn't want him to, living with him and Tomás in the quiet stability of their modernist Polanco apartment, she began to feel the satisfying of a desire that she hadn't known was still there—perhaps it had resurfaced only just then. She was a part of this family.

At the same time, Tomás, too, felt the return of an old desire: to have another child. He and Bianca had planned on having several, he told Marisol, and Rafael had very much wanted younger siblings, but he'd stopped asking for them after his mother's death when it became clear that it pained Tomás. And now Tomás was married again. As he told Marisol about his hopeful vision of their future—"it's a love you must experience in your life, it will humble you how much you will love your baby," and "having a child will make you become your fullest self, as a human and a woman and an artist, all"—Marisol became more intrigued by the prospect than she had been, but she was still not fully persuaded. The idea of having a baby with Tomás brought pleasant images to mind, yet she believed it was far more likely the baby would diminish all aspects of her rather than enhance them. This was what she'd seen happen to her artist friends who'd chosen to have children: their days became unrecognizably dull and intricate and heavy, and they became servants, if altogether happy ones, to maintaining the life they'd given themselves.

As if providing an answer to the question she hadn't yet thought to ask, her body began to change, subtly at first, then drastically. Her periods were often late, or missing altogether, and she felt tearful and tired and strange. She knew what was happening to her, she'd just thought it wouldn't happen now, maybe in a few more years. Though she hadn't spoken to her mother in decades, and she hadn't wanted to,

Marisol now wished she could call her and speak only of this, as if they were still mother and daughter, she'd ask when she went through menopause, how she felt afterwards, and if she still felt like a woman.

I was near sleep, and I sensed she was, too, her breathing now quiet and slow. Recorded guitar music started playing from the room next door—laughter, man and woman. I pictured the bartender and the strawberry-blond singer, dancing close, a kiss on a neck. I wanted to move closer to Marisol, press against her, see how she would react if I kissed her arm, or if I lay my hand across her chest. I stayed still, waiting for her to go on. I wondered if Tomás knew where she was now, if Rafael was asking for her, and if she would tell them about me.

"So, it's too late," said Marisol. "Even if I wanted a baby now."

I opened my eyes and looked over at her. She lay as she was before, eyes closed, hands resting on her stomach. I touched her arm, lightly, as she'd laid her hand on mine at the bar. Her skin was warm and it rose with her breaths. She let my hand rest where it was. We stayed like this for a little while.

"Does your husband know?" I asked.

She sighed, barely nodded.

"He didn't want to give up so easily. He came up with alternative explanations for what was happening to me, none of which made much sense, and he talked about adoption, or egg donation—but I didn't want to do any of that. I didn't know what else there was to say about it—and I wished he would be able to grieve what wasn't going to happen rather than fight it, and fight me on it. I finally told him I needed to go away for a while and when I came back we will have put it all behind us.

"I'm ready to go back now," she said after a long pause. "This country doesn't feel like home to me, and I don't know that it ever did.

I feel all the anger and the hate, there is beauty here but not enough. It's a good feeling—missing them, I mean. I've never had the feeling of wanting to go back home."

I woke up next to her some time later. She was sleeping, the light was still on, the music from the room next door had stopped. I found my shoes and looked for a piece of paper, finding none, but a crumpled receipt in the trash—gas and coffee—and a pencil in my purse. I stood by the door, unsure what to write, if I wanted to write anything. *Thank you,* I wrote. Then, below: *I'm glad I met you.* I paused before writing my full name and phone number, and decided against it, not wanting to wonder if she would ever contact me. I left the note on the bedside table, turned off the light, and left the room as quietly as I could. I was relieved to find the keys in my pocket with the room number on them, and I lay in bed without taking off my clothes and fell back asleep until dawn, when the sun was sharp through the eastern window.

When I woke I checked my phone for the first time since I'd left for the Rimrock Saloon the night before. Isaac had called three times and texted, *you make it? you OK? Anna? I'm gonna assume you're out of service . . . plz let me know you're OK when you get this.* Margot had called, too, and my mother. I responded only to Isaac. *I'm OK.*

I brushed my teeth and washed my face, ate dried mango from my bag and drank three plastic cups of water from the sink, packed up the room and dropped the key in the box outside the main office. I drove deep into the park, empty except for a few cars pulled off on the shoulders. I drove slowly with the windows down, though it was cold, passing the cliffs and boulders and Joshua trees, wanting to touch them all. There were hardly any young trees left in the park, I'd heard somewhere. It was too hot; in one generation the park would be all but barren.

I drove until the road forked, and to the right the land fell into a wide, flat valley pocked with tall boulder outcrops, cut off by purple rock mountains some immeasurable distance away, and I knew this was the place I wanted to be. I parked along the side of the road and put on my backpack and walked in the sand until I couldn't see the road, only the glinting roof of my car, as the sun rose above the mountains and heated the land below it. When I found a small enclave in a boulder that looked like nobody had ever been before and would never be, I sat down on the sand, cool in the rock's tall shadow. I took from my backpack the seashells Isaac had collected from Crystal Beach shortly after the surgery, when I could walk without much cramping and bleeding, and a few wildflowers a friend had left at our doorstep in a jam jar. The petals were now dried, but they still held their color, they were still intact.

I set the shells and flowers down in the sand, arranging and rearranging, then I let them alone and sat there for a long time, hugging my knees with my eyes closed, feeling the sun cutting into the shadow and warming my toes, then calves, then hands. The mountains and sky and sand all brightened, and in the quiet I could hear soft sounds of small creatures moving in the sand. I sat there for a while longer, then picked a few stones with shapes and colors that pleased me, dropped them in my pocket and walked back the way I had come.

I called Margot back after I started to drive back out of the park, expecting her not to answer, hoping she wouldn't answer. She picked up on the second ring, just as I was about to hang up.

"Hey," she said. "I was just thinking of you."

"You're not at work?"

"Nope, home today and tomorrow. I just finished three night-shifts in a row."

"You must be exhausted. I was exhausted pregnant when I was sleeping twelve hours a night. With a nap."

"I'm all right," she said. "It's not so bad."

She never spoke of her pregnancy to me, never complained, though I knew she must be sore, tired, her back must ache from standing. By now she might even be having some Braxton Hicks. You can whine to me, you know, I wanted to tell her. Please, whine to me about your second perfect pregnancy so I can say well I'm sure that's uncomfortable but at least your baby isn't dead.

Alex was saying something I couldn't comprehend.

"Shh, love," she said to him. "I'm talking to aunt Anna. Do you want to say hi?"

"Hi," he said, barely above a whisper. "Hi. Hi."

"He's waving to the phone," she said. "Can you say I love you aunt Anna?"

He murmured in protest.

"I love you, Alex!" I said.

No response.

"I'm sorry," Margot laughed. "He's been in such a weird mood. I think he's constipated."

"It's okay."

"Honey, please," she said. "Please stop pulling that. It's not supposed to come off."

"I can call another time."

"No, no, now is perfect."

A short silence followed, in which I heard Alex's voice fading away. Margot was waiting for me to speak.

"I saw Elizabeth had her baby," I said.

A few days before, Margot had posted pictures of Elizabeth,

round-faced and red-cheeked, holding a bundle of muslin cloth with a little face. The picture was taken on a leather couch, at Elizabeth's house, I assumed. Phin was sitting next to her, one hand resting on the baby's belly. His hair had darkened since I'd seen him last summer; he looked like Patrick. Elizabeth wore a tired smile.

"Yeah," Margot said. "It was a really rough labor. She was induced since her blood pressure was so high, and the baby had some trouble breathing at first. Had to be in the NICU for a little while."

"But they're both okay now."

"Yup, they're both fine. We just saw them earlier, actually. We've been watching Phin a few afternoons a week."

"Boy or girl?"

"Girl. Evelyn. I forget the middle name. It's Patrick's godmother's name. Frances, maybe."

"Tell her I say congratulations," I said. "If she remembers me."

"I will."

I drove through the park's exit. There was a small line to get in now, but nobody else coming out.

"I've been thinking of you all week," she said. "I want you to know I haven't forgotten. I'm sure yesterday must've been, I don't know, I—"

"I have to go," I said, unable to listen to whatever else she had to say. "I'm sorry. I'm driving and I have to pull over and get gas."

"Let's talk more soon? I want to hear how you're doing."

"I'm okay," I said, and I meant it.

"Love you," she said.

"We'll talk soon."

When we hung up I thought of calling my mother back, I wanted to tell her that I'd found a place in the park and I'd kept a stone, now the weekend was over, and I was glad it was over, but I didn't want to talk anymore. I'd call her later, on a walk back at home, with the drive behind me. I turned the radio to the Top 40 station and made it so loud I could hear nothing else, and it felt good, driving like that. I wished I had a sweetened bottled tea, a bag of Skittles, things I hadn't bought for myself in years. Marisol would be waking up now, or she might be on the 10 with me, not far away, heading to LAX. I could go there, too, I thought. I could just keep driving and go to the airport and buy a ticket to Mexico City, or New York, or Prague. I noticed the idea and the fleet of images that accompanied it—me buying a paperback at Hudson News, sleeping restlessly on the flight, finding a hotel in the new place and falling asleep while it was still light, waking up to night.

But I didn't want to go, I wanted to go home. I missed my pile of books on the coffee table, our couch pillows and place mats. I missed Isaac suddenly and acutely, thinking of him waking up, turning on his side, his fingers searching for his glasses on the nightstand.

I kept driving, passing plazas and orchards of windmills and miles and miles of terra cotta roofs, and after some time the buildings disappeared and the road was framed only by dry hills, nearly green in parts after the rain from the week before, then the land sloped down, subtly at first, then steeper, and I let the car glide toward the ocean.

Summer

MARGOT CALLED ME in July to say that her college friend, Vanessa, was getting married in Lake Tahoe the last weekend in August, and she hadn't mentioned it to me earlier because she didn't think they'd be able to make it.

"But I have more vacation than I realized," she said to me on the phone, "and it won't roll over. We thought we might try to all come down, the four of us. Alex has been totally obsessed with airplanes lately, and I think it would be good for us to take a short trip."

A few weeks before, she'd texted the family thread a video of Alex in their living room, flying plastic planes up and over the coffee table, mumbling incoherently to himself. Nick had taken the video; he was the family documentarian, Margot said, he's the one with two free hands and two free breasts. On the couch behind Alex, in the upper corner of the screen before it moves to follow the flight path, you could see Margot's legs in floral pajamas, and baby Zoe's feet, kicking idly in cobalt booties. I'd watched the video over and over, stopping at the moment when Margot's hand held the baby's feet, squeezing gently, calming them to stillness.

"Would you be able to come up and see us?" she asked.

When I saw it was her calling I'd taken the phone outside to walk in a circle around the parking lot. The yellow film of a faraway fire eclipsed the sun. The summer had been another season of hungry fires—the worst of them were far enough north that we couldn't smell the smoke, but the air was still tinged, dirty, the sky like sunset by midafternoon. We hadn't spoken on the phone since my ride back from Joshua Tree two months earlier, though she'd called me once while I was teaching and we'd texted a little about Billie Eilish and *Los Espookys*. The texts soon tapered off, and I didn't expect to hear from her.

"I know Tahoe isn't exactly close to Irvine," Margot added. "But it'll be closer than we've been in a long time."

I didn't answer right away. Alex was pleading in the background, "Who you talking to? Who you talking to?" I listened for Zoe but couldn't hear her.

I told Margot I'd talk to Isaac about it, but it probably wouldn't work out.

She paused, exhaled. Fabric ruffled.

"We'd only go if you came to see us," she said.

She said it as though it were obvious, of course she was really coming to visit me. I didn't know what to say.

There—a soft coo, lolling vowels.

"Hey baby," Margot said in a tender tone I'd never heard her use before, not even with Alex. "You got it, girl. C'mon, that's it. Try to take just a little more."

I passed the grills and picnic tables, shaded by bougainvillea on trellises. There was a family barbecue, maybe a birthday party. Two teenage girls were doing cartwheels in short shorts, sweeping their feathery hair out of their eyes as their feet found the earth beneath them.

"The wedding is on Saturday, but Nick has to work that Friday," Margot continued. "We were thinking maybe we would fly back late on Sunday, skip the brunch and spend the day with you and Isaac before we fly back.

"I really want to see you before you get even farther away," she said. "I've been thinking lately, we might want to move back East sometime too, especially now that you and Isaac are going to be there. I want Alex and Zoe to know their cousins and grandparents better than we knew ours. We don't want to live in Alaska forever. But that wouldn't be for a couple of years, at least."

Cousins. I said nothing. She wasn't thinking, but she wasn't being thoughtless.

"If you don't come up to see us," she said, now with a small bite in her voice, "I don't know when we'll see each other again."

Isaac and I would be leaving California at the end of the summer, going East, back to my home but farther away from his. We weren't sure where to go—we had never not been students. I'd lived in Boston before; I'd shared an apartment above a vegan ice cream parlor with a college friend and a couple on Centre Street in Jamaica Plain, and I remembered running through the Arboretum in foliage on paths of mulch, stopping to stretch at the garden of Bonsai trees, some older than the country itself, one a survivor of the bomb on Nagasaki. I'd been happy there.

Isaac would be teaching at Emerson and I'd be at Simmons, both in composition, adjunct lecturers, with no benefits and no guarantee we'd be hired for a second semester. But it was enough for us, for now, it'd pay rent on our two-bedroom apartment with hardwood floors on Burroughs Street, a short walk to Jamaica Pond.

When I came back inside after talking to Margot and told Isaac what she'd told me, and I said it's a long way to go for a short visit, he set his book down on his lap and said, "We should go. We've been wanting to make a trip north for years and we never have. This is the time to do it—just think of it as a road trip with a lunch with them in the middle.

"Maybe it won't be so hard," he said, seeing my face change. "Meeting her baby could be good, even, for you—for both of you. I don't know. I think it could be. I think I'd like to meet her."

We drove there in four days, leaving the afternoon after our last class let out, driving the long way, along the 1, the ocean to our left and the hills to our right. We'd go through Yosemite on the way back, we decided, with the hopeful logic that it might be less crowded during the week. In San Luis Obispo a family friend of Isaac's hosted us in the pool house of their prefab villa; we car camped in Big Sur at the foot of redwoods, our tent flanked by trailers smelling of septic; we stayed at a La Quinta in Sacramento near the airport, watched the second half of *The Truman Show* in bed and fell asleep under the hush of engines falling from the sky.

I drove most of the way. Isaac navigated on his phone, selected the podcasts and music. Sometimes, for a long time, when the light was low and soft, the shadows long, we drove in silence.

It was early afternoon on Sunday when we arrived in Tahoe City. We'd planned to meet them at Commons Beach, where none of us had ever been before. The air was hot and dry, mountain air, perfect and clear, and the water was a deep, pleasing blue. The beach was small, not far from the main street, and it looked artificial next to a lawn of trimmed grass and a playground busy with children.

Isaac and I scanned the narrow shore for them, packed with families staking their space with vibrant towels and shade tents, some with music blaring from Bluetooth speakers, clashing against the breeze off the lake. Margot had texted *by the big family with the pink umbrellas*. I didn't see them when we passed the only party that seemed to match that description, so we walked to the end of the sand and then turned around, and I felt something just short of hope that we'd gone to the wrong beach, or they had, and we'd miss one another after all, and I wouldn't have to meet Zoe and see Margot holding her and nursing her and watching Nick playing with Alex, praising all his new skills and vocabulary, her healthy baby boy, no longer a baby.

When I saw them, retracing our path along the shore and looking more carefully, I didn't wave right away, and I didn't tell Isaac. I watched Nick, sitting on the sand with his legs outstretched as Alex buried his feet. Nick wiggled his toes, breaking free, and Alex laughed, scrambling to cover them again. Margot sat in the shade of an umbrella in a folding chair, wearing a large office shirt and a drooping sunhat. She looked strikingly like our mother did on the summer trips to the Cape we'd taken as children, always the one to stay in the shade, covered in an old poplin shirt of my father's, watching over us and our bags while we crept shivering into the waves and dug holes to China.

Margot saw us, waved and called our names, beaming. Across her lap, Zoe lay in a bundle of turquoise.

Nick stood to greet us and hugged us both as sand fell from

his legs. Alex looked up at us with recognition, first vague, and then when Nick prompted him—"You know who these people are, remember?"—his face sharpened and he took the cue, said confidently: "Aunt Anna and Uncle Isaac from California."

Margot remained seated in the folding chair, weighted by Zoe, nursing at her breast. She beckoned us over. I hugged her, still standing, leaning over her, and she gave Isaac an enthusiastic high five.

"Hey beautiful strangers," she said.

It was clear she was still thin, even under the large shirt—the trace of her sternum was visible above the top button—though there was a new softness about her, in her chin and cheeks. I hadn't seen her in person since our honeymoon in Alaska, which was, suddenly, two years before, and she did look changed by the time, and the pregnancy, as I likely did, too.

Zoe fretted at the disruption, threatened a cry. She lay on a nursing pillow I recognized as the backdrop of most of Margot's pictures: simple sketches of foxes, bears, bunnies. Margot lifted her breast, revealing the edge of her areola, darker than mine, and eased it back into the baby's mouth with the tired grace of a gesture many times repeated.

"Baby Zoe, Aunt Anna. Aunt Anna, baby Zoe."

Her face was buried in Margot's breast and her eyes were closed. I took the baby's hand, held in a tight fist, and kissed it lightly. The black hair I'd seen in photos after birth was nearly gone, and finer, lighter hairs were coming in. She didn't look much like either of them, rounder in the face, though the spacing between the eyes—just a touch further apart than most, in a way that suggested an active mind—I recognized from Nick's mother.

I felt a swell of all feelings; I let them rise and level within me.

"She's so lovely," I said. I squeezed her hand gently and let it go.

"Do you want to hold her?" Margot asked.

"That's okay. She looks very comfortable there."

"She's almost done with this breast; she can take a little break."

"I probably smell like sunscreen."

"So do I," she said. "I don't think she minds."

But Margot understood; she didn't press.

Zoe unlatched again and her hand found the top of the turquoise muslin. She was pulling it up to her chin, covering her open, searching mouth. Margot slid the cloth down to her waist, making sure it was still protecting her legs and feet from the sun. Isaac complimented Zoe, too, and said he couldn't believe how tiny a person could be. Alex interrupted then, requesting to bury Isaac now, and Isaac complied, took the seat next to Nick, and Alex went to work. I sat down next to Margot in the shade on a towel she'd laid out for me, hugging my knees and digging my toes into the sand.

"I love her top," I said. Zoe wore a cream eyelet onesie that revealed her arms, pale and chubby.

"I do too," said Margot, rubbing the fabric with her thumb, then holding the baby's arm and repeating the same gesture on her skin. "It's a hand-me-down from Elizabeth. Most of her girly clothes are. Evie is an absolute giant with an incredible wardrobe. Patrick's parents buy her all these clothes from fancy baby boutiques in New York, and she grows out of half of them before wearing them even once. Elizabeth gave me this one with the tag still on."

I'd sent Zoe a gift soon after she was born, a hat like a polar bear, though it wouldn't be cold enough for her to wear for months, and by then it'd likely be too small. I didn't know what Margot's friends had given her and what of Alex's she'd kept for his future sibling, now arrived and real—and I didn't know what a baby needed. I'd only just begun to research bassinets and cribs and co-sleepers during my pregnancy, and I'd become so overwhelmed within minutes that I shut all browsers and decided to wait until my third trimester before giving it another thought. I'd bought the polar bear hat online after many irritated hours over several days spent browsing baby websites, then I purchased it impulsively, without considering the season or the size. It was expensive to ship. I filled the cart with other gifts for Margot, her belated birthday presents—Epsom salt, a lavender-scented heating pad for her shoulders, witch hazel. I didn't know if she ever used them.

We watched the boys against the water.

"How was the wedding?" I asked her.

"Incredible," she said. "Her mother's family owns Bishop Hotels, so I knew it would be very nice, but it was even more extravagant than I'd expected. There must have been over three hundred guests there, and they were the most gorgeous people I'd ever seen—we were by far the worst dressed. Luckily for them they didn't have to look at us too long; we were so exhausted we left by nine."

I asked her about our parents, and it soon became clear that my mother had been talking to Margot more than she'd been talking to me, or at least she'd been talking more candidly to her about my father and his health. He'd had another spring of mysterious and violent fevers, night sweats that soaked his sheets, and a fatigue so debilitating he was unable to ascend the stairs without pausing for breath. He didn't talk to Margot on the phone, as he never talked to me on the phone; he didn't seem to know what to say to us, what to keep to himself—"I'll hand you back to Mom now," he was always quick to say, not wanting to take up any more of our finite time.

My mother had told me about my father's health after they knew he was okay, feeling better though still not completely well; the doctors thought it was just a strange allergic reaction that came with the change of season. But she'd been talking to Margot before they knew what it was, and what it wasn't. She told Margot she was sleeping in my room, since his shivering and rasping breathing kept her up at night. It was the first time they'd ever slept apart, alone, since all the nights he'd spent in the hospital when he was young.

"She said it feels like a dress rehearsal for widowhood," Margot told me. "She was laughing when she said it. She said she'd been having great bedtime chats with the dog."

My mother said something else to Margot that had stuck with her, that she didn't like; she hadn't said it to me. My mother said she felt that now the doctors thought of my father as a sick man—an old, sick man—she could tell by how they now addressed her rather than him directly when they explained their findings, next steps. They seemed tired just looking at him. This meant, my mother knew, that they would forget him when he left the room, they would not press their minds to think of how else to help him, not like the doctors had when he was young, when being sick was not the way of things. What hurt her more was that my father was now thinking of himself the same way.

"I wish she would've told me before they knew he was okay," I said. "I would've liked to be there for them, somehow, do something."

Zoe unlatched, exhaled a deep, long breath, and fell asleep against Margot's breast. Margot absently stroked her hair, then traced her eyebrows, as our father had done to us when we were unable to sleep as children, haunted by nightmares.

"I told her to tell you sooner," said Margot. "She's been feeling protective of you, I think. Well, I know. She's said as much."

I bristled at the thought of my mother thinking I needed to be protected, and saying so to Margot. Yet it was true that I had been weakened, for a while, anyway, unsure if grief would ever make me more resilient and compassionate to the suffering of others, or if it would only turn me angry and bitter. My mother would have heard the fragility in my voice when we talked and decided to keep it from me, to confide in Margot instead. My mother had a different love for Margot than she had for me—no less strong, but different, and that was all right. I was the baby who lived after the baby who died, I was the baby she didn't think she'd ever have. But I'd never been my mother's only child.

No, they were right to not tell me, I thought. I was grateful that Margot had kept it from me, too, but that she told me now.

Alex called to her then to show her how he had successfully submerged Isaac and Nick's legs in the sand. Isaac shook his leg a little, creating a small earthquake above his knees, saying, "Oh no, it might be the big one!" and Alex scrambled to pile the sand back in place, patting it frantically for a firmer hold.

"You look gorgeous," Margot said after a pause, appraising me.

I blushed, despite myself. She didn't say things like this to me. Then her eyes changed, playfully suspicious—she was asking if I was pregnant, it was clear—and I felt as though she had skinned me with her gaze, leaving me bloody and bare-boned. While I didn't like that she could see into me like this, without my permission, in a way I could never see into her, I was relieved that I didn't have to summon the words and find a way to speak the maybe-truth that it was.

"I don't know," I said, finding it difficult to stifle a smile. "Maybe."

Her face brightened, and she looked as though she might cry, then regained control of her mouth. She was trying to read my cues, unsure, it seemed, whether or not I wanted her to show excitement, or something else, a more reserved understanding. I hadn't planned to say anything to her; I hadn't wanted to say anything at all, to keep it a secret, even from myself, if I could, until the baby was out of me and the cord cut, breathing with a beating heart.

"I mean, I really don't know," I said. "Probably not. I just feel a little off, not unlike last time, but it could be anything. It's too soon."

For the past few months, Isaac and I had entered into a silent agreement that we were no longer trying to not get pregnant, nor were we explicitly trying, either. We agreed the night I returned from Joshua Tree and he didn't take the condoms from the nightstand and I didn't either, and I pulled him into me with my hand, feeling him bare for the first time since I'd been pregnant. And we agreed again a few nights later when I used my mouth on him, and he asked if he could finish inside me, and I took him from my mouth and moved on top of him, and we agreed again, and again, each time we lay together for some time after sex, and he would rise to bring me a glass of water, and I would stay in bed on my back, hearing the pulse of blood in my ears and the sound of my breath.

I didn't count the minutes on my back; I didn't take my temperature in the morning; I didn't open the app; I didn't study my toilet paper or the calendar. I didn't need to. I knew when it was time. I felt it, the warmth in my blood, and we found each other in the dark.

"I haven't said anything to Isaac," I said to Margot. He was burying Alex now, up to his skinny thighs, and drawing giant feet in the sand with his finger, sending Alex into fits of laughter.

"I won't tell," she said, and I trusted her. I knew she'd tell Nick; that was okay. "Mom doesn't know anything?"

"No, not yet. When there's something to tell."

I didn't know what day my period was supposed to come, not precisely, but I knew it would be soon. I'd been feeling hungry, wanting gas station jerky, anything with salt and grease, and uninterested in the fresh fruits sold in cardboard boxes on the side of the mountain roads that Isaac lusted after. He ate so many strawberries he felt sick. And I hadn't been able to sleep since we'd left. I lay awake in the strange new places with my eyes closed, unsure if the churning in my gut was dread, hope, something real or nothing at all. I tried to remember what I'd felt last time, before I knew for sure, the heavy ache of my breasts, or the pulsing in my temples.

I couldn't remember it well; it felt like a long time ago.

"I don't know that I'd be able to do it again," Margot said as she took Zoe over her shoulder in one fluid motion and patted her back firmly. "You're braver than I am. After what you went through, I could hardly manage this," she said, laying Zoe down to her other breast.

She watched Zoe nurse for a few moments, lifted her breast slightly for a better latch, then turned back to me and said, "You know I'm keeping all her things to give to you. Alex's, too. I can't imagine giving them to anyone else. So you'll be seeing this top again."

She smiled at me with a warmth I hadn't ever felt from her before, so naked with affection it was hard to meet her eyes.

Zoe let out a cry, an unconvincing plea of discontentment that made us both laugh.

"You're okay, baby," Margot said, calming her. "How about you go back to lunch and save the screams for the plane ride."

"I'm really glad you came," she said, looking back to me. "I know it's a long drive."

Her expression was still affectionate, but more serious now, in a way that made me anxious, waiting for her next words.

"I didn't think you'd come," she said. "I almost didn't even ask."

"Of course I came," I said.

"It's not an 'of course.'" She paused and looked at the boys, and I could see the effort it took to say what she was saying, to speak to the thing we had always felt but never named. "I feel like you haven't wanted to talk to me in a long time. I don't know if I did something wrong, or said something to offend you—I feel like you don't want me in your life. And I want to be in your life. I want us to be in each other's lives."

She spoke calmly, without anger, but with hurt. I thought she must have weighed her words, debated whether or not to say anything at all. She'd decided to ask me to come, and she'd decided to say this to me, now—she wanted to make it right, whatever it was.

The wind off the lake blew cold, and I pulled my hands into my shirt and Margot held Zoe tighter. Alex was telling Isaac about all the states he knew, and that Tahoe is both the name of a city and a lake. The ten tallest mountains in the United States were all in Alaska and he planned to climb them all.

"No," I said. "You have it wrong, that's not how it is at all. You've never done anything wrong."

I'd been the one who had it all wrong. The realization of it began to bloom in me, a sensation like nausea, not yet thought.

"I'm sorry," I said, unable to look at her directly for more than a moment. "If I ever made you feel like you've done anything wrong."

She shook her head. "You haven't, really. I just get this sense from you, sometimes, like you don't want to be in touch with me. And I get it, I mean, we've lived apart for a very long time. That's not how it's supposed to be.

"I know it's not easy seeing me and Zoe right now," she said. "The timing of all this—it's just cruel, how it happened. I want you to know I wish so badly it didn't happen this way."

"I'm glad I came," I said. "I mean it. Zoe is only a good thing."

Margot smiled at me, and then stared down at the baby in her arms. I wasn't sure if there was more to say, she seemed to be thinking of something else to say, but Zoe started to cry, really cry this time, Margot held her tighter and rocked, but couldn't calm her. Nick, hearing her, came to us and unwrapped the muslin and peaked inside her diaper.

"She's soaked," he said. "I'll go change her," and he carried her and the diaper bag to the grass lawn behind us. Alex came and lay himself at Margot's feet, grumpy and sun-weary, and we all decided it was time to eat.

The afternoon passed quickly. We ate the sandwiches Margot had bought us from the deli in town; we tested the cold lake water with our toes; Alex told us about the plane ride, how he saw the tops of clouds and the whole ocean. Isaac offered to hold Zoe while Margot and Nick ate, and when they said thanks but it's okay, we're used to eating in shifts, Isaac said he'd really love to hold her, if it was all right with them. Nick lay the baby into Isaac's arms, where she soon fell asleep, and so he held her there for a while longer, walking back and forth along a small stretch of shade by the playground.

When the sun began to lower, and the air cooled, it was time for them to go, pack up, head to the airport. Margot and I hugged deeply, said I love you, let's talk more often, please. Alex asked Isaac to lift him up again, and again, before finally agreeing to say goodbye and give us both a hug around our necks. I kissed Zoe's forehead and gently squeezed her feet. She was freshly asleep, Nick was still holding her, her brows were furrowed, lips parted, all the muscles in her face moving, tensing, then relaxing, as she dreamed.

Isaac and I stayed on the sand for a little longer, watching the water reflect the fading sky and families packing up, older couples walking together. Then we went back, walking the long way to our car, down the main street, Highway 28. There were many white tents set up, an art festival wrapping up. The vendors were talking idly to one another, comparing sales of the day and how they preferred this to the scenes at Truckee and Palo Alto, as they loaded the framed work into boxes for the night. A few tents were still open with all the art hanging up and the artists sitting on stools, hoping for last-minute business, and we stopped in several, glancing at the originals and leafing through the cards and prints.

I looked for Marisol. I'd searched for her online when I came back from the desert in May, and after some time I found her in the *Past Fellows* section of the website for Casa Cuadrado in Mexico City. Marisol Silvia Lizalde. She had a clean, professional website, with large photographs of her art, a list of past and upcoming shows, an evasively concise *About* section, and a portrait of herself on an urban street taken too far away to see the details of her face. Her paintings surprised me, though I hadn't been aware, until seeing them, that I'd conjured images of what sort of paintings they might be. They were rich with red, brown, and blond tones that resembled both earth and flesh—it took me some time to realize that in the abstract landscapes were hands, hips, breasts, hair, and the faces of women. It was not the same woman in each painting—some were thin in the waist, others wide, one had hair so long it became a river and another's was so short it showed the curvature of her skull—but there was a sharedness to them all I couldn't quite place, something in the angles of their bodies, their degree of abstraction and the faint resemblance to Marisol herself.

As Isaac examined a small woodprint of a fox in the last tent in the row, checked the back for the price and returned it to the table, I pulled out my phone, found Marisol's website and clicked on *Past & Upcoming Shows*. The link was slow to load, and when it did, the configuration of the site was messy, incompatible with my phone. I zoomed in and saw the most recent date was *Kleiner / Cage Gallery*, Victoria, B.C., December 2017: nearly two years ago.

It wasn't long after seeing her paintings that I began to write again. I hadn't been able to write after losing Scout, only scattered fragments that never cohered, nothing came easily, and I was tired, preferring to consume the stories of others rather than create them myself. Isaac didn't want to write our story, not directly—but now I did, I felt unable to write anything else until I wrote that.

(This was never supposed to be part of this novel. The novel I'd started writing in the first weeks of my pregnancy with Scout did not end with the character named Anna in Tahoe City with no baby on her hip and no milk in her breasts. I will not end this novel by granting her a healthy baby, because her baby, like mine, is lost—and she, like me, does not yet know if she will ever have the baby she'd so easily imagined not long ago. But I will leave you with the knowledge that the character named Anna will try again—she has already begun—because this young couple now knows not only that their baby can die, but their baby can die and they can still walk down Highway 28 in a summer evening, they can notice the sky and the water, and they can believe the story of the family they will create together may begin with death, but that is not how the story will end.)

"Are you looking for somewhere to eat?" asked Isaac.

He was watching me looking at my phone.

"I can," I said, closing the browser. "Are you hungry?"

"Not yet, that was a big sandwich. But if you are I can eat soon."

He draped his arm around me and we said to the artist, thanks, these are beautiful, take care. Isaac held me close, sensing I was growing cold.

We kept walking through the rows of white tents, as more of the artists packed up and said to their neighbors have a good night, hope to see you again. I wasn't hungry either, and I felt a rush of gratitude for Margot for the sandwiches, for her forethought. I should have made my gratitude known to her in the moment, before they had left, in the flurry of hugs and goodbyes and folding the towels into their tote bag.

"You'll let me know, either way?" She'd asked me before we parted, when our husbands couldn't hear, and I nodded that I would.

I could see it more clearly now, now that I was no longer with her, the ways I'd been the one imposing the distance between us, not her; I'd thought it was her choice and I was honoring it, always waiting for her to call me, never making the first gesture, but that was not so— and for how long had it been this way? Her gestures were so plainly there, and I hadn't recognized them as such, stymied by my grief, my envy, my stale rancor. She'd invited us to stay with her after our wedding, threw the barbecue so we could meet her friends, bought the Shakti Yoga pass, confided in me about her miscarriage and her troubles with Elizabeth and texted and called me throughout my pregnancy, and after, sent gift certificates for Postmates and two boxes of sage and parsley tea to stop my milk, and now, she flew to us for an afternoon, she'd been saving her children's clothes for their cousin who had not yet been born.

I'd even been the one to tell her to go to the wedding brunch, saying we'd be driving in the morning, anyway, and wouldn't be there until at least one. I'd orchestrated it that way, desperate to cut the hours with her and with the baby to one afternoon, one meal, no more.

I was no longer a sensitive child and she was no longer a peppery adolescent; now we were adults and mothers; we were sisters. I would call her soon, I vowed to myself, after we were all back home, rather than wait for her to call me, and say to her what I hadn't said then. I wanted to tell her that she was the sort of mother I hoped to become.

By then I would know if I was pregnant. My period would have arrived, or not. The thought gave me a blooming warm feeling, deep inside, a teenage sensation of requited crushes and first kisses.

I was still looking for Marisol, passively, without hope or expectation, in the crowd of young and old tourists, growing as the main street livened with restaurants and bars. Women of all ages were wearing short dresses, sheer tops, heels and platforms, moving gracefully up and down the street. I felt chilled as the sun set behind the Sierra Nevadas, and I regretted that I had left my thick scarf and fleece in the car. I was wondering at what point I had become a woman who would rather be comfortable than beautiful, I was still too young for that, I thought, though perhaps just barely—when ahead on the street I saw a woman carrying a baby in a wrap with an elaborate pattern. My eyes still found them, women with babies, women with bellies—but this woman was striking, both in her familiarity and in the sharpness of her thin figure, her white-blond hair, pulled into a high ponytail. The woman was walking ahead of us, and I couldn't see her face. It was just the two of them, from what I could tell, the woman and the baby, Zoe's size, it seemed, too far away to see more clearly.

Corrie—that's who she looked like—though she didn't turn for more than a moment to check the traffic before crossing the street, away from us and toward the lake. I couldn't make out her face. I didn't call her name to check; I didn't quicken my pace to see more clearly. I watched her weave through the families and couples on the sidewalk, now adjusting the wrap and holding her baby in a hug, moving north, until the crowd filled her wake and blotted her, step by step, out of sight.

It wasn't her, I decided. Corrie would have stopped and said Hello, remember me? How strange this is to find one another here, now, where neither of us have ever lived.

I should've given her my number before I left her on Briarcrest

Drive, I thought, and I should've written it on my note to Marisol. They were gone now, off in their lives, I would very likely never see them again, I'd all but assured as much. But there were other women, how many other women, who had felt and wanted what I'd felt and wanted, and felt and wanted differently, too, how many were walking on this street in Tahoe City, what was the story of the white-blond woman who was not Corrie, and the woman who passed me now, and now. Anywhere I've been and will go next, there they will be. And when I meet them I will ask, Do you want to see each other again?

"What do you think?" Isaac asked.

"Sorry?"

"I said maybe we should try to go to a grocery store before it closes, get some things for the drive tomorrow."

"Good idea."

"There's a Safeway behind us," he said, reading his phone, and we agreed to walk a little more, until the restaurants and shops thinned out, then go back to the grocery store, buy something simple to make for dinner at the Airbnb, sleep early, wake early, drive south. We walked slowly, without agenda or hurry, commenting on the retro style of the buildings, the odd natures of tourist towns, and what the land would look like if nobody lived here.

We would never return to California, I thought. Isaac said otherwise. He said he had felt more like home here than he had anywhere else—even more than in Laramie, Wyoming, where he grew up— and California would have a way of bringing us back. He didn't want to stay now any more than I did—it was no place to live without money, real money, the kind we would very likely never earn—and our friends would be leaving as we did, starting fellowships abroad or reuniting with long-distance lovers.

He could think we would return, if it helped him to leave now, but

I chose to believe that the land would close up behind us as we left, sealing within it everything we had lost. I would not tell him, when we flew east in a few weeks, as all our belongings we hadn't sold or donated or left to the students taking our place were on a trailer, moving far below us, that I would never come here again, to this beautiful place of mountains, ocean, fire, death, and desert.

It was dark now.

After several blocks, when all we passed were hotels and gas stations and we could no longer see the black of the lake, we turned around. We moved more quickly than we had before, with a destination in mind, back to the main street, now lit by gas lamps and headlights, loud with laughter, the clashing music from bars and bistros, and the shrieks of children.

ACKNOWLEDGMENTS

I could never have become a writer without the immeasurable amount of love, encouragement, and trust given to me by many incredible people I am so fortunate to have in my life.

To everyone at Riverhead—I am so happy and honored to be a part of your family. I'm especially thankful to Sarah McGrath for believing in the book, to Shailyn Tavella for the lovely way she's brought the book into the world, and to Alison Fairbrother for her incisive edits and for being my patient guide through the book's journey. I couldn't imagine a better team.

Warren Frazier, you are the most attentive and supportive agent I could imagine. With you, I always know I am in the very best of hands.

Thank you to the teachers and friends who made me believe I could be a writer: Tracy-Ann Spencer, who gave me a notebook and told me to fill it with anything I wanted; Erika Krouse and Jennifer Wortman and the entire

Lighthouse Writers Workshop family; Rachel Edelman, Sara Fardi, and Joel Cuthbertson for reading my first stories and allowing me to read yours. Josh Goldman: thank you for your ten million letters of recommendation! You are my eternal supervisor on all things, clinical and otherwise.

Michelle Latiolais, Sarah Shun-lien Bynum, and Amy Gerstler: you are my guardian angels. I didn't know what a story was, and what it could be, before I met you three. Thank you to Richard Bausch and the Chapman workshop, who read the first pages of this novel in its infancy. I deeply appreciate my UCI cohort, with particular gratitude for Sarah Beth Ryther, Justine Yan, Dillon Sefic, Lara Fitzgerald, Rebecca Sacks, Jamie Lalinde, Ross Green, Michael Andreasen, and Corinna Rosendahl. Miles Parnegg, thank you for your friendship and your brilliant edits; I'm so lucky to have you in my life. Chris Spaide: your feedback and encouragement helped me when I needed it desperately.

To my clients, thank you for trusting me with your stories, for showing me your resilience and vulnerability and bravery every day. You don't know how much you all inspire me.

Madison Newbound, my great old and new friend both: you are my most trusted reader, and I'm so happy we've found each other again! I hope we will be trading work and walking Sloan Road together for many more years to come.

I am deeply and forever grateful for my parents, who have never ceased to be supportive of my writing and all else. Thank you for all the books you've ever given me, for the journals and pens, for letting me write in the shed for hours without interruption, for my education, and for far more kindnesses than I could possibly list. Thank you for sharing your stories with me and granting your permission to write them however I wanted. Emily: You don't know how much your friendship and sistership have meant to me over the years, over the course of my life. Natalie, I'm so proud to call you my little sister. I love you both immeasurably. Ciaran, Matt, Andy, and Rosalie—thank you for making our family full of love and joy.

Shelby—how can I thank you for all you've given me? You saw me as a writer long before I did. I have both the greatest friendship and romance with you; I didn't know this could exist between two people, much less become better with time. You are a partner in all ways, my first and last reader, my true love. We are much too fortunate to have found each other.

Dearest Faye, thank you for keeping me company while I wrote this, squirming at all hours to assure me you were alive and well, and for waiting to be born until the book was done—if barely! I am perpetually in awe of you. I love you, Faybelina. I love you, I love you, I love you.